MAGGIE CHRISTENSEN

A New Dawn in Pelican Crossing

Cover and interior design: J D Smith Design
Editing: John Hudspith Editing Services

Dedication

To my scuba-diving granddaughter, Lara.

Also by Maggie Christensen

Oregon Coast Series
The Sand Dollar
The Dreamcatcher
Madeline House

Sunshine Coast books
A Brahminy Sunrise
Champagne for Breakfast

Sydney Collection
Band of Gold
Broken Threads
Isobel's Promise
A Model Wife

Scottish Collection
The Good Sister
Isobel's Promise
A Single Woman

Granite Springs
The Life She Deserves
The Life She Chooses
The Life She Wants
The Life She Finds
The Life She Imagines
A Granite Springs Christmas
The Life She Creates
The Life She Regrets
The Life She Dreams

A Mother's Story

Bellbird Bay
Summer in Bellbird Bay
Coming Home to Bellbird Bay
Starting Over in Bellbird Bay
Christmas in Bellbird Bay
Finding Refuge in Bellbird Bay
Escape to Bellbird Bay
Second Chances in Bellbird Bay
Celebrations in Bellbird Bay
Happy Ever After in Bellbird Bay

Pelican Crossing
The Restaurant in Pelican Crossing
Secrets in Pelican Crossing

One

It was a glorious morning, the first of July, the middle of winter, but winter in Pelican Crossing was like a British summer day. Gill Dickson powered across the bay as she did every morning, her arms slicing through the waves like a well-oiled machine. It was only here in the ocean she was able to forget her worries, forget Max's ridiculous demands, forget the fact her daughter refused to talk to her, forget the tiny blister on the underside of her tongue which had appeared several days earlier.

She had discovered this group of women who participated in what they called wild swimming soon after Max left, and the idea appealed to her. Now, it was the one time of the day when she could be herself, before she donned her work persona and became Gillian Dickson, divorce and family lawyer.

These days she felt her life was a joke. How had she, who helped other women navigate the hazards of divorce, become embroiled in such an acrimonious dispute with Max? Her ex, not content with leaving her, claiming she spent more time with her clients and the various local organisations she belonged to than with him, had instituted a legal battle to not only stake a claim on half of their mutual assets but to garner a proportion of her future income.

When they met and married, Gill had been in her early twenties, madly in love with Max and unable to imagine life without him. Freya had been born soon after, and life had been good. It had all started to go wrong when her law practice had taken off, and her income exceeded his. As a high school teacher, he was on a fixed salary while she was able to set her own fees.

Gill turned on her back to float for a while before returning to the shore, unsure why this morning the ocean had failed to bring her its customary solace. She gazed up at the sky, turning pink and gold as the sun rose over the horizon. How she loved this place.

She had grown up in the city and only moved to Pelican Crossing when she and Max married. He'd been offered a position at Pelican Crossing High School, and they'd jumped at the opportunity to move to the coastal town. Max had started at the school, and Gill had joined a local solicitor's practice. Their daughter, Freya, had been in her teens when Gill was made a partner in the firm and decided to specialise in divorce and family law, after realising how difficult it often was for women to deal with a male lawyer at such times.

She gave a sigh and, turning over, headed back to the shore. She had a busy day ahead.

'Thought we'd lost you,' one of her companions called, as Gill walked up the beach to grab her towel. Olivia had become a good friend over the years. Her experience as a counsellor had helped Gill when Max left, and when Freya stopped communicating with her.

'Sorry, I was lost in thought.' Gill shook her head as if by doing so she could shake away her worries. 'All good now,' she lied as she towelled herself dry.

'See you at book club tonight?'

'Wouldn't miss it.' But as she spoke, Gill realised she hadn't made time to read this month's book. Maybe she could get away with reading the reviews on Amazon and Goodreads. She always felt it was cheating to do this and vowed never to do it again. Then work got in the way...

Perhaps Max had been right when he said she didn't make time for him, but her clients needed her too. How much she was beginning to realise; she was in touch with her own solicitor almost every day as Max's demands grew. Then there were the organisations she belonged to, crucial to maintain her professional standing in the town, and which proved so useful in networking.

Driving home, Gill pondered again when things had started to go wrong. Was it only when Freya left for university, when they purchased the townhouse on the far side of the marina? Or had it started long before that, when Max was turned down for the principal's position around the same time as her practice started to flourish?

Arriving at the townhouse which she was determined to keep in whatever settlement could be agreed on with Max, she threw off the tee-shirt and shorts she was wearing, before stepping into the shower. As the water flowed over her, Gill automatically itemised what she had to do today.

First there was the weekly conference with other partners in the firm, then a meeting with her PA. The rest of the day was filled with client appointments, leaving her little time to grab a coffee or lunch. It was to be a typical Monday, and she should feel rested after the weekend, but she'd spent most of it wrestling with the latest missive from her solicitor and hadn't got much sleep. At least she had a day off on Wednesday when she'd be lunching with the three friends she'd met when they were all new mothers. It was thirty years ago now, but sometimes it seemed as if it was only yesterday. What if she could go back? Would she do anything differently?

Dismissing the thought before it could take root, Gill stepped out of the shower. A few minutes later, dressed in one of the four pants-suits she kept for work, today the navy one with a bright pink shirt, she applied the subtle makeup she deemed suitable for the day ahead and pulled a comb through her cropped black hair. As she did, she frowned at the streaks of grey which had appeared recently – maybe she should ask her hairdresser to take care of them. But, although she hated the signs she was getting older, she remembered how elegant her mother had looked with silver hair.

*

Gill was tired when she arrived home that evening. It was almost seven, and all she wanted to do was pour herself a glass of wine, defrost one of the frozen dinners which packed her freezer and drop into bed. She used to enjoy cooking, but these days she had neither the inclination nor the energy after a busy day.

But it was book club night, and she'd promised Olivia she'd be there. So, taking a quick shower and changing into a pair of casual pants and a linen shirt, she made herself a cheese sandwich, and browsed reviews while she ate. This month's book choice, *Happy Place* by Emily Henry, didn't seem to be her sort of book. She couldn't imagine spending time with Max and being able to fake they were still a couple. The reviews were varied too, but she liked the one which referred to the author's sarcastic wit. She sounded like Gill who often found herself making sarcastic comments – though they might not be witty. It might make for an interesting discussion.

Before leaving, Gill checked her phone – something she hadn't had time to do all day – but as she'd expected there was nothing from Freya. How long was her headstrong daughter going to continue ignoring her? She'd tried calling too, only to reach her voicemail. She'd given up leaving messages there, suspecting they only succeeded in irritating Freya.

Did Freya feel Gill had spent too much time at work too? Was that why she sided with Max when they separated? If only she'd reply or answer her phone, Gill could ask her.

Tonight, the book club was meeting at Olivia's, and the others were already there when Gill arrived. Olivia handed her a very welcome glass of wine, and she took a seat in the comfortable living room of Olivia's renovated fisherman's cottage. Like many such buildings in Pelican Crossing, the house had gone through several makeovers before now, when the original small rooms had been opened up to make one large living/dining area with floor-to-ceiling windows which during the day let in lots of light.

'Glad you could make it,' Olivia whispered, as she handed her the wine. Gill smiled. She always kept her word. It was something her mother had instilled in her as she was growing up and it had served her well.

The others were already chatting among themselves, suddenly falling silent when Olivia held up the book and asked, 'What did we think?'

Comfortably ensconced in one of Olivia's deep armchairs, Gill relaxed for the first time that day. She took a sip of wine, declined a refill since she was driving, and let the discussion flow over her, feeling pleased when she managed to make a comment about the author's sarcastic wit, before drifting off again, her eyes beginning to close. She came back into the present to discover Olivia had asked each of them to close their eyes and describe their happy place. Gill supposed she should have expected something like that given the title of the book. When it was her turn, Gill closed her eyes. She immediately visualised herself floating weightlessly in the ocean, the only sound the lapping of the waves and the shriek of the seagulls, the pink and gold of the sunrise, the…

'Is that where you were this morning?' Olivia's voice broke through Gill's thoughts.

Had she spoken out loud?

'When you took so long to swim back,' Olivia said.

'I guess.' Embarrassed, Gill picked up her glass and drained it. What had she said? But everyone was nodding, so it couldn't have been too bad. She sat up straighter, determined to listen to what the others had to say. How awful if she'd actually fallen asleep.

'Your turn next month, Gill,' Olivia smiled at her, waiting for her to name the book she'd chosen.

Completely unaware it was her turn next – she should have checked the list stuck on her fridge – Gill was lost for words, then remembering a book she'd enjoyed recently said, '*Time's Prisoner* by Linda Gillard. She's a Scottish author. The book's available on Amazon.'

As the others noted down the title, Gill breathed a sigh of relief. She'd be able to talk about this one, and it should engender a discussion about belief in ghosts. She looked forward to it.

Driving home, she reflected how little she had in common with most other women. While she belonged to a number of local groups and organisations – mostly for business or professional reasons – she had few close friends. She could probably count them on one hand. There was Olivia and the friends she met for lunch each month, and… She couldn't think of any others. Had she become so focussed on her work, she'd cut everyone and everything else out of her life? Was it too late to change? Perhaps once things with Max were settled, she could turn over a new leaf?

Two

In the office of the new *Crossing Echo*, festivities were winding down from the morning's celebration. Joe Harris drained his glass of champagne, set it down on a table and glanced around the room. The event designed to farewell the old paper and welcome the new one had been a success. The tables set up for the occasion, which had been groaning with food, were now almost empty and were being cleared by the staff from *Crossings*, the local restaurant which had catered the event.

'It went well.' Finn Hunter, the editor of both the old and the new newspapers joined him. 'It's all thanks to you, Joe.'

Joe shook his head. While as mayor of Pelican Crossing, he'd spearheaded the campaign to save the paper after the consortium that owned it decided to close it, along with a number of other regional papers, it had been the community – and a very generous anonymous donor – which had provided the necessary funding. The funding thermometer outside the town hall had now reached the top.

'I must be getting back. I left Coco in the office,' he said, referring to the chocolate labrador who had been his sole companion since his wife died.

'Catch you later, and thanks again.'

Embarrassed at the outpouring of thanks he'd already received, Joe left and made his way back to the mayoral office. He had only been doing his job. The town needed its newspaper. But was that all it had been, he wondered as he walked through the town. The campaign to save the newspaper had been a way of helping him get through each day, something that had become difficult after Barb passed away. They had been childhood sweethearts, neither looking at anyone else after they met at high school. They'd married young, intending to have a large family. But the children they both longed for had never eventuated. Instead, they had found comfort in each other's company, enjoying their home and garden, even taking a year off to travel around Australia in an old caravan.

Now all he had were his memories.

When he'd been voted in as mayor, he and Barb had thought it the pinnacle of their life together and he had joked about how she'd be the most elegant lady mayoress Pelican Crossing had ever seen. The diagnosis of her ovarian cancer soon after his inauguration had been a terrible shock, and the following years a challenge. Then he was alone.

Joe had thrown himself into his work with the council but coming home each night to an empty house had threatened to send him out of his mind, so he'd bought a dog. Now, he couldn't imagine life without Coco. The dog was the perfect companion and seemed to sense his every mood.

When he opened his office door, Coco rose to greet him, emitting a gentle 'Woof', her wet nose pushing into his hand.

'Sorry, Coco,' he said. 'I'll take you for a walk at lunchtime to make up.'

Seeming to understand, the dog padded over to lie in her favourite spot under the desk.

The rest of the morning passed quickly, as Joe scrolled through his emails, deleting some, and answering others, and gave instructions to his PA regarding the agenda for the next council meeting. Then, with a sigh of relief, he picked up Coco's leash.

Once outside, there was no question in his mind where they would go. He'd been so tied up with the campaign to save the paper, it was some time since he'd spoken to his friend, Cam Mitchell, who owned and managed *Pelican Marine*. But it was no excuse for ignoring an old mate.

It was good to get out into the fresh air. Coco enjoyed it too, after being cooped up in Joe's office all morning, excited by the sight of a group of seagulls fighting over a scrap of food and pulling on his leash. There was a stiff breeze coming off the sea when they reached the marina, making many of the vessels rock in their moorings. It was good to be alive, but Joe wondered what he could find to occupy him now the campaign was over. Being mayor was all very well, but he needed a project to keep his mind occupied in the lonely nights.

'Joe, good to see you again. A great success this morning,' Cam greeted him before reaching down to pat Coco.

Joe had forgotten Cam had been there, as had many other local businesspeople. 'It did go well, didn't it? But it's not why I'm here. I want to apologise for being so out of touch the past couple of months.'

'No worries.' Cam grinned. 'You had other things on your mind. And it was all worth it. You must be very proud of what you've achieved.'

Joe flinched. If one more person tried to congratulate him for what had been a community effort, he'd either scream or dock them one. But this was Cam. They'd known each other most of their lives. So, he smiled and said nothing.

'Fancy lunch?' Cam asked. 'I often go across to *The Blue Dolphin.* We can sit at one of the outside tables to accommodate Coco.'

'Sounds good.'

The pair were soon seated outside the café, Coco happily lying at their feet, a bowl of water having been provided for her.

'How's life?' Joe asked, when they'd been served with coffee and the ploughman's lunch Cam had insisted on, telling Joe it was a new item on the menu.

'Better than ever.' Cam grinned again. 'Life with Poppy is never dull, that's for sure. And now, with the grandkids… We don't have a moment to ourselves, but we wouldn't have it any other way.'

Joe winced. He envied Cam who had got together with Poppy, the owner of *Crossings*, only a year earlier. Between them, they now had two grandchildren and two more on the way. Interestingly, one of them, a little boy called Taylor, was the son of Poppy's daughter and Cam's son. No wonder Cam was enjoying life.

Joe's one regret was that he and Barb had never had any children. He had no children or grandchildren to fill his life. As if reading his mind, Coco nudged Joe's leg. He looked down affectionately at the dog and patted her head. If only she could speak.

'So, what's new?' Cam asked. 'Now the campaign's over, you must feel relieved.'

'Not really.' Joe sighed. 'After fighting the development, then setting up the campaign, life will seem pretty empty.' He chuckled, but it sounded hollow, even to himself. He shrugged. He didn't want Cam's pity, but there it was. Since Barb died, he'd been lonely, needing something to fill his life. The fight to save the town from a developer, then the paper, had filled the empty hours. Now they were both over, he'd be back to spending all his time on town business.

'I'm sorry. I didn't realise.' Cam was silent for a few moments. 'You must come to dinner,' he said, injecting a note of enthusiasm into his voice. 'I'll talk to Poppy and get back to you.'

'Thanks.' It was good of Cam, but a dinner with the loved-up couple wasn't going to cure what ailed Joe. He needed a purpose in life, a project he could get his teeth into.

Three

Today was the monthly lunch with her three friends, and Gill hoped they wouldn't ask about Max again. The four women had met as young mothers and their friendship had continued over the years, now having evolved into lunch once a month with each of them taking turns to host. She had become accustomed to their not-so-subtle enquiries about the progress of her divorce and, although Gill knew they only did it out of concern for her, it made her feel uncomfortable.

None of them knew what it was like. Liz was the only other one of them to have undergone a divorce and hers hadn't been nearly as bitter as Gill's. Both Poppy and Rachel had been widowed and while she empathised for their loss, they had no idea of her pain.

Today they were meeting at Poppy's, and Gill wasn't sure if she was looking forward to seeing them all again.

It was strange, she thought, as she drove to Poppy's clifftop home, how only a year ago, all four of them were single. Now Poppy and Cam were a couple and Liz had recently paired up with Finn, the editor of the local newspaper. Only Gill and Rachel were still on their own and likely to remain so. Gill had no desire – or room – for a man in her life, too caught up in the divorce battle with her hopefully soon-to-be-ex-husband. She couldn't imagine wanting to become involved with a man ever again.

Poppy's home was so different to Gill's. It was built on a clifftop with views to the marina in one direction and to the Boodalang River on the other. The river, whose name was the Aboriginal word for pelican, was what gave the town its name, that and the large number of pelicans who made it their home. The house hadn't changed much since Poppy and Jack built it and raised their three girls there. All three were now married, but they still lived in Pelican Crossing, as did Rachel and Liz's daughters. Gill's daughter was the only one of the three babies who had brought the women together to have chosen to live overseas, though Rachel's younger child, her son, did too. But, unlike Freya, he kept in touch with his mother and even made it home from time to time.

Gill and Rachel arrived together. 'You okay?' Rachel asked, making Gill wonder if her distress was showing on her face, despite her attempt to hide the dark shadows under her eyes with makeup. She wasn't getting much sleep these days and rose early for her morning swim, the only thing that helped her get through the day.

'Any word from Amber?' Rachel asked Poppy, once they were inside, the three had greeted each other with hugs, and Rachel was petting Poppy's West Highland Terrier, Angus, who sniffed at her ankles, no doubt scenting Molly, her own little Westie.

'Not yet. I'm carrying my phone with me everywhere,' Poppy said, holding up her iPhone. 'Chris has promised to call me as soon as there's any sign. Let's hope I don't get a call during lunch.'

'Excited?'

'You have no idea… though maybe you do. You've already gone through this with Jess's twins. I know Megan and Scarlett have already given birth, and I have two perfect grandchildren, but Amber was my first baby and it's been so difficult for her.' Poppy wiped away the tear which slid down her cheek. 'Oh, I don't know why I'm crying.' She gave a weak laugh. 'Look at me, and I haven't offered either of you a glass of wine.'

Poppy took a bottle of semillon blanc out of the fridge and filled three glasses. 'To grandchildren,' she said raising her glass.

'To grandchildren,' Rachel replied.

Gill raised her glass too and took a gulp of the chilled wine. She always felt awkward when the others talked about grandchildren. Poppy's oldest daughter, Amber, who was the same age as Freya, was due to give birth to twins any day, adding to the two grandchildren she already had. Rachel had three grandchildren too, and now Liz's daughter, Mandy was pregnant, and Liz had recently discovered a teenage granddaughter from the daughter she'd given up adoption for in her own teenage years. Gill was the only one of the group without grandchildren, and with a daughter who refused to communicate with her. It made her feel as if she didn't belong in the group anymore.

Maybe if she and Max had had more children… But she had never become pregnant again, and once her practice took off, she had been glad there had been no more babies to take care of.

There was a knock at the door, and Liz arrived.

'Ooh, you've started already,' Liz said, seeing the glasses of wine.

'Toasting grandchildren,' Rachel said.

'Oh, has Amber…?' Liz turned to Poppy.

'Not yet,' Poppy laughed, 'but any time now. We were just toasting them in general.'

'I'll drink to that,' Liz said as Poppy poured her a glass. 'I'm sorry, Gill,' she said, turning to Gill. She and Liz had been in the same boat till Liz discovered her teenage grandchild, then her youngest daughter announced she was pregnant. 'Your turn will come.'

Gill grimaced.

'Still no word from Freya?' Rachel asked.

Gill shook her head and took another gulp of wine. Freya was overseas and had cut off all communication with her mother. There was nothing any of them could do or say to make it better.

'Let's go into the dining room,' Poppy said. 'I thought we'd eat inside today since it's turned cooler.'

They all trooped into Poppy's large dining room where the table was already set with red and green table napkins. It looked very much as if…

'You didn't!' Rachel said as she spied a Christmas garland sitting in the centre of the table.

'Christmas in July? I did.' Poppy laughed. 'I know it's a bit early, but we're planning to make a big thing of it at *Crossings* later in the month, and I thought why not? I love all the Christmas food and trimmings.'

'If we'd known, we could have had another Secret Santa too,' Liz said, referring to their Christmas lunch the previous year.

'Just as well not,' Gill said. 'I'm not sure I agree with all the Christmas in July stuff. It seems so American. But, like Poppy, I do like turkey and all the trimmings. I assume…?' She looked at Poppy.

'Turkey, roast potatoes and pumpkin,' Poppy confirmed, 'but I'm afraid I stopped there. Dessert is a lemon meringue pie from the bakery.'

As expected, the meal was delicious, and the conversation revolved around the new newspaper, the first edition of which was eagerly awaited. Although Liz was now close to the editor, she was unable to tell them when it would appear, and she took their friendly bantering in good part. Gill wondered if Liz now regretted her previous tendency to gossip about others, having recently been the subject of it herself when the daughter she'd given up for adoption at fifteen had arrived in town.

Gill was just heaving a sigh of relief when Liz asked, 'What word on your divorce, Gill?'

Gill took a deep breath. 'Still nothing to report. It must be the longest divorce proceedings on record,' she said trying to inject a note of humour. It fell flat.

'Oh, Gill. I'm sorry. It must be hard,' Rachel said, her face etched with concern.

Gill shrugged in an attempt to make light of what kept her awake at night. 'It is what it is,' she said. 'Worse things happen at sea.' She looked down at her hands to avoid the sympathetic expressions she knew she'd see if she met her friends' eyes. She didn't need their pity. She just needed Max to come to his senses and agree to a settlement… and Freya to talk to her. She had never been clear on exactly why her daughter had taken Max's side in the divorce proceedings.

Four

'I've left him!'

Joe's sister's broken voice resounded in his ears. It was two years since he'd seen Erica, not since Barb's funeral, when she and her husband had left abruptly immediately after the service. Since then, he'd hardly heard from her and their calls had been brief with her sounding guarded and not her usual self, often ending the call suddenly.

He'd never taken to Geoff, always felt there was something odd about him, despite his success as the owner of what appeared to be a thriving car dealership. Now this!

'Calm down, Erica, and tell me what's happened,' he said, as his sister burst into tears, making anything she said inaudible.

'Sorry, Joe. I just couldn't take it any longer. I didn't know who else to call.'

'That's okay.' Joe was reminded of how, when they were growing up, his little sister always brought her worries to him. He would pat her on the back and give her a cuddle to make it all better. If only she were here in Pelican Crossing, he'd do that now. 'Where are you?'

'I'm still in Perth,' she sobbed. 'I don't know what to do. Geoff's at a motor show. I didn't want to be there when he got back. I've booked into a hotel, but I can't...'

Joe thought quickly. He had no doubt Geoff would be furious when he realised Erica had left him. He'd seen his temper years ago when he and Barb had visited the couple in Western Australia. The two couples had gone out for a meal and the steak hadn't been cooked to

Geoff's satisfaction. Joe had been embarrassed and managed to calm his brother-in-law down before it turned into a nasty incident. He'd wondered then if everything was okay in his sister's marriage, but Barb had told him to leave it, that it was Erica's life, and her choice.

Coco padded over to nudge Joe, as if telling him what to do. 'Why don't you come here?' he said, the words bursting out before he could stop them. But as soon as he'd said them, he knew it was a good idea.

'You mean… to Pelican Crossing?'

'Of course. I have plenty of room here. There's just me and Coco. I've been rattling around in this big house since Barb's been gone.' It would be good to have some company, he thought, and he was the only family Erica had.

'Coco?'

'My dog. After Barb… It was lonely, so I got myself a chocolate labrador for company. You'll love her too.' Joe remembered how much Erica had loved the mutt they'd rescued when he was only ten and she six. She'd spent hours with that dog, even dressing it up in her doll's clothes. 'How are you for money? Can you afford the fare?' It suddenly occurred to him Geoff might have kept control of the purse strings. He wouldn't be surprised to learn Erica had no money of her own.

'No, I'm fine. I had a little put away and I have some jewellery I can sell. Geoff was always very generous like that,' she said bitterly.

They chatted a little more, ending with Erica promising to text Joe details of her flight. Then Joe sat, his hand on Coco's head – the dog sensing his mood, remained still – thinking about what Erica hadn't said. She hadn't explained exactly why she had made the decision to leave Geoff after twenty years of marriage, and why now.

*

Joe was still thinking about Erica next morning when he walked into the office, Coco at his heels. He'd fallen into the habit of taking her to work with him, knowing how she fretted when left at home on her own. It was something Joe understood. He often felt lonely too. The dog was good company, but their conversations were very one-sided. He sighed, wondering what it would be like to share his home with his sister.

As children they had got along, often arguing as siblings did. But they'd never lived together as adults. He expected it would take a bit of getting used to, and she'd given no indication of how long she might stay.

The day started with a series of meetings, each one more tedious than the last. Then there was the usual assortment of emails, many of which he was able to pass on to his PA. Debbie was a godsend, a middle-aged woman he'd inherited from the previous mayor. She had been with the council since she left school and was *au fait* with all the nuances of running the council. She had quickly become Joe's right-hand person, and he would be lost without her. She knew more about the workings of the council than he did and had steered him right on many occasions. She also loved Coco which was a big plus in Joe's books. Although the dog spent her day lying under Joe's desk, she was not averse to the treats Debbie offered her.

Joe was glad when lunchtime came around. Coco, sensing it was time for her walk, rose to her feet and stretched, uttering a gentle 'Woof' when Joe attached her leash. He was meeting Finn for lunch in *The Grand*. The old hotel was an institution in Pelican Crossing and had managed to retain both its original frontage and its name despite several changes in ownership. It was a favourite with Joe who had recently become a devotee of the craft beers from a local brewery set up by two enterprising young men.

Joe found it was good to stretch his legs after sitting all morning, and Coco enjoyed it too. She was well-behaved, only pulling on her leash when they walked past the marina, and she was distracted by the sight of two pelicans coming in to land.

Finn was already seated at an outside table when Joe and Coco arrived. After making a fuss of the dog, he asked, 'Your usual?'

Joe nodded. Finn knew his taste in beer, and they both enjoyed the hotel's pie and chips. 'Thanks.'

Coco settled at his master's feet, his nose almost touching a bowl of water supplied by the hotel. Joe's phone pinged with a text.

Booked my flight. Arriving 2.15 tomorrow. Can you meet me? E

Although he'd been expecting it, Joe was still stunned Erica was arriving so soon. He visualised the meagre offerings in his fridge and pantry. He lived on frozen meals, sandwiches, fruit and yoghurt these days, with no inclination to cook for himself; he missed Barb's home cooking and knew he couldn't compete. He'd need to do some grocery shopping and make up the bed in the spare room. He typed a brief reply.

Will be there.

'Problem?' As Finn placed two frothing glasses beaded with moisture on the table, Joe realised he was still staring at his phone and must be frowning.

'Not really. It's my sister. She's coming to stay. She's left her husband.'

'Oh! Are you close… you and her?'

Joe rubbed his chin. 'She's my little sister. We were close growing up, grew apart in our teens, then she married Geoff.' He grimaced. 'I could never understand what she saw in him, nor could Barb. We didn't see much of them and when we did, it always seemed to end with us disagreeing. I haven't seen Erica since Barb passed. I hadn't realised she was unhappy, unhappy enough to leave him.'

'You don't like your brother-in-law?'

'How can you tell?' Joe grimaced. 'He's done well for himself, owns a big car yard in Perth, but I never trusted him.' He sighed. 'But he was Erica's choice. I thought she was happy.'

'Children?'

'A boy, married now. I haven't seen Kieren for years, not since his wedding when Barb and I flew over to Perth. He seemed a good kid but took after his dad. I wonder how he'll feel about Erica leaving Geoff, leaving Perth too.' Joe shook his head. Erica's decision was going to impact a few lives.

Their meals arrived, and the conversation moved on to how Finn was managing with the newspaper. Joe was keen to know when they might expect the first issue of *The Crossing Echo* to appear, but Finn was being cautious.

'There's no sense in rushing it,' he said. 'I want our first issue to reflect the new ownership, for the community to feel it's their paper. I've been thinking of a colour supplement for some time and have been working on several pieces – one featuring old Agnes and her pelican rescue centre. Seems the time might be right to launch it with one of the first issues of *The Echo*. What do you think, Joe?'

'I think it sounds bloody marvellous. You never cease to amaze me,

Finn. But don't leave it too long. A lot of people worked hard to make this happen and they want to see a result. We need our paper.'

'I know, I know. But even *I* can't put a new paper together overnight. We've had to replace much of the equipment, and the staff we lost when they thought we were going to close.'

Joe nodded. He was aware Finn had almost left too. If it hadn't been for a very generous last-minute donation, there would be no local paper in Pelican Crossing, and the town would be forced to access news online or on the television. 'I'll try to be patient. Just don't leave it too long.'

'I won't. Now, another beer?'

'My shout.' Joe rose and picked up their empty glasses, before heading inside to the bar. Finn was a good guy. Although he wouldn't admit it, it was mostly thanks to him they still had a local newspaper. Another editor might have jumped at the opportunity of a production position with a regional television station, but Finn had stuck by Pelican Crossing. Though his friendship with local woman, Liz Phillips, might have had something to do with it, Joe mused.

Joe was glad he'd been lucky. He and Barb had enjoyed thirty years of married life before she'd been taken from him. Not many could boast of that, and while he was happy to see his friend finding a second chance at love, he knew it wasn't for him. He'd never find a woman to replace what he'd had with Barb, even if he did sometimes get lonely and wish Coco could talk.

Five

As always, Gill returned refreshed from her early morning swim, arriving home just as the resident pair of kookaburras were starting their morning chorus. Rising before sunrise had become a habit, and she loved driving to the beach before the sky turned light, while most of the residents of Pelican Crossing were still asleep. It gave her a sense of freedom, a feeling of being at one with the universe.

The water had been cold on this winter morning, so as soon as she was back in her apartment, Gill headed for the shower. Standing under the blast of hot water, which felt like needles on her chilled skin, she began to warm up. It was a great way to start the day.

Dressing in one of her workaday suits, black today, she chose a bright green shirt, drew a brush through her hair and headed into the kitchen. She boiled water for her morning herbal tea, choosing strawberry and echinacea this morning, dropped an egg into a pot of boiling water and a slice of sourdough bread into the toaster, before opening her iPad to check the day's news.

There were the usual news items about fighting overseas, the ongoing issue of youth crime, and the upcoming state election. Then Gill's eyes were drawn to an item about domestic violence. One more woman was reported to be missing, believed dead. She shook her head. When would men stop harassing and killing their wives? It was an ongoing challenge and what she saw in her practice was only the tip of the iceberg. At least Max had never been violent towards her or Freya.

She was eating her breakfast, when she recalled an earlier news item. It had been a few years ago but had impressed her at the time and she'd vowed to do something about it. But things got in the way. It had been about a development down the coast in Bellbird Bay which combined a women's centre with a rape crisis centre and women's refuge. It had made the news when a new director had been appointed, the previous one having passed away suddenly.

Googling *Women's Centre, Bellbird Bay*, Gill found the website. It had been revamped from the one she remembered, and there was a bio of the current director. Alison Wells had a background in teaching Women's Studies at a university in Perth and had followed in the footsteps of the previous much-loved director, Maxine Henderson, a woman Gill had heard of, and whose work she admired.

Reading about the centre again reinforced Gill's previous decision, but this time she was going to do something about it. She'd make time in her busy schedule to visit the centre, she decided. She was interested in meeting Alison Wells to find out if there was some way they could collaborate; perhaps Alison would be willing to come to talk to one of the groups Gill belonged to in Pelican Crossing. Zonta was an organisation dear to Gill's heart, perhaps more so than any of the others she belonged to and used for networking. It promoted women's rights, advocating for equality, education and an end to child marriage and gender-based violence, making it a perfect fit for Gill's own beliefs.

Deciding not to delay any longer, she sent an email to Alison Wells, detailing her background, her interest in the centre and asking if she might visit and have a chat with the director.

Then she sent her daily text to Freya in the hope that this time she'd receive a reply, though in her darkest moments she doubted her daughter even opened the texts. At least Freya hadn't blocked her... yet.

*

The morning passed uneventfully, a partner's meeting, two new clients and a lot of paperwork. It was a relief when one o'clock rolled round, and Gill was able to take a break. Sometimes, she ate at her desk, but today, she felt like getting away from the office. She pulled on her suit jacket, slid her bag over her shoulder and headed out, telling her PA to leave any messages on her desk.

Outside the office, she stood still for a moment, breathing in the fresh air. Although she loved her job, she sometimes hated being stuck in an office all day. The street was empty save for a man walking his dog. The chocolate-coloured labrador reminded her of a pet she'd had when she was growing up. Brownie had been a faithful friend, the repository of all her dreams and goals, things she'd never share with her parents or schoolfriends. She'd cried buckets when the animal was run down by a careless driver, refusing to get another pet as none could replace Brownie in her life. She felt her eyes moisten at the memory, before dismissing it as the sort of sentimentality that had no place in her present life.

Gill quickly made her way to her favourite lunch spot. *Books and Coffee* was close to her office and was a combined bookshop and café. It was located on a corner, with each part having a separate entrance. The bookshop was managed by the owner, Lou, a lively woman in her sixties, and the café by Ron and Denny, a couple who cooked the most delicious food and who, in Gill's opinion, brewed the best coffee in Pelican Crossing.

Breezing through the bookshop with a wave to Lou, who was busy with a customer, Gill entered the café section to be met with the mouthwatering aroma of coffee. While she preferred her herbal tea with breakfast, there was nothing like a good cup of coffee to rejuvenate her.

'What'll it be today?' Denny asked, when it was her turn to be served. 'We have the vegetable lasagne you like, and strawberry and white chocolate muffins just out of the oven.'

'Hmm.' Gill checked out the blackboard menu on the wall behind Denny. The muffins sounded yummy, but she didn't feel like lasagne, more like... 'I'll have the pumpkin soup with sourdough,' she said, then after a moment's hesitation added, 'and a muffin.' She could always take it back to the office for later.

As Gill turned from the counter, she noticed a familiar face at a corner table. 'I didn't know you lunched here,' she said to Olivia. 'Mind if I join you?'

'Please do. I love the atmosphere here, and today I just needed to get away from work.'

'You, too?' Gill chuckled. 'I love what I do but sometimes…' She grimaced.

'I know what you mean. I'm guessing that, like me, your clients tend to drain you.'

Gill looked at her friend in surprise. This wasn't something they'd ever discussed. Gill had never revealed to anyone how she often felt like banging her head against her office wall, especially if the other party was being particularly stubborn. Then there were the times when she came off the phone to her own solicitor…

Although she knew how as a counsellor, Olivia must deal with some difficult situations, Gill hadn't gone to her professionally, merely discussing her predicament with Max and Freya over coffee. Now she felt guilty for unloading her problems on her friend, who was probably tired of dealing with the challenges of her clients. Her concern must have shown on her face – although she could maintain a poker face with her clients, it often let her down with friends.

'I was happy to be of assistance to you, Gill,' Olivia said. 'Don't imagine I wasn't.'

'Thanks.' But Gill still felt guilty. 'Don't interrupt your lunch for me,' she said, noting Olivia had put down her cutlery while they were speaking.

'Not a problem. I was almost finished anyway.' She forked up a few more pieces of her pasta.

Gill's soup arrived, the pumpkin soup topped with a generous dollop of sour cream and accompanied by a chunk of sourdough bread and a tiny dish of butter. The muffin sat on a separate plate.

'Can you bag the muffin for me, Denny?' Gill asked.

'Sure thing. Would either of you ladies like coffee?'

'Yes, for me,' Olivia said. 'Gill?'

'Yes, please.' She didn't think she could face the afternoon without a caffeine hit.

'How are things with you and Max?' Olivia asked, harking back to their earlier conversation once Denny had left.

'Don't ask!'

'That bad?'

Gill nodded. She didn't want to talk about it. 'What's happening with you?' she asked, knowing Olivia's life was no picnic either.

To her surprise, Olivia smiled. 'Nancy's pregnant again,' she said.

'Your oldest?'

'Yes. This will be grandchild number three,' she said. 'It's such a pity they're all living so far away. At least Dylan is still in Queensland, though…' she sighed. 'I know how difficult it must be for you with Freya. Still no word?'

Gill shook her head, her heart contracting as it always did when the subject of Freya came up. Olivia's daughter and grandchildren might live on the other side of the world, but they were in regular contact via Facetime, and her son made frequent trips back to Pelican Crossing to visit his mum.

She picked up her spoon and started on her soup. 'This is delicious,' she said, hoping to change the subject.

But Olivia hadn't finished. 'Nancy wants me to visit them,' she said.

'And will you?' How Gill wished Freya wanted to see her.

'I'm thinking about it. It's a long time since I took a proper holiday. But it's a long way, and I'd have to arrange for a locum to look after my clients. It wouldn't be easy.'

'But possible?'

'Anything's possible.' She checked her watch. 'I'm sorry. I need to go. I have a client coming in fifteen minutes.'

'Good to see you,' Gill said. But was it? Talking with Olivia, hearing about her daughter, only emphasised the rift between her and Freya, a rift her daughter showed no signs of attempting to heal.

Six

Joe poured his coffee and spread his toast with the lemon, lime and ginger marmalade which had been Barb's favourite, before settling down with Coco at his feet to read the newspaper.

The first edition of *The Crossing Echo* had arrived on his doorstep that morning, weeks before Finn's predicted date, and Joe was eager to see what it was like. The masthead was different to that of the previous paper, of course, and he grimaced at the sight of his photo on the front page, with the editorial thanking him for his foresight and persistence in turning an idea into reality. He quickly turned the page.

Joe's coffee grew cold as he read through what was a completely new style of local paper. Finn had really gone to town to make this a newspaper for Pelican Crossing to be proud of, a paper worthy of the community to which it belonged. He should be proud of what he'd achieved. While Finn – and others – might give credit to Joe, it was the editor and staff of the new *Echo* who had produced the paper. He picked up his phone.

Ten minutes later, he had congratulated Finn on his achievement and arranged to meet him for lunch.

'Sorry, Coco,' he said to his dog, 'you'll have to stay home today. I have to meet Erica's plane this afternoon and they don't permit dogs in the airport unless they are working dogs or in a safe kennel.'

Coco looked at Joe, her sad eyes telling him she understood but didn't like it.

'I'll take you for a walk when we get back. Erica will want to stretch her legs and she's going to love you.'

Coco gave a soft 'Woof' and padded to where her bed lay just inside the back door.

'Good dog.' Joe went over and scratched her ears, before picking up his keys and checking he had his wallet. He planned to spend a quiet morning in the office, then head to the airport immediately after lunch.

But the best laid plans… Almost as soon as he arrived at work, he was drawn into a disagreement with two councillors about their desire to restrict access at the town's most popular off-leash beach. They were two of the most belligerent councillors, and Joe was hard put to maintain his cool when they accused him of being biased and even had the temerity to suggest it was an offense to bring Coco into the office.

Luckily, he was saved by his PA reminding him of an appointment. He followed Debbie out of his office, confused. It wasn't like him to forget an appointment.

'I heard raised voices and thought you might need rescuing,' she said, when they were out of hearing of the two troublemakers.

'Thanks,' Joe said.

'Were they hassling about the dog beach again?'

'How did you guess?'

'They've been going on about it for ages, long before your time. But the dogs don't do any harm and it's good for them to be able to run free. It's far enough away from surf beach, where the surf lifesavers are and where families go to swim. All dogs are on the leash there. I wouldn't let it worry you.'

But Joe *was* worried. If these two felt that way, how did other members of the community feel? Was this something he needed to put to the council as a whole?

'Coco,' he said with a sigh.

'Oh, dear. They didn't… did they? How dare they? We all love Coco. It's not as if they're in the office every day like we are. Pay no attention to them, Joe.'

But Joe knew it wasn't so easy. They were elected members of council and, until they were voted out – or retired – he had to listen to their views. But it was true what Debbie said, Coco was popular with the office staff who always spoke to her and petted her. Debbie wasn't the only one who offered the dog treats when they thought Joe wasn't looking.

'Thanks, anyway, Deb.' Joe's forehead creased. This was just one more thing to worry about. He didn't want to be on bad terms with any of the councillors, especially these two who had the reputation of being difficult.

By the time lunchtime came around, Joe had calmed down, but he was glad to get out into the fresh air. He walked smartly along the street and down towards the harbour, glad he had arranged to meet Finn. Seeing the inevitable pelicans perched on the bollards, waiting for a fishing boat to be unloaded, Joe grinned. It was difficult to feel down in the presence of these magnificent birds with their elastic throat pouches. He'd read how, contrary to common opinion, the birds didn't use the pouch to store fish, but as a dip net to catch the fish which they swallowed immediately.

He arrived at the hotel before Finn and, greeting the barman, he ordered two glasses of beer and automatically checked his phone. There was a message from Erica to say she'd spent the night in Sydney and was on her way to the airport. He was glad she'd broken her journey and hoped she'd managed to get a good night's sleep. She had still given him no indication of her reasons for leaving Geoff.

'Joe!'

Joe looked up to see Finn smiling at him.

'This for me?' Finn gestured to the untouched glass of beer, still beaded with condensation.

'It is.' Joe slipped his phone into his pocket and took a gulp from his own glass.

'Your sister?'

'Yeah. She's arriving this afternoon.'

'Why don't the two of you join Liz and me for dinner?'

'Thanks, mate. But maybe not today. Give Erica time to settle in first. Can I let you know?'

'Sure.'

Joe took another drink. 'Congratulations again on the first edition of *The Crossing Echo*. It's a ripper.'

'Glad you like it. When we redesigned the masthead, we decided to revamp the entire design. Hope you liked the front page.' Finn chuckled.

Joe grimaced. 'I'm sure you could have found a better image. But the rest of the paper is pretty amazing.'

'Thanks, I can't take all the credit. I'll pass on your compliments to the staff.'

'Please do.' But Joe knew Finn was the driving force behind the new look. It was his vision which had set it all in motion. Like Joe, he tended to deflect compliments. It was what made Finn a good manager. 'What's next?'

'You'll find out next week. We're finally going to publish the colour supplement I've been talking about for ages but couldn't get the consortium to agree to. I'm glad I kept back the feature about old Agnes and her pelican rescue centre. The photos Coop took there are amazing, and after some negotiation – and a donation to the centre – Agnes has agreed to allow us to put one of her on the cover.'

'You must have done some fast talking there.' Joe chuckled.

'I've got to know her since Coop and I were out there taking photos. Sandy and I often see her when we're walking on the beach,' he said, referring to his grandson. 'Sandy's dog, Bluey, and Agnes's Lady have become friends.'

The mention of dogs on the beach reminded Joe of the dispute he'd become embroiled in earlier. 'About that.' He cleared his throat. 'I got into a bit of a disagreement with morning… about restricting dog access to the beach.'

'What?'

'Would you like to order, Joe?' the barman asked, interrupting their conversation.

'I'll have my usual pie and chips. Finn?'

'Same for me.'

'My shout, I invited you.' Joe took out his credit card and swiped it.

The bar was becoming busier, so the pair made their way to a free table before continuing their discussion.

'Tell me again… dog access to the beach,' Finn said.

'It's the usual story,' Joe said. 'A couple of disgruntled councillors with not enough to do have decided to take aim at me and Coco. They're prettying it up with pretend concern for beachgoers. Though Debbie says they've brought it up with the previous council too.' He pulled on one ear. 'Anyway, they want all dogs to be on leash, supposedly for the safety of everyone else on the beach.'

'But it's on the open beach not the bathing part, isn't it?' Finn frowned, as if trying to recall the different stretches of beach.

'It is. They brought up Coco's presence in the office too.' Joe felt a resurgence of the anger which had engulfed him when Coco's name had been mentioned.

'Bloody hell!' Finn seemed to think for a moment then, 'I can't do anything about the office, but why doesn't *The Echo* do a feature on the dog beach and how important it is for our four-legged friends? I'm sure I can persuade Agnes to let us photograph her and Lady, and Sandy would be thrilled to see Bluey and him in the paper. No doubt we could bring on board a few other dog owners, too.'

'What a brilliant idea. I know Poppy Taylor and one of her friends own Westies. They'd know other dog owners too.'

'Great! I can talk with Rhana Black, the breeder where we bought Sandy's spaniel. Then there's the local vet… And we should include a mention of you and Coco. We can't leave out our local mayor.' He chuckled.

'Maybe,' Joe said cautiously. He didn't want to inflame the two councillors. They were upset enough with him already.

'I suppose we need to give both sides. You willing to let me have the names of the guys who spoke to you?'

'Sure. I'll get Debbie to send you their contact details.' Joe could sense Finn's rising excitement. He'd seen it before when the editor got the bit between his teeth.

Their meals arrived, and the conversation stalled as they enjoyed the food, served with the hotel's usual flair.

After coffee, Joe checked the time and realised he'd need to leave if he was to make it to the airport in time.

'Thanks, Finn. Good talking with you as always, and congratulations again.'

'No worries. Thanks for lunch. I'll be in touch re getting a shot of you and Coco, and don't forget your promise to have dinner with Liz and me once your sister feels ready.'

'I won't, thanks.'

*

Joe arrived at the airport with only a few minutes to spare, glad he'd left *The Grand* when he did. He parked the car and hurried into the terminal just as the passengers from Sydney were disembarking.

When he saw Erica coming towards him, he caught his breath. Instead of the elegant woman he remembered, he was looking at an older, more worn version of his sister. What had happened to her in the two years since they last met?

'Erica!' Joe pulled her into a hug, feeling her sag against him.

'Oh, Joe. It's so good to see you. Thanks so much for agreeing to my coming to stay.'

Releasing his sister, Joe thought he could detect the trace of tears on her cheeks, but the Erica he knew never cried. Even when she had fallen out of a tree when she was eight, she'd refused to give in to tears. 'Let's get your luggage,' he said gruffly, hiding the emotion he was feeling at the sign of her unfamiliar weakness.

'I just have one small case. It was all I could manage to pack.'

'Right.' Taking Erica's arm, he led her across to the luggage carousel where, after only a few minutes, the luggage began to emerge.

'There it is,' she said, pointing to a small black case.

Joe picked it up. She hadn't brought much. How long did she intend to stay? It wasn't like Erica to travel so light. He glanced at his sister. There were dark circles under her eyes, a sign she hadn't been sleeping well. He needed to know what was wrong but now wasn't the time to ask.

Erica didn't speak on the drive home. To break the silence, Joe found himself babbling on about what was happening in Pelican Crossing – the new newspaper, the dispute about the dog beach, Coco. He was glad to finally reach the house he and Barb had lived in all their married life and which he couldn't bear to leave. It was filled with memories.

As soon as he opened the door, Coco bounded up to greet them, pushing her nose into Joe first, then moving on to investigate Erica.

'Down, Coco,' Joe said, worried she might upset Erica.

'She's fine,' Erica said, bending down to stroke the dog, her lips turning up into the first smile Joe had seen that day. 'What a lovely girl you are,' she said to the dog who reacted to her affection by licking her hand. 'Thanks for this, Joe,' she said again. 'You don't know how much it means to me.'

Embarrassed, Joe cleared his throat. 'Coco has been in all day. She needs a walk. Do you…?' He looked at Erica, unsure if she had the energy to join them.

'I'd rather have a lie down, if it's all right with you. I didn't get much sleep last night… or the night before.'

Or even before then, Joe thought. 'No worries,' he said. 'We won't be gone for long, then we can have a bite to eat.' He showed her to her room and, taking down Coco's leash, headed out.

As he and the dog made their way in the direction of the beach, Joe was more distracted than usual, failing to enjoy the sights which normally gave him pleasure. He was concerned about his sister. There was something very wrong, and he was determined to get to the bottom of it.

Joe waited till after dinner, a dinner of which Erica ate very little, pushing the steak and salad around her plate before saying, 'I'm sorry, Joe. I'm not very hungry.' He made them both coffee and carried it through to the living room, Coco following as usual and dropping into her usual spot at Joe's feet.

Erica took a seat opposite Joe in one of the comfy armchairs.

'Erica,' he said gently. 'I can see you're unhappy. Won't you tell me what's wrong?'

To his surprise, his normally self-contained sister broke into a flood of tears.

Seven

Gill had cleared her diary for Monday and spent the weekend catching up on paperwork, including a terse reply to her solicitor regarding Max's latest litany of claims. Now she was free to make the trip to Bellbird Bay to visit the Women's Centre. Alison Wells had been most welcoming when Gill contacted her about a visit, and she was looking forward to meeting this woman she'd read so much about.

It was a pleasant drive down the coast. Unable to bear what she considered as time doing nothing, Gill tuned into one of her favourite podcasts. *A Podcast of One's Own*, produced by The Global Institute for Women, was a series of podcasts hosted by former Australian Prime Minister, Julia Gillard, each episode featuring her in conversation with prominent female leaders. In this episode Julia was chatting with feminist icon, Gloria Steinem, on *what feminism means today*. It proved to be uplifting listening and most appropriate as a precursor to her visit.

Soon Gill was turning into the entrance to draw up in a spacious car park close to two long single-storey buildings surrounded by trees and bushes. When she got out of the car, she saw a sign pointing to the office and a board which appeared to show a map of the centre.

She was about to examine it when she caught sight of a tall, elegant woman walking towards her. As the woman came closer, Gill could see she had short, grey-streaked hair brushed back from her face and was casually dressed in a pair of jeans and a loose white shirt. The woman offered her hand. 'You must be Gill Dickson. Welcome to *Bellbird Women's Centre*. I'm Ali Wells.'

'Hello, Ali. Thanks for agreeing to see me.' Gill shook the outstretched hand.

'I'm always delighted to show off what we do here. You said you're a divorce and family lawyer. I'm guessing you're pretty familiar with the issues the women here have had to deal with.'

Gill nodded.

'Why don't we have a cup of tea first, then I can show you around?'

'Thanks, that would be great.'

As Ali led her into the building, Gill gazed around, seeing several women and small children. The only male in sight was busy trimming a tall hedge.

The office into which Ali led her was a comfortable room with a lived-in feel, one wall filled with shelves overflowing with books. Along another was a sofa. There was also a low coffee table and several plants in colourful pots. On yet another wall were a series of watercolours and a number of framed photographs.

Seeing Gill gazing around, Ali chuckled. 'I know what you're thinking. This doesn't look much like the sort of office you're familiar with. It was what I thought on my first visit. It was nothing like my university office. I've kept it exactly the same as Maxine Henderson, the previous director had it, partly in her memory and partly because it makes the women feel more at home. Now, peppermint tea okay for you?' she asked, as a young woman appeared in the doorway.

'Lovely, thanks.' Gill understood what she meant. She was beginning to feel quite at home here too, although the furnishings were very different from those in her apartment.

Over tea, accompanied by tasty slices of banana bread, Ali outlined the work of the centre and the affiliated women's refuge, providing Gill with more information than she could have hoped for. She filed much of it away for future reference, knowing a time would come when one or more of her clients would have need of the support Ali and the centre offered. Sadly, for some, divorce alone wasn't the answer.

After a tour of the facility, Gill and Ali shook hands again. Ali had readily agreed to speak to the members of Gill's Zonta group, and the visit had given Gill much food for thought, making her realise that, despite her challenges with Max, she was a lot better off than many others.

Driving home, Gill didn't need the distraction of a podcast. Her mind was filled with what Ali had told her and what she'd seen. She wished there was something she could do to assist the centre and the women who sought help there. Ali had filled her in on its history and on the story of Maxine Henderson who had been director for a number of years before her untimely death. The centre had been operating in one form or another since the 1990's and offered a variety of services to women – not only those who had experienced rape or were suffering from domestic abuse. The centre itself dealt with sexual assault, homelessness and women's health and ran a number of workshops, including sessions for yoga, music, gardening, cooking, and even a writing group.

There hadn't been time to visit the women's refuge which was located separately from the centre to provide the security its clients needed, but Ali had suggested Gill could visit it at another time.

It was all so much more than what Gill had to offer. It made her feel her work on assisting her clients with their divorce or family law disputes was merely a drop in the ocean.

As she approached Pelican Crossing, Gill debated with herself whether to go into the office, but it was mid-afternoon and she knew if she did, she'd only get caught up in whatever had come in that day. She had the urge to talk with someone, someone unrelated to the stories of domestic violence she'd just left, someone who could help her recover a sense of normality. She found herself heading for the house on the bluff belonging to Rachel. Of all the friends she lunched with, Rachel was the one to whom they all gravitated when they needed to let off steam or to ask for advice. Right now, Gill needed neither. She just needed to see a friendly face.

Two small children and one small, white dog were playing a game on Rachel's front lawn. At the sight of them Gill felt the familiar ache at the thought she might never have grandchildren of her own, might never even know if Freya gave birth. She'd forgotten Rachel often looked after the girls during the week. She was about to turn the car around when Rachel came out of the house and looked towards her.

Gill sighed and got out of the car.

'Gill. This is a lovely surprise. Not working today?'

'I had a meeting in Bellbird Bay.' Gill knew this didn't explain why she was here, but she knew it would satisfy Rachel. She was the least curious of her friends.

'I was about to call the girls in for afternoon tea. You'll join us? I've just taken a batch of ginger scones out of the oven.'

'Yum,' called the girls in unison as they almost fell over each other and the dog, rushing past Gill to be first into the house.

'Hands washed first,' Rachel called after them, shaking her head. 'Those two terrors will be the death of me,' she said to Gill, 'but I'm going to miss them when they start school next year. I don't know what I'm going to do with myself. Emily's too little to be much company as yet,' she added, picking up her youngest grandchild who was only a year old, and had been playing happily with her toys, unconcerned with what her older sisters were doing.

Once inside, Rachel settled Emily in her highchair, made lemon and ginger tea for herself and Gill and poured two glasses of milk for the girls, and water into a Sippy cup for Emily. The girls drank their milk down quickly, then each taking a ginger scone, liberally spread with butter, dashed off again followed by the little dog.

'Peace again,' Rachel sighed. 'But I wouldn't be without them.' She peered at Gill. 'You look as if you've something on your mind. Want to talk about it?'

'Not really.' Gill took a sip of tea. But the urge to confide in Rachel was too strong. 'I've spent the day at the *Bellbird Women's Centre*. I initially only went there to meet the director and persuade her to give a talk to the Pelican Crossing Zonta group… and I admit I was curious to see the place. I'd heard a lot about it, about the previous director and how the new one was carrying on her mission.'

'And did you… persuade her to do a talk?'

'Yes, that was the least of it. Seeing all those women, Rach. And the children… It was… I hadn't realised.' She took another sip of tea. 'I get the easy bit… helping women end a difficult marriage, obtain a fair settlement, gain custody of their children. Today I saw the other side of it, the women who have nowhere to go. And I didn't even visit the women's refuge. They have women come there from all over the state. And I thought my situation was bad.' She muttered the final words under her breath.

'Don't put yourself down. You do good work. Everyone has a different cross to bear.' Rachel's eyes clouded.

'Oh, Rach, I'm sorry. I didn't mean....' How could Gill have forgotten Rachel's husband's drawn-out death.

'I wasn't talking about myself. I've read a lot about domestic violence, how it can happen even in the wealthiest of homes, and the violence isn't always physical.'

'It made me wish there was more I could do,' Gill said.

'As I said, you do good work. You provide a necessary service to the women in Pelican Crossing. And it sounds as if what the *Bellbird Women's Centre* provides is a different and equally necessary service. You complement each other. Can you look at it like that?'

The two women sat in silence for a moment, each lost in thought.

'You're right,' Gill said at last with a sigh. While she might want to do more for the women she'd seen and heard about today, there were only so many hours in the day, and hers were fully taken up. She could still hear Max's complaints about the amount of time she spent at work and in what he referred to as her *good causes*, and it had increased exponentially since he left.

Gill and Rachel chatted on about more inconsequential matters, the children running in and out, pursued by the little white dog, till Rachel said, 'Jess will be here soon to pick those two and Emily up. Would you like to stay to dinner? I don't have any guests at the moment,' she said, referring to the visitors who regularly stayed with her since she'd turned her home into a B&B.

Gill checked her watch, shocked to discover how much time had passed since she arrived. 'Thanks, but no, Rach. I need to check in on things. I've been out of touch all day. It's been good to talk with you. You've helped me get things into perspective.' She rose and hugged her friend. 'Thanks again.'

'Any time. Are you sure you'll be all right?' Rachel's forehead creased. 'You can't help everyone, Gill. Remember that and be sure to look after yourself.'

'I will.' Gill smiled as she left Rachel and made her way to the car, sorry to leave the comfort of Rachel's family kitchen.

It was only when she stepped into her own spartan apartment that Gill realised how, over the years, even before she and Max went their separate ways, she had built a barrier around her emotions, preferring to put her energy into helping others while ignoring her own needs. Maybe it was time to change.

Eight

Erica had been in Pelican Crossing for three days now and had spent most of them either in tears or lying in bed, her eyes tightly closed. So far, she'd refused to talk about what prompted her sudden decision to leave her husband. Joe was determined that, when he returned home from the office tonight, he was going to try to get to the bottom of it. He wanted to help his sister, but as long as she refused to disclose what was worrying her, he felt helpless.

Coco's presence was the only thing that appeared to soothe her. The dog seeming to sense her distress had started following her around.

So, Joe had left his pet at home and missed her comforting presence in the office, as did the office staff who wanted to know where she was and why Joe hadn't brought her into work. It was confirmation, if any was needed, that Coco was welcome there.

Joe had been in meetings most of the day, so it was a relief when Debbie popped her head round his door in the late afternoon to say Cam Mitchell wanted to see him. 'Show him in,' he said, rising and coming out from behind the desk.

'Cam,' he greeted his old friend, 'what can I do for you?' It was a few weeks since they'd had lunch together, after the launch of the new paper.

'Joe, good to see you too. I've come on a mission, from Poppy.'

Joe was puzzled.

'You may remember last time we met, when we had lunch, I mentioned you coming to dinner.'

Joe nodded, having only the vague recollection he hadn't been keen on the idea.

'I said as much to Poppy and she's been on at me, telling me it was time we set a date. So here I am, to fix a time with you.'

'Oh!'

'Problem?'

Joe hesitated. 'It's Erica, my sister.'

'How is she?'

Of course, Cam would remember her. They all grew up together here in Pelican Crossing. Erica was younger and used to want to tag along with Joe and his mates.

'Not good. She's here in Pelican Crossing. She's left the no-good man she married. Got here several days ago, and I haven't gotten to the bottom of it yet. But I intend to.'

'Oh! Well, maybe you could bring her along… to dinner. I'm sure Poppy would remember her too. And Erica would know Poppy.'

Joe smiled. Everyone in Pelican Crossing knew Poppy. She had been such a livewire as a teenager… her and Jack, her late husband, Cam's best friend. There had been the four of them, Jack and Cam. Poppy and Gail. He and Jamie Whittaker had been around too, but never part of their tightknit group. 'Maybe…' he said, wondering if perhaps the prospect of dinner with a couple of old friends would pull Erica out of her depression. 'Can I let you know?'

'Sure. Poppy was thinking of Saturday. Now she's given up going into the restaurant so often, we can enjoy our weekends.' He chuckled.

Joe smiled. He knew how, after her husband's death, Poppy had thrown herself into building up *Crossings*, the restaurant she and Jack had built together. It was only after she and Cam got together, that she'd begun to ease off and take time to herself. 'I'll talk to her tonight and call you,' he promised.

'Good man.' He looked around the office. 'Are you tied up here or have you time for a beer? No Coco, today?'

'She's home with Erica, and…' Joe looked across at his desk, at the pile of paperwork sitting there. There was nothing that wouldn't keep till tomorrow, and he'd welcome a break before going home to face Erica. 'A beer sounds good,' he said.

*

By the time he reached home, Joe was feeling mellow. One beer had morphed into two as he and Cam proceeded to put the world to rights, and Joe shared the dispute about the dog beach and Finn's plans to feature it in *The Echo*.

To his surprise, the aroma of cooking greeted him. For a moment, the years fell away. It was as if Barb had come back. But it wasn't Barb; it never would be again. Erica was in the kitchen, Coco at her feet, hoping for some titbit to come her way.

'Feeling better?' he asked.

'Yes, thanks. Sorry I've been such a misery. It was…'

'It's okay. You can tell me later.' Joe patted Erica's arm awkwardly. 'Something smells good.'

'I thought it was time I earned my keep. It's good of you to…'

'Don't be daft. Where else would you go?' Joe wondered why he had been Erica's first port of call, not her son. Perhaps she wasn't on good terms with her daughter-in-law, or had she wanted to get as far away from Geoff as possible? You couldn't get much farther from Perth than Pelican Crossing, unless you left the country.

'I had a beer with Cam Mitchell after work,' Joe said after they'd enjoyed the spaghetti Bolognese Erica had prepared from what Joe had in the fridge. 'Remember him?'

'The awesome foursome.' Erica smiled. 'That's what we used to call them. Cam, Jack, Poppy and Gail. They were in your year, three years older than me, always together. Didn't Poppy and Jack marry, and Cam and Gail?' Her brow furrowed.

'They did. You may not have caught up, but Jack died almost six years ago now, and Gail and Cam divorced. She formed a relationship with a woman she taught with. She's passed now too. And Cam and Poppy are together.'

'Wow, I am out of touch. It's been a while.'

'Too long.' Pelican Crossing was a long way from Perth, but that was no excuse for brother and sister not seeing each other, unless Geoff… 'I've been remiss since Barb passed,' Joe said. 'I should have made the effort to visit.'

'Best you didn't.' Erica's lips tightened.

'Want to talk about it?'

'Not really,' she sighed, 'but you deserve to know. Geoff… he… he wasn't violent… not at first. But when it escalated, it's when I knew I had to leave. It started with the little things, finding fault with me, refusing to allow me to see my friends – they didn't stay friends for long once they'd got the edge of his tongue – keeping a tight grip of our finances, telling me I couldn't understand them, forcing me to give up work. The list goes on. But when he started to hit me, it was the final straw. Then…' Her voice broke. 'That's when I left and called you.'

'Kieren?'

'He's in his dad's pocket, works in the car yard with him. He doesn't know.'

'Any of it, or that you've left?'

'Geoff's his hero, always has been. I didn't dare tell him I was leaving, but…' she bit her lip. 'Briony, Kieren's wife… she's pregnant… my first grandchild. I wish…' A tear trickled down her cheek.

'Come here.' Joe pulled Erica into a hug while she sobbed.

'Sorry. I promised myself I wouldn't do this again.'

'Sometimes it's good to cry, to let it out.'

'Thanks, Joe,' Erica sniffed. 'You always did know the right thing to say. Barb was a lucky woman.'

'I was the lucky one.'

Coco, clearly feeling she was being ignored, let out a low whine, breaking the sombre mood.

'Coffee?' Joe asked.

'Please.'

'You were telling me about having a beer with Cam Mitchell,' Erica said, when they had moved into the living room with coffee, and Coco was settled happily at Joe's feet, her head on her paws.

'Yeah, he's invited us to dinner on Saturday, or rather, Poppy has.'

'But she didn't know I was here.'

'I may have mentioned it. He talked about my going to dinner some time back, and I wasn't keen, but it was difficult to refuse this time. You'd be doing me a big favour if you come with me. I feel out of it with couples these days. You will come?'

'I remember thinking Poppy was the epitome of what I wanted to be like when I was older,' Erica chuckled, her earlier distress seemingly forgotten as the memory surfaced. 'It will be interesting to see what she's like now.'

'Still elegant, even though she's now a grandmother.'

'She and Jack took over her parents' restaurant, didn't they?'

'*Crossings*.' Joe nodded. 'She still owns it, though isn't so active in it these days since she and Cam got together. He manages the marina and owns *Pelican Marine* – boat sales and chandlery.'

'I wonder who else is still around,' Erica mused.

'From the old crowd? Jamie Whittaker from my year plus a few others… and…' Joe closed his eyes and tried to think, '… you used to go around with the Grace girl, didn't you?'

'Livvy Grace? She's still here? We lost touch when… Oh, I'd love to catch up with her.'

'She works as a counsellor in the Medical Centre.' Over the past few days, it had crossed Joe's mind to suggest Erica visit her professionally. Till now, he'd forgotten they used to be friends.

'Livvy Grace,' Erica said again. 'We used to do everything together, Livvy, me and Rhana Gordon. I suppose she's married now and moved on.'

'There's a Rhana Black breeds spaniels in the hinterland,' Joe said, remembering Finn telling him where he bought a pup for his grandson. 'It's not a common name.'

'It could be her. She always wanted to work with animals. Imagine if we all got together again?' Erica's face lightened, and Joe saw a trace of the Erica he remembered.

'Thanks again, Joe,' Erica said, when they rose to go to bed. 'It's been a tough, few weeks, few years actually, but I'm glad I'm here in Pelican Crossing. I'm glad I've come home.'

Joe was glad too. It had taken his sister's misfortune for it to happen, but for the first time since Barb died, he felt he might have a future.

Nine

When she wasn't immersed in work, Gill had spent time over the past two days thinking about her conversation with Rachel, the conclusion she had come to about her own behaviour, and her resolve to change. But it was easier to decide to change than to actually do it.

The previous evening, over a glass of wine, she made a list of things she needed to change, first of which was to take more care of herself. While her early morning swims provided her with much needed exercise, the rest of the day was spent sitting behind a desk, and she was aware her diet left a lot to be desired. While she enjoyed cooking, these days she only did it when it was her turn to provide lunch for her group of friends. She put an asterisk beside meals on her list.

The next area she could change was friends, which were few. There were the three she had lunch with who she'd met all those years ago when they were all struggling with a new baby, and… she thought for a moment, Olivia and the other members of the book club. She saw Olivia at the beach every morning, and they occasionally bumped into each other in town, but she always avoided making any arrangement to meet her – or anyone else – socially. Reflecting on her life since Max left, Gill concluded that she had become almost completely isolated, preferring her own company and hiding her emotions behind an impenetrable expression. She'd become a very private person, unable or unwilling to show her feelings.

Except with Rachel, she thought, but that had been different, related to work, and Rachel was a friend, one of her few friends.

Over coffee, instead of checking the news on her iPad, Gill re-read what she had written. Top of her list was her health, and the small bump which had appeared on the underside of her tongue.

Before applying her makeup, Gill peered into the magnifying mirror. The little bump was still there. It appeared to be the same as it had last time she looked, and the time before. Was it a good sign it hadn't grown? She remembered the google search she'd done before going to bed, and the horrific story of a woman who'd left what she thought was an ulcer on her tongue untreated, only to be diagnosed with stage four tongue cancer. She peered at her tongue again. It couldn't be cancer, could it? Her stomach shrivelled. Maybe she should get it checked out, just in case. A rush of fear prompted her to pick up the phone and call the medical centre.

*

Gill's mouth was dry, and her legs were shaking as she sat in the waiting room. She was sure it was nothing, but she couldn't dismiss the article she'd read, the article which had kept her awake most of the night worrying. She'd been glad to get an appointment so quickly and to have a free slot in her diary.

'Gill? I don't often see you here. Everything all right?'

Gill looked up to see her friend, Liz. How could she have forgotten Liz worked here as practice manager? 'Just a routine checkup,' she lied, hoping her eyes didn't give her away.

'Time for a coffee after?' Liz smiled.

'Probably not. Maybe another time?'

'Sure. Give me a call.'

Gill nodded. She and Gill had a lot in common. They were the two divorcees in their lunch group, both Rachel and Poppy being widows. But their commonality had ended when Liz formed a relationship with the local newspaper editor. Gill couldn't understand how Liz had managed to trust another man after what she'd been through.

'Gill?' Mary Bolton, Gill's GP, popped her head into the waiting room, relieving Gill of any further conversation.

Once inside the doctor's office, Gill explained why she was there.

As she opened her mouth so the bump could be examined, she was hoping to be told she was worrying unnecessarily. She was already regretting having made the appointment when she could have been at work, and the doctor could have been dealing with more deserving patients.

'Hmm,' Mary said, stepping away from Gill. 'I think we need to have a biopsy. I'll refer you to an oral pathologist.'

Gill's heart dropped. She barely heard Mary describe the process and tell her to make another appointment after the follow up with the pathologist, leaving the office with Mary's final words, 'Don't lose any sleep over it,' ringing in her ears.

She was glad there was no sign of Liz while she paid and walked through the door and out into the street. Her senses were reeling. Cancer. What if it was cancer? What if she died? Who would miss her? Not Max, that was for sure. Freya? Would she even care? The wild swimming group, her clients, the group she met for lunch on a monthly basis? They'd notice her absence for a time, then for them life would go on; it would be as if she'd never existed. She had isolated herself so completely, no one would care. For the first time, Gill acknowledged she was lonely.

Gill's eyes blurred with tears. She didn't see where she was going, till she bumped into someone. She looked up into a pair of concerned brown eyes, and felt a wet nose push into her hand.

*

Erica seemed to be feeling better this morning. Over breakfast, she'd announced her intention to spend the day refamiliarising herself with Pelican Crossing, revisiting her old haunts and maybe even checking out the hospital for nursing vacancies. Although it was years since she'd done any nursing, it seemed she'd retained her registration in the hope one day Geoff might relent and allow her to work again.

As a result, and to the delight of his staff, Joe had taken Coco to the office again. After a contentious meeting with the planning department, he'd felt the need for fresh air, and was walking along the street with Coco when they were almost bowled over by the tall, dark-haired woman.

'Woah!' he said, letting go of Coco's leash and putting out both hands to grasp the woman by the shoulders – he knew the dog wouldn't run off. 'Almost knocked you down. Steady, Coco,' he said to his dog, who seemed eager to make friends.

'Sorry, I wasn't looking where I was going.' The woman raised her head to meet his eyes. Hers were red, as if she'd been crying.

Joe recognised her. She was a partner in the large law practice in town, the one who specialised in divorce and family law. He'd heard good things about her but couldn't recall her name. They'd never met. 'Are you all right?' he asked. She clearly wasn't, but he was a stranger to her, even though she probably knew who he was. Everyone knew the mayor.

She looked so lost, so bereft, without thinking he said, 'You look as if you could do with something to pick you up. I was about to have a coffee. Join me?'

The woman's eyes widened, and he thought she was about to refuse. Then she said, 'Thanks. It's kind of you, but…' She gestured to where Coco was patiently waiting.

'*Books and Coffee* is just along the way. We can sit outside, and they'll provide a bowl of water for Coco.'

'Coco, what a nice name.' Her voice was low and melodious, but flat. She sounded defeated. Joe wondered what had happened to make her so distressed.

She didn't say any more till they were seated at one of the tables outside the café, her hands wrapped around a cup of coffee. 'Whatever must you think of me?' she said, holding out a hand. 'Gill Dickson. I'm sorry. I just received some bad news and wasn't thinking straight.'

'Joe Harris.' Joe took her outstretched hand.

'I know who you are,' she said with the hint of a smile, making Joe realise with a shock what an attractive woman she was. He couldn't remember when he'd last taken enough notice of a woman to find her attractive.

He wondered what the bad news she'd received was, suddenly transported back to the day of Barb's diagnosis of ovarian cancer. Best not to ask, he decided. He didn't know why, but he had the impression Gill Dickson was someone who didn't want to disclose too much about herself. He tried to remember what he'd heard about her. She'd made partner early in her career, belonged to a number of local organisations known for their good works. He thought there was a daughter, and hadn't she been married to a schoolteacher? She was probably divorced.

All of this passed through his mind as the woman sitting opposite sipped her coffee in silence.

'What a friendly dog.' Her words came as a surprise.

Joe looked down to see that Coco's head was now in Gill's lap and she was stroking it. True to form, Coco had sensed the woman's distress and was doing her best to comfort her.

'She has her moments,' he said, unsure what else to say, aware of the anxious vibes Gill was giving off, as if she had no intention of revealing anything about herself. Well, that suited him. He had enough on his plate with Erica's problems. But he had to admit to being curious as to what had caused Gill to be so upset, and why she'd agreed so readily to have coffee with him. Perhaps she was regretting it already?

As if reading his mind, Gill drained her cup and gently pushed Coco's head from her lap. 'I need to go now. Thanks for the coffee, for your sympathy. but I'm fine now. I'm sorry to have troubled you.' She rose.

'It was no…' Joe began, but before he could finish his sentence, she was off, walking smartly along the street, no longer the vulnerable woman he'd rescued outside the medical centre, but an elegant career woman intent on putting as much distance between them as she could, as quickly as possible.

'What was that about, Coco?' Joe asked the dog who seemed as bewildered as he was at the sudden change in her. But, as usual, Coco had no reply.

Ten

By the time Saturday came around, Joe had almost forgotten his meeting with Gill Dickson, almost but not quite. There were times, during the odd moment in his office, when the memory of the vulnerable woman who'd burst into his life came back to haunt him, and he wondered anew what had caused her to be so distressed she agreed to have coffee with him, an act which he was sure was out of character for her.

He'd made a few discreet enquiries which only reinforced his view she was not the type of woman to have coffee with someone she'd just met – even if he was the town mayor with an impeccable reputation. From what he could gather, she was a very private person with few friends, one of which was Poppy Taylor, the woman with whom he and Erica were having dinner that very evening. It wasn't such a coincidence. Pelican Crossing was a small town. It was inevitable people knew each other. What surprised him was how he and Gill Dickson had never crossed paths before now.

Each day this week, Joe had noticed a change in his sister. Imperceptible as it might be to others, he knew Erica so well it was easy for him to spot how every day it seemed as if the load she'd been carrying lightened. It was as if Pelican Crossing was working its magic on her, restoring the old Erica, the sister he remembered, the young girl she'd been before she left to take up a nursing position in Sydney, before she met Geoff and moved with him to Perth in Western Australia.

They'd spent the day on the beach with Coco. With the sounds of the sea and the scent of the ocean, it was easy to forget the cares of the working week, and to pretend all was well with his sister. Joe knew they'd soon have to face the fact she'd left her husband, a husband who might well decide to follow her. But for now, it was enough they were here together in the place they'd both grown up, throwing a ball for his dog.

There were a few other dog owners on the beach, reminding Joe of the challenge he was facing with the two difficult councillors. Earlier in the week, he and Coco had joined several other dog owners to pose for photographs which would accompany the article Finn had promised would appear in *The Echo*. Joe hoped it would raise the community's awareness of the value of the dog beach and would influence the council's decision if it ever came to a vote on ongoing access.

Joe raked his fingers through his still thick hair which was fast turning grey, and grimaced at his face in the mirror. There seemed to be more wrinkles each time he looked, but he supposed it was to be expected at his age. He'd never see fifty again. Then he felt the familiar pang. Barb had never reached her fiftieth birthday, despite all the plans they'd made to make it special.

He took a deep breath, headed out of the bedroom and popped his head into Erica's room. 'Ready?' he asked.

'Almost. Do you think this will do?' Erica turned from the mirror where she'd been examining herself, and Joe was struck again how, despite the improvement he'd noticed since she arrived, Erica's self-confidence was at an all-time low. Geoff had a lot to answer for. He'd managed to change the feisty girl he'd married into a shadow of her former self.

'You look lovely,' Joe said. And she did. The pink, wool dress suited her to perfection, and she'd done something different with her hair.

'Thanks,' she smiled. 'It's a while since anyone called me that.'

Joe smiled back, vowing to say it as often as he could. 'Let's go then.'

*

As soon as the door opened, Poppy's little West Highland Terrier ran out to sniff at Joe's ankles. He leant down to pat him, glad he'd left

Coco at home. Although the dogs got along well when they met on the beach, this was Angus's territory, and it was best not to tempt fate.

'Come on in,' Cam said. 'Poppy's in the kitchen. Good to see you again, Erica. It's been a while.'

'Thirty years since I lived here,' Erica said. 'I was back for Barb's funeral, but only briefly.'

Joe frowned, remembering how Geoff had insisted they leave immediately the ceremony was over. He'd have liked to spend more time with his sister.

'Poppy's looking forward to seeing you again,' Cam said, leading them into the kitchen, Angus padding along at their heels.

'Oh, this is lovely,' Erica said, when they entered the large family kitchen with the French window through which they could catch glimpses of the sky filled with stars, and the lights of a distant ship on the ocean.

'Thanks.' Poppy came forward to hug Joe and Erica. 'Jack and I built it. I could never leave. I'm so glad Cam had no qualms about living here too.' She sent an affectionate glance in his direction.

Joe flinched. This is what he'd been afraid of when Cam first mentioned him coming to dinner. But somehow, it didn't feel as bad as he'd expected. Maybe it was Erica's presence which mitigated the effect, or maybe… Why did the image of Gill Dickson suddenly appear in his mind's eye?

'It's lovely to see you back in Pelican Crossing, Erica,' Poppy continued, clearly oblivious to Joe's discomfort. 'We must see more of you while you're here. Do you plan to stay for long?'

There was an uncomfortable silence during which Joe looked at Erica, and she looked at the floor. Then she said, 'I'm back for good. I've left Geoff.'

'Oh, I'm sorry. Oh, is that the right thing to say? It's good you have Joe to come to.'

'He's been wonderful.' Erica said, smiling at Joe. 'I don't know what I'd have done if he hadn't taken me in.'

There was another awkward pause, then Cam said, 'Sorry, guys. I haven't offered you a drink. What'll you have?' And in the kerfuffle of pouring beer for himself and Joe, and wine for Poppy and Erica, the uncomfortable moment passed.

Over dinner, the conversation focussed on how Pelican Crossing had changed over the years, with Poppy reminiscing about the plans she and Jack had had for *Crossings* and how she had thrown herself into the restaurant after his death.

Joe marvelled at how she could talk about this in Cam's presence.

Then she took Cam's hand, smiled at him and said, 'Then Cam came along and persuaded me to take things easier.'

Joe wondered if he'd ever be able to speak about Barb in this way, as if she was a dear friend, who somehow was no longer with him.

'You must bring Erica for a meal at *Crossings*,' Poppy said, when Erica expressed an interest in how the restaurant looked now; she could only remember what it was like in Poppy's parents' day.

'Good idea,' Joe said, 'if you're up for it, Erica.'

'I'd love it,' she said, a sure sign to Joe she was on the mend.

After dinner, Cam and Joe went out onto the deck, ostensibly to sample a special Scotch Cam had obtained through a contact he'd met on the marina, leaving the women to chat.

'I could tell Poppy wanted a quiet word with Erica,' Cam said. 'Women's business.' He tapped the side of his nose.

Joe hadn't seen or heard any communication between Cam and Poppy but understood what he meant. He and Barb had been able to communicate silently too. Something else he missed. He wondered what the two women were saying to each other.

When the men returned inside, he heard Erica say to Poppy, 'Thanks. I'll contact her. I'll probably need her help.'

Despite being curious to know who and what Erica meant, he had the sense not to ask. But when they were driving home, Erica said, 'Poppy has suggested I talk with a solicitor to work out what my options are. She's given me the name of a friend of hers, a Gill Dickson. Do you know of her?'

Joe swallowed. 'As it happens, I met Gill recently,' he said.

Eleven

Since the appointment at the medical centre, thoughts had been swirling around in Gill's head. She had found it difficult to sleep, visions of what might happen if the bump was cancerous preying on her. Eventually she had found the light sedative she'd been prescribed when Max left – and which she'd refused to take. It helped. She slept. But the nightmares were even more horrific than her waking fears.

She was glad the appointment with the oral pathologist was only a week away. Then she would know the worst. Meantime life went on, and Gill forced herself to carry on as usual, swimming in the early morning, dealing with clients and spending her evenings on paperwork. It didn't help matters when she received notification Max's solicitor had requested a new valuation on the apartment, citing the increase in values since the last one. She sent back a terse reply via her solicitor but knew she couldn't prevent it happening. He seemed determined to bleed her dry.

But this morning as she ploughed through the ocean, she had other things on her mind. Today it was her turn to host the monthly lunch with her three friends, and she was looking forward to it. She planned to cook a favourite Nigella Lawson recipe. Italian chicken with peppers and olives was one she used to cook as a special birthday treat for Max and Freya, and she hoped that concentrating on cooking would help her forget about her worries for a time, at least.

Gill felt invigorated as she towelled herself dry, listening to the other women discuss a television programme most of them seemed to have watched the previous evening when she'd been poring over her client files and silently raging about Max's latest demand.

'Heading to another day at the office?' Olivia asked, as they walked up to the car park together.

'Not today. Lunch with friends,' Gill said.

'Half your luck. Well, see you tomorrow.'

'Yes.' Lucky… was that how others viewed her, Gill wondered as she started up the engine of her Prius. It was the car she'd treated herself to after Max left and took the Subaru Outback with him, telling her she'd be able to replace it. He probably wanted to count it among her assets too, she sighed.

She supposed, to many, she would appear lucky. She was a successful lawyer, lived in an expensive apartment, dressed smartly. They had no idea of what went on behind the elegant image she presented in public, the sleepless nights, the loneliness…

As she left the car park, she almost collided with another car, a white Jeep. There was a dog leaning out the passenger window, a vaguely familiar chocolate labrador who looked happy, its tongue hanging out as if it was grinning at her. She found herself smiling automatically and wishing her life was as simple as the dog's clearly was.

Back home, Gill showered and changed into a pair of black pants with a grey and white patterned top. She headed to the kitchen where she donned an apron, turned on the oven, then took the chicken out of the fridge, pausing only to set up her iPad and turn on the audiobook she'd started listening to in the small hours when she couldn't sleep. It was the one chosen for next month's book club, *The Dry* by Jane Harper – a very different choice from hers the previous month – and she'd managed to lose herself in the tale of the murder/suicide in a small country town until the sound of the narrator's voice had finally put her to sleep.

Now, she picked up where she left off, following Aaron Falk's adventures as she placed the lemon halves and sprigs of rosemary into the cavity of the chicken which was sitting in the roasting pan, and added the sliced leek and peppers. Once she'd added the olives and oil, she slid the pan into the oven and set the timer for the required one and a quarter hours.

Gill had set the table the night before, and dessert was a pear frangipani tart from the local patisserie, so there was nothing left to do. She poured herself a glass of wine and went out to sit on the balcony to continue to listen to the audiobook.

*

Exactly one and a quarter hours later, Gill reluctantly turned off her iPad. She took the chicken out of the oven, leaving it to rest, and was in the process of sliding the tray of vegetables back into the oven when she heard the door. Rachel and Poppy arrived together. They hugged Gill, told her she was looking well and sniffed appreciatively.

'Mmm, roast chicken,' Poppy said.

Gill smiled. It was good to have people to cook for again. Perhaps she should make time to cook properly for herself, but despite her resolve it didn't seem worth the effort. 'Wine?' she asked.

She had just poured three glasses of wine and cut the chicken into chunks for serving, when Liz arrived. 'Sorry I'm late,' she said. 'I got caught up.' She blushed. 'Finn's moving in, and I was tidying up. I know it's very sudden, but… when you know, you know.' She looked around the group as if seeking their approval.

'We're happy for you,' Poppy said, 'aren't we?' She glanced at the others.

'Of course,' Rachel said warmly.

Gill didn't speak. She was at a loss to understand how Liz could fall in love again so quickly. It was true Finn Hunter was a good man. Look at how he had managed to get the entire community around him, how he'd revived the local paper, how he'd provided support to his daughter and grandson when his son-in-law died. He'd become a legend in their small community. But for Liz who, like Gill, had experienced how duplicitous men could be, to get involved in a new relationship so quickly, to give up her independence… Gill mentally shook her head.

'Gill?' Poppy said.

'Of course,' Gill said. 'But it is rather sudden. Are you sure?'

'I'm sure.' Liz beamed. There was no other word to describe the glow on her face. 'The girls are all happy about it too,' she said, referring to her three daughters, 'and Finn's family. I can understand your reluctance, Gill. I was like you for ages after Tommy. I never expected to find someone like Finn. There may be someone out there for you too. You never know what the future has in store.'

'The future!' Gill scoffed. 'My future seems to be entangled with Max and his never-ending demands.' *And do I even have a future?* 'Sorry, I didn't mean to put a downer on the conversation. Lunch is ready. Why don't you all go through to the table, and I'll bring in the food?'

The three women trooped through to the other room and, by the time Gill carried in a tray containing the chicken and vegetables, she had calmed down and the others were chatting about a photo shoot which had taken place on the beach the day before.

'You should have seen it, Gill,' Poppy said laughing. 'Rachel and I were there with our dogs, Finn was there with his grandson and his dog, Rhana Black brought along a pair of her spaniels, and the mayor had his labrador. There were several others too, and it took ages for the photographer to get all the animals to sit nicely.'

'What was it about?' Gill asked.

'Oh, of course, you wouldn't know,' Liz said. 'It seems a couple of the councillors have been speaking out against allowing dogs to access the beach off leash, so our mayor and Finn got their heads together and *The Echo* is going to feature a group of some of the dog owners who use the beach.'

'Oh!' It seemed a lot of fuss about nothing to Gill, but she supposed it was an important issue for dog owners. Dogs had been free to run on the beach for as long as she could remember, and they didn't do any harm.

Then something Liz had said, caught her attention, something about the mayor and his labrador. It had been a labrador in the car which she had almost run into on her way home from her morning swim, a chocolate labrador, and a chocolate labrador which had comforted her when the mayor had found her in tears outside the medical centre. She hadn't paid any attention to the driver of the car. Could it have been him? Had she made a fool of herself in front of him again?

Twelve

Joe cursed as the Prius came flying out of the car park. 'Sorry, Coco,' he said as he swerved to avoid the car, causing Coco to pull her head in from the window from where she'd been enjoying the view and the breeze. Then he recognised the driver. It was Gill Dickson, driving like a madwoman. What was wrong with her? One day in tears, the next driving dangerously. Although not exactly the next day. It was strange, he mused, how you might never bump into someone for years, then your paths started to cross. Some would call it fate. He just called it bad luck… or was it good luck? And what was she doing down here at this time in the morning? Was she one of the crazy group of wild swimmers, mostly women, who braved the ocean at dawn regardless of the weather?

Joe didn't normally come to the beach as early as this, but he hadn't been sleeping well since Erica arrived. Since Barb died, he'd become used to the emptiness of the house, to the familiar sounds. The presence of another person changed things. It took a bit of getting used to. This morning, when he found himself unable to get back to sleep, he'd gone to the kitchen to make himself a cup of tea. Coco had wakened and decided it was time for a walk. As a result, here he was, arriving at the beach at an ungodly hour, just as the early morning swimmers were leaving.

Unclipping Coco's leash, Joe wandered across the beach to the edge of the water and gazed out towards the horizon. It was beautiful at this time of the morning. He could understand why people chose to rise early and greet the dawn in the ocean. But it wasn't for him.

His thoughts turned to the woman whose car he'd almost collided with. He wondered what made her tick. She was a friend of Poppy's. He supposed he could ask Cam about her. But then Cam might think he was interested in her, and he wasn't, was he? He was just curious. He knew of her reputation as a lawyer. It was good of Poppy to suggest Erica speak with her. His sister needed advice, more advice than he could give her. And Gill Dickson was the person to provide it.

By the time he and Coco arrived home, Erica was up and bustling around in the kitchen.

'I guessed you'd taken Coco for a walk,' she said. 'I bet you're hungry. Scrambled eggs and bacon?'

'Sounds good. I'll take a shower while you're making them.' Since Coco was standing over her empty bowl, Joe filled it and her water bowl, before heading to the ensuite.

Washing himself in the shower, his thoughts went again to Gill Dickson. It wasn't good, seeing her in tears, or driving like a madwoman. He wondered what was ailing her. Something intrigued him about the elegant woman with the cropped black hair. He wondered also if fate would cause their paths to cross again. He also wondered, as he was drying off, if he would like to bump into her again. But Erica shouting that breakfast was ready left that thought unanswered.

'What are you doing today?' Joe asked when he had demolished the large breakfast Erica had prepared. He could get used to eating like this. Since he'd been living alone, breakfast had consisted of toast with vegemite or marmalade.

'I'm meeting Livvy for lunch,' Erica said. 'I decided it's time I made an effort to catch up with old friends. I bumped into her when I went in to register with the local medical centre.' She hesitated. 'And I've made an appointment with the solicitor Poppy recommended.'

Joe paused, his cup partway to his mouth. 'Gill Dickson?' He wasn't sure why he suddenly felt a rush of heat to his face.

'That's her. I called her office and I'm seeing her tomorrow at nine.' She twisted her hands. 'I'm not sure how she can help me, but…'

'She has a good reputation. She'll be able to steer you in the right direction.' He had a sudden thought. 'Does Geoff know you've come here?'

'He might guess, but…' Erica bit her lip, '… I'm not sure what he'll do. I don't…' The colour drained from her face.

Joe wished he hadn't asked about Geoff. Erica had been doing so well. 'You'll enjoy seeing Olivia again,' he said, 'and why don't we go out to dinner? You've been doing a lot of cooking since you got here. It's time I treated you. How about I book a table at the yacht club?'

'The yacht club? It's still a thing? Remember how we used to think it would be so grown up to go there on a date?'

Joe chuckled. It was when they were all in their teens, and the yacht club was where their parents went, only taking the children there for special occasions like birthdays. 'It's very much a thing. I eat there a lot. It's undergone a few renovations since then. You'd barely recognise it. The food's pretty good too. Maybe not quite up to the standard of *Crossings*,' he said, remembering he'd promised to take Erica there.

'Let's start with the club and work up to *Crossings*,' Erica said with a smile.

'Let's.'

*

Joe was glad he'd had the foresight to book a table. The yacht club was packed. There were two large tables of groups who looked like they were celebrating birthdays, plus the usual collection of families out for a mid-week dinner. There was a lot of loud chatter and laughter coming from the larger groups as several of the diners were taking photos with their phones.

To Joe's relief, he and Erica were shown to a table at the other side of the restaurant, close to the window which faced the marina.

'This is nice,' Erica said, gazing out at the rows of vessels, many of which were lit up. 'It's grown a lot since I lived here.'

'The whole of Pelican Crossing has grown,' Joe said, 'but luckily, we've managed to retain the unique atmosphere which the tourists love. It was touch and go there for a bit last year when a developer tried to ruin it.'

'What happened?'

'You don't want to know. But suffice to say, he didn't succeed and has since got his comeuppance.' Joe tapped the side of his nose. He had no intention of going into the gory details. It was over and best forgotten.

After they'd placed their orders, chilli prawn pasta for Erica, and smoked eye fillet for Joe, he asked, 'How did your lunch with Olivia go?' He'd been unable to ask her earlier because the planning committee meeting had gone on longer than he anticipated, and he'd been late home, leaving him only enough time to have a quick shower and change before leaving.

'Good.' Erica took a sip of the Seppelt Jaluka chardonnay Joe had ordered. 'It was as if we'd only seen each other yesterday. I'm glad she's still around. And,' she took another sip of wine, 'you'll never guess...' She grinned.

Joe raised an eyebrow and took a sip from his own glass. It was good to see Erica looking so happy.

'She knows Gill Dickson. You know, the solicitor Poppy recommended, the one I'm seeing tomorrow. She and Olivia are in the same book club, and they swim together every morning. Livvy's invited me to go along.'

'To the book club?'

'No, silly. At least, not yet. Swimming. She says it's amazing to be out on the ocean as the sun is rising.'

Joe stared at his sister in amazement. So, he'd been right about Gill. She *was* one of those wild swimmers. But... 'Will you?' he asked.

'Maybe, but not tomorrow. I don't want the first time I meet my future solicitor to be on the beach... and I'm not sure I'm a strong enough swimmer.' She chuckled. 'But it does sound fun. Don't you think so?' she added, when Joe didn't immediately respond.

'Sure,' Joe said, but he knew he didn't sound enthusiastic. It appeared that fate was ensuring Gill Dickson's life was going to become entangled in that of his family, one way or another, and he wasn't really sure how he felt about it.

Thirteen

Gill opened her computer, glad to be starting another busy day. She'd been awake half the night googling images of bumps on tongues and reading about tongue biopsies till she'd finally closed her iPad, disappointed with herself. Her GP had told her not to worry; it was a routine procedure and probably benign. But what if…?

She checked the calendar to see she had a new client coming in at nine. It was always interesting to meet another woman who had decided to leave her marriage. Now Gill was undergoing a divorce herself, she felt more akin to these women, many of whom came to her as a last resort, having tried everything they could think of to save their marriage. Others were fleeing abusive or faithless husbands, eager to be free of their clutches. She wondered which criteria this poor woman would fall under.

The woman who walked into Gill's office looked vaguely familiar. She was tall with grey streaks in her dark hair and striking angular features. Gill checked the note on her desk, but she hadn't met Erica Masters before.

'Hello.' Gill rose to shake hands. 'Please take a seat.' She moved from behind her desk to join the woman on one of the comfortable chairs which sat by a low coffee table. She always took pains to put her clients at ease. 'Would you like coffee or tea?'

Seeming surprised, Erica gave a stiff smile. 'Tea would be lovely, herbal if you have it.'

'No problem.'

As if on cue, Gill's PA appeared in the doorway. 'Two lemon and ginger teas, please, Josie,' she said.

'Thanks.' Erica seemed to relax, but she was still grasping her hands together tightly in her lap.

'I'm Gill, and I'm here to help you in any way I can.' Gill smiled encouragingly. She really felt more at home here, in her office with clients, than she did anywhere else.

Josie appeared again carrying two mugs of tea and a plate of chocolate and ginger biscuits which she placed on the coffee table.

'Thanks, Josie.'

Josie left, closing the door behind her.

Gill picked up one of the mugs and took a sip.

Erica picked up the other and, her hands trembling, did the same.

'Would you like to tell me why you're here?'

'It's difficult... Poppy Taylor recommended you...' Erica took another sip of tea.

'You live in Pelican Crossing?' If Poppy knew her, she must do, but Gill was sure she hadn't seen her before.

'I used to. I grew up here. I've recently returned. I... I left my husband. I'm staying with my brother, Joe Harris.' The words came out in a rush.

Joe Harris's sister. That was why she looked familiar. She had the same angular features as the mayor, the same, grey-streaked dark hair. She was a female version of the man had been so kind to her when he found her in tears, the man whose jeep she'd almost bumped, she reminded herself. And she knew Poppy.

'Poppy's a good friend,' Gill said. 'It was kind of her to recommend me.'

'I'm not sure how you can help me. My husband...' Erica's eyes began to fill.

Gill reached for the box of tissues she kept on the coffee table for this very purpose.

'Thanks. I'm sorry.' Erica wiped her eyes.

'There's nothing to be sorry about. Your husband... do you want to talk about it?'

'Not... I don't... He... We lived in Perth. I didn't tell him I was leaving.' She started to sob again.

Gill waited till the tears had stopped. 'Poppy knew that I could advise you what steps you might take… if you want to.'

Erica raised her eyes to meet Gill's, eyes the same shade of deep brown she remembered gazing into hers with such compassion. Her stomach fluttered. She stifled the memory.

'I want to end my marriage,' Erica said, her voice becoming stronger. 'Geoff has become more and more controlling over the years, especially since Kieren married. My son,' she said, clearly seeing the question in Gill's eyes. 'He and his dad…' She held up two crossed fingers. 'He started to hit me, only in places no one would see, and only when I annoyed him. I thought I could cope, that it was my fault. Then it got worse, it started to happen when things went bad at work. It happened once too often. I waited till he was out of town, then I packed a case and left.'

'Has he tried to contact you?'

'I don't know. I turned off my phone. I didn't want…' She looked down.

'It's okay. I understand.'

'I suppose you've heard it all before,' Erica said bitterly. 'I'm not the first woman to sit here in tears.' She took another tissue from the box and wiped her eyes.

'Women who are happy in their marriages have no need to see me,' Gill said, 'but everyone is different. Now, let me take down some details.' She drew an A4 pad towards her. She always found it to be less inhibiting to her clients for her to write things down. She would set up the file on her computer later.

It was almost an hour later before Erica was ready to leave. By that time, Gill had provided her with information about the length of time she would need to wait before filing for divorce and suggested taking out an AVO – an Aggravated Violence Order – in case her husband decided to follow her to Pelican Crossing.

'I'd also strongly recommend you make an appointment to talk with a therapist,' she said, when Erica rose to leave. 'We have a very good one attached to our local medical centre. I can vouch for Olivia's professionalism.'

'Oh, I know Livvy. We went to school together and were in the same crowd. We had lunch together yesterday. Do you think, because we're friends…?'

'It's up to Olivia. I didn't realise you were friends. She may recommend you see someone else.'

'Thanks. I'll speak with her. And thanks for your help. I feel much better about everything now. I plan to find work here. I was a nurse before Geoff decided he didn't want me to work outside the home. I've applied for a position at the hospital.'

'I'm sure they'll be delighted to have you. It's good to keep busy.'

'Thanks. Joe said he knows you too.'

Gill caught her breath. *He did?* She smiled. 'Pelican Crossing is a small town. Everyone knows everyone else. You must remember that, growing up here.'

'Of course. It was a long time ago. It's easy to forget. But it's good to be back. Thanks, again.'

When Erica had gone, Gill sat for a time, staring into space, the memory of Joe Harris filling her thoughts. What were the chances, she wondered, of his sister walking into her office, a sister who looked so like him that her presence conjured up memories of Gill's own shortcomings and vulnerability, memories she'd rather forget.

Fourteen

Erica was seated at the kitchen table with a cup of the herbal tea she enjoyed when Joe and Coco got home. Now she seemed to be settling down, he had begun taking Coco to the office again, though he could no longer pretend it was to stop the dog from fretting at home.

'How did it go with Gill Dickson?' he asked, pulling a beer out of the fridge after he had filled Coco's bowls, and she was munching down her dinner.

'Good. She was everything you and Poppy said she was. It's as I thought. I won't be able to file for divorce until we've been apart for a year. But she suggested taking out an AVO in the event he decides to turn up.'

'Here?' Automatically, Joe looked around the room.

'Where else? But I can't imagine he would. How would he know?'

'Where else would you go? He knows where I live. He was here for Barb's funeral.' The possibility had been at the back of Joe's mind, but he hadn't wanted to mention it. He was glad Gill had.

'Coco would see him off. Wouldn't you?' she said to the dog who, now she had finished eating, padded over to Erica's side at the sound of her name. 'She also suggested I talk to a therapist. She recommended Livvy.'

'Olivia? Wouldn't she have a conflict of interest?'

'I wondered that too, but Gill said it was up to Livvy. So I dropped into the medical centre afterwards. She recommended I see her colleague. I've made an appointment. We'll see how it goes. I'm not sure how I'll feel, talking to a stranger.'

Joe shrugged. 'Gill's a stranger.'

'Yes, but… she didn't feel like one. I liked her.'

'Good.' Joe didn't know what else to say. The woman he'd only met briefly, to whom he'd felt an immediate attraction, was now his sister's solicitor, privy to all her secrets. It felt odd. He took a swig of beer to cover his confusion.

'I did a shop on the way back. Thought I'd cook some pasta for dinner.' Erica said.

'You don't have to. I can cook.' Erica had fallen into the habit of making dinner and, while Joe enjoyed her cooking, he didn't want her to feel she had to earn her keep. He wasn't sure how much money she had, suspecting she and Geoff had a joint account to which she no longer had access.

'I enjoy it. It's the least I can do when you're letting me stay here rent free.'

'As if I could charge you.' Joe put down his beer to give Erica a hug. 'You're my little sister, always will be. It's my job to take care of you.'

'Maybe when we were growing up, but I'll be fifty next year, Joe. I need to learn to look after myself. Speaking of which, I have an interview at the hospital next week. It sounds promising. So, I'll be out of your hair soon enough.'

'I enjoy having you here. It's been lonely since Barb…'

'Sorry! I didn't mean it like that. I'm glad if me being here has helped.'

'It has,' Joe said, realising it was true. While at first, it had seemed strange to have another person in the house, he was becoming accustomed to Erica's presence. It was different to having Barb there but comforting in an odd sort of way. And Coco liked her. 'You can stay as long as you like.'

'Thanks, Joe.' Erica threw her arms around his neck and kissed his cheek.

Coco stretched, then rose to her feet and nudged Joe.

'Looks like she wants a walk. Some fresh air would do me good too. Want to join us? We can eat when we get back.'

'Love to. I haven't had much exercise today.'

A few minutes later, they were climbing down to the beach, the very section which was to be featured in the paper. A few other dog owners were there too. Finn with his grandson and their young spaniel were making their way across the beach. And old Agnes with her spaniel was strolling along at the edge of the sea her long skirt trailing in the water.

'Joe!' Finn stopped beside Joe and Erica, while the little boy ran on with his dog.

'Finn, this is my sister, Erica. Erica, this is Finn, our local editor.'

'Hello, Erica. Joe's told me about you. Welcome back to Pelican Crossing. I understand you grew up here. I'm very much an incomer.'

'But a very welcome one, from what I've heard. It's good to meet you. I'm looking forward to your column in next week's paper. It would be a great pity to lose this.' She gestured to where the three dogs were now tearing along the beach together.

'It would be a disaster.'

Just then, Sandy returned. 'Can we visit the pelicans on the weekend, Grandy?' he asked. 'Agnes says she's looking after two baby ones.'

'If Agnes says it's okay,' Finn said. 'The old lady with the other spaniel manages the pelican rescue centre,' he explained to a clearly puzzled Erica. 'She's a marvel with the birds, does it all herself with a few volunteers. Sandy has made friends with her over the dogs, and she helped him feel safe in the water again after he suffered a traumatic incident.'

'Grandy says we can,' Sandy yelled, running back to join the old woman.

Finn and Joe laughed, and Erica joined in.

Joe, Erica and Finn chatted for a few more minutes, until Sandy returned with his dog. Then Joe and Erica continued their walk, Coco running ahead.

Agnes had almost disappeared into the distance, her long white hair flying in the breeze.

'How old is she?' Erica asked.

'No one knows. She seems to have been here for ever and old for as long as I remember. Don't you remember her?'

'Vaguely. I guess I was interested in other things.'

They walked on in silence, Coco running back and forth. It was pleasant, the only sounds the waves lapping on the beach and a distant siren.

Then Erica said, 'The wild swimming Olivia talked about. I think I'll join them.'

Joe stared at her in the growing darkness. 'Are you sure? They go out very early.'

'I'm sure.' Erica nodded.

*

The pasta turned out to be delicious, the sauce an unusual mix of broccoli and kale with ranch dressing and parmesan cheese, a recipe Erica said she'd discovered on the internet, and which Geoff had hated when she cooked it for him. One more black mark against his brother-in-law. Erica was a good cook. She'd learned from their mother and enjoyed perfecting her skills in the kitchen during her marriage.

'How was *your* day?' she asked when they had progressed to coffee in the living room, Coco in her usual spot at Joe's feet.

'Okay. Not a lot happening at the moment.' Joe paused to take a sip of coffee and ruffle Coco's ears. 'I did catch up with Finn for a beer at lunchtime. I told you about the article he's putting together promoting the dog beach.'

'Yes, the one you and Coco had your photos taken for?

'Seems we're to be featured in next week's edition of *The Echo*. I'm not too sure how two of my fellow councillors will react.'

'I thought that was the point… to get community support.'

'Yes.' Joe scratched his head. It had been Finn's idea, but Joe had put it there. Now he wondered if it would all backfire on him. 'We'll have to see,' he said. 'There's a council meeting next week and I'd not be surprised to see it on the agenda.'

'Don't you make up the agenda?'

'Not all of it. Each councillor is able to add items which they deem relevant.'

'Oh! Not so easy being mayor, then?'

'It has its moments.'

'About the swimming, Joe. I waken early. It would be better than lying awake thinking. You wouldn't mind, would you?'

'It's up to you.' It should have occurred to Joe Erica might still be troubled by thoughts about Geoff. 'I might come with you,' he said. 'Not to swim,' he added, before she could remind him it was a group of mostly women swimmers. 'Coco would enjoy an early morning walk.' *And I'd enjoy the opportunity to bump into Gill Dickson again.*

Fifteen

Gill was startled to see her latest client at the beach. Then she remembered… Erica was a friend of Olivia's. No doubt it was she who had invited her. Then her eyes moved to where another familiar figure and a chocolate-coloured dog were getting out of a car. It couldn't be, but it was… Joe Harris and his dog.

Gill shouldn't have been surprised. Erica was his sister, after all. It was only natural he'd accompany her to the beach. But Gill was suddenly very aware of her old black swimsuit, the one she'd dragged out from the back of a drawer when she'd begun these early morning swims, reasoning no one would care what she wore. And no one had. But the thought that Joe Harris who'd already seen her at a disadvantage – twice – might see her like this, made her want to disappear.

She dropped her towel on the beach and, leaping into the ocean, and gasping at the shock of the temperature, she swam out to sea as fast as her arms would take her. Once out there, far from the beach, she turned on her back as she usually did and gazed up at the sky, waiting for the sense of peace to envelop her. But all she could think of was the man who, even now, would be walking along the beach with his dog.

It was a nice dog, from what she could remember from their meeting over coffee and seeing its head hanging out of the window of the car with which she'd had a near miss. She liked dogs. It was the dog's owner who she was unsure about. Joe Harris was the mayor, a respected member of the community, a widower. She'd known his wife before her illness took over her life. Barb Harris had been a member of Gill's book club, always one of the first to comment on the book of the month which, unlike Gill, she always read. You could always tell who had actually read the book, and who, like Gill often did, relied on repeating what they had read in the reviews from other readers.

The sky changed colour. The day had begun. It was time to return to the beach. With a bit of luck, Joe and his dog would have gone.

'Hello, Gill,' Erica said shyly, picking up her towel which lay next to Gill's. 'I didn't know you were part of this group.'

Before Gill could reply, Olivia joined them. 'What did you think, Erica? Isn't it amazing to be out here as the sun's rising? You've met Gill?' she asked, as if suddenly noticing Gill.

'I have, and yes, it is,' Erica replied, towelling her hair. 'It's so peaceful out there, as if you're the only person in the world.'

Gill nodded. She knew exactly what Erica meant. Even if she didn't always manage to achieve that sense of peace, it was something she continued to strive for, wonderful when she attained it. She was glad if Erica had managed to put her worries aside while she was swimming. Maybe, Gill thought, she should introduce some of the other clients to the group. But then it wouldn't feel the same, a tiny voice in the back of her mind told her. She preferred to keep the different parts of her life separate, compartmentalised. This was the first time her work life had impinged on her personal one.

Gill was on her way to her car, wearing a loose robe, a towel around her neck, when she became aware of a panting sound behind her. Turning quickly, she was shocked to see the chocolate-coloured labrador and its owner close behind her.

She stopped, flustered, her hand going to her wet hair which was plastered to her head. All she wanted to do was get into her car, drive home, and take a hot shower. She didn't want to speak with Joe Harris, to have him see her like this. But it was too late.

'I thought it was you,' Joe said, as the dog sniffed at Gill's ankles, her tongue tickling her toes. 'I wanted to thank you for being so helpful to Erica yesterday.'

'I was glad to be of help, but I was just doing my job.' She shuffled her feet. She was eager to get away but didn't want to appear rude. He was the mayor, after all, and his sister was her client. This wasn't a situation in which she felt at ease. Couldn't the man sense her discomfort, that she was wet, barely dressed, and needed to get home?

Evidently not, because he continued, 'I thought it was you I saw the other morning… In the Prius,' he added with a grin when she didn't immediately respond.

'Sorry about that. My mind was elsewhere. If I caused any damage…' Was this what it was about? Gill was sure her car hadn't made contact with his.

'Not at all.' It was his turn to look ill at ease. 'When Erica said she was coming to the beach this morning to join the swimmers, I took the opportunity to join her. Oh, not to swim,' he chuckled, clearly seeing her surprised expression. 'I thought it would give me the opportunity to meet you again.'

Gill stared at him as if he was mad. He wanted to meet her again? After seeing her in tears, after she almost ran into him? 'But…' she began.

'I know. I could have contacted you at your office, even checked out your phone number, but this…' he scratched his head, and gave a lopsided grin, '… it seemed like a good idea at the time. I'm sorry if I took you unawares. The point is…' He kicked at the sand by his feet, causing the dog to shy away. 'I wondered if you'd like to have a drink with me sometime… or dinner?'

Stunned, Gill was lost for words. She looked down to where the dog was gazing up at her with soulful eyes, then up to where Joe's eyes held a similar expression. 'I… I…' she stammered, her only desire to get away from this awkward situation as quickly as possible. 'Y… yes, of course,' she found herself saying, only to see his face light up.

'Great, I'll call you.' Joe turned away, pressing his car key as he went, the dog loping along behind him.

Gill stared after him in dismay. *What had she done?*

Sixteen

Joe was humming to himself when Erica joined him in the car.

'You sound happy. Good walk?' Erica asked, rubbing her hair with the towel.

'Very good. How was your swim?'

'Amazing. I can't believe the sense of peace I experienced out there just as the sun was rising. It's magical. And they seem to be a nice group. Gill Dickson was there too. I told you she and Livvy are friends.'

'You did.' Joe decided to keep his exchange with Gill to himself for now. He had the impression she'd agreed to see him as a way of ending the conversation. She had looked so vulnerable standing there, water trickling down her face from her wet hair, hair which was plastered to her skull showing off her sharp features. He was sure she had no idea how attractive she looked. 'So, you intend to make this a daily occurrence?'

'I think so. Out there on the ocean, the sky above, it's easy to forget...'

Joe felt humbled. Erica was still worrying about Geoff... even though he was on the other side of the country.

'Will you and Coco be joining me?'

'Probably not. I enjoyed today, but it's a bit early for us.' And he'd done what he set out to do.

Erica laughed. 'I thought you might decide that. If I can have the car...'

'Of course. I don't need it till later. You might want to think about getting one for yourself.'

'I would if…' Erica bit her lip.

'If it's a matter of money. I can lend you the price of a car.'

'Thanks, Joe, but I don't want to be beholden to you. It's enough you've put a roof over my head.'

'It's no trouble. How about I ask around, see if anyone has an old one they want to sell?'

Erica smiled. 'There's no stopping you, is there? But it would be good to have my own wheels.'

'Especially if you get a job at the hospital.'

'You're right. I'll be able to pay you back then. Okay, thanks.'

'Good.'

They had just reached home, and Erica was sliding out of the car when the loose garment she was wearing slid off her shoulder.

'What's that?' Joe asked, seeing what looked like a large bruise on his sister's upper arm.

'I didn't want you to see,' she said, quickly pulling the garment up to cover it, her eyes filling with tears.

'Did Geoff do that?' Joe pulled Erica to him and pushed down the loose top to reveal more bruising on her arms. 'Why didn't you tell me?'

Erica pulled away and covered herself up again. 'There was no point,' she said, her voice flat. 'What could you do? I'm fine now.'

Joe felt a flash of anger threaten to erupt. He wished Geoff was here right now. He'd like to make him pay for how he'd treated Erica. But he supposed she was right. What could he have done? 'You were right to leave him,' he said. 'If I'd known…'

'But you didn't, no one did. And I'm here now. I'm safe.'

Joe pulled his sister into a warm hug. She was right. She was safe here, and he meant to ensure she remained that way.

*

Despite the revelations about Geoff's treatment of Erica, Joe was smiling to himself when he arrived at the office. After their converstion about her bruises, Erica had become more cheerful over breakfast, planning to check out some other old schoolfriends Olivia had told her were still living in Pelican Crossing, and he had plans to call Gill before she had time to change her mind.

Settling behind his desk, he picked up the photo which had sat there for ages. It was of him and Barb, taken on the evening of his inauguration as mayor. He had been so proud that night, proud he'd been the choice of Pelican Crossing and proud to have Barb by his side.

Barb would have liked Gill. They were similar in some ways. When they'd first met, Barb had been a bit like Gill – prickly, proud… and vulnerable. Over the years she'd mellowed. She always said it was Joe's influence, that he'd given her the confidence she lacked, completed her. He remembered how, in the final days of her illness, she'd told him not to be lonely, encouraged him to find someone to love, someone to spend the rest of his life with.

He hadn't thought of her words till now, content with his own company, with his memories, despite the loneliness that often overtook him… until he got Coco. It was a strange quirk of fate that, now he was no longer alone, now Erica was living with him, was when he'd finally met someone who might be a cure for the loneliness that had plagued him since Barb's death.

Joe checked his diary, an idea occurring to him. He picked up his phone.

*

Gill had been annoyed with herself ever since she left the beach. Standing in the shower, she blushed at the memory of how she had stammered like a schoolgirl at Joe Harris's invitation. Why did he always seem to see her at her worst? And why had he invited her on a date?

Maybe he wouldn't call, she consoled herself. Surely the invitation had been a spur of the moment thing, something he'd already be regretting. But hadn't he mentioned wanting to bump into her again? She rinsed the shampoo from her hair wishing she could rinse away the memory of her embarrassment just as easily.

By the time Gill arrived in the office, she had almost persuaded herself Joe wouldn't call, despite a tiny part of her wondering what it would be like to spend time with him, time which she'd prepared for, instead of being caught at a disadvantage. It was years since she'd been on a date; she'd avoided men ever since Max left and had only dated a few before him. She wouldn't know how to behave.

Scrolling through her emails, Gill discovered her first client had cancelled. She sighed. It happened, more often than she'd like. Either the woman had second thoughts, the husband persuaded her to reconsider, or she just got cold feet. Gill could understand the last. She often wished she could call off the whole divorce process, forget about Max, and pretend the marriage had never happened. But it had. There was Freya. She could never regret having her daughter, even if she did refuse to communicate. Gill checked her phone – it had become a habit – but there was still nothing from her daughter.

Luckily, there was no new email from her solicitor either, which meant no new demands from Max. She was still waiting to hear his response to the last communication, the rebuttal to his demands, which had gone to his solicitor through hers.

She was about to immerse herself in the file she was setting up for Erica Masters when her phone rang.

'Gill Dickson, how may I help you?'

There was a moment's silence, then, 'Gill, it's Joe, Joe Harris.'

Gill felt her stomach flutter. Her mouth went dry. 'Hello,' she said, annoyed he'd caught her unprepared again. *Did he do it deliberately?* Even as the thought crossed her mind, she knew how ridiculous it was.

'I promised I'd call and thought it best to do it right away… before you forgot about me.' He chuckled.

At the sound, the tension in her stomach began to uncoil. What was she fussed about? Joe Harris wasn't Max. He was the town mayor, a man of good character. He'd been a good husband to Barb until her untimely death. And he was the brother of a client, she reminded herself. She'd always vowed to keep her personal and professional life separate and till now had succeeded. It had been easy, since she had no personal life to speak of.

She grasped the phone tighter, aware he was going to repeat his invitation. Should she decline? Would it be rude? Or could she break the vow she'd made to herself never to let another man into her life?

'Look, this may seem like a strange request,' Joe said, 'but I've been invited to attend a Chamber of Commerce dinner in Bellbird Bay. It's tomorrow evening. Sorry about the short notice. The invite includes a plus one, and I don't have one. I wondered if… I'll understand if you say no.'

'What about your sister?' *Surely he could take Erica?*

'She's still pretty shell-shocked from what happened and not up to facing a room full of strangers.'

But I am?

Gill could almost hear him holding his breath as he waited for her response.

'I suppose…' It wasn't an agreement but wasn't a refusal either. Bellbird Bay was some distance down the coast. Gill didn't know anyone there, apart from Ali Wells, and it was unlikely she'd be attending a Chamber of Commerce dinner. Thinking of Ali reminded Gill she had still to arrange a date for the director of the women's centre to speak to her Zonta group.

While she'd been thinking, Joe had obviously taken her words for agreement.

'Oh, good. The dinner should be decent, and you might find it interesting. We've done a few joint activities with Bellbird Bay over the years. Their mayor is quite a character, a local surfing hero.'

Gill recalled hearing something about him, how he'd been the local surfing champion three years running. A strange choice for mayor, she'd thought at the time. It could be an interesting evening.

Joe was still speaking. 'It's to be held at *The Leonard Family Resort*, the local hotel which was renovated by Leo Carlson a few years ago. He used to own the Leonard international chain of hotels before moving to Bellbird Bay.'

'Oh!' It was too late to refuse now, and Gill was curious to see the hotel which she'd heard of, along with its owner. It had made the local and national news when Leo Carlson had sold the chain of hotels to move to the small coastal town. 'Dress code?'

'It's black tie, I'm afraid, so something smart. And we need to allow enough time for travel in case of traffic, since it's the weekend. Can I pick you up around five-thirty?'

'That'll be fine. I'll email you my address.'

'That would be good. Thanks for saying "yes".'

'No problem.'

As Gill hung up, she felt an unexpected flutter of excitement. It might be fun. There had been little of that in her life recently. And at least it might take her mind off her worries.

Seventeen

Gill pulled the little black dress out of the wardrobe. It was her standby for formal occasions. Was it too formal for the Chamber of Commerce dinner? If only she could ask someone, but then they'd know she was attending with Joe Harris – she, who had sworn off men.

It would have to do, she decided. Joe had said black tie, and this was the most appropriate outfit she owned. Since his phone call the day before, Gill had lost count of the times her hand had reached for her phone to tell him she'd changed her mind. But each time, she had stopped before making the call. She must be mad.

Now it was five o'clock. In half an hour he'd be here, and they'd be on their way down the coast. It wasn't a long trip, but long enough to spend with someone who was practically a stranger. What would they talk about? She wasn't good at small talk, unless it was about work or one of the charitable organisations she belonged to. Maybe she could encourage him to talk about himself. Wasn't that what you were supposed to do on a date? A date? She was going on a date. Gill got that fluttery feeling in her stomach again, the one she'd felt in her office when the call from Joe ended.

While all this was going through her mind, Gill had managed to get dressed, apply makeup and brush her hair into its usual style. Now she slipped her feet into a pair of black high-heeled sandals – thank goodness Joe was taller than her – and examined herself in the mirror. She nodded and smiled at the image she presented. She looked, as always, the consummate professional. She was ready for whatever the evening had to offer.

The trip down the coast to Bellbird Bay was easier than Gill had expected. While at first, she asked Joe questions about his role as mayor, the conversation soon turned to books and music, and she discovered they had a lot in common.

'Barb belonged to a book club,' he said, when she expressed her surprise at his eclectic taste in books, 'and I always read them too. It gave us a common interest, and I discovered authors I'd never have found otherwise.'

'It's my book club too.'

'Really? I didn't know.'

'Barb was a lovely lady. You must miss her.'

'Yes.' Joe sighed heavily, and Gill wondered if it had been the wrong thing to say. What did one say to a widower about his deceased wife?

'Thanks. It's good to hear you speak of Barb. So many people avoid mentioning her. It's as if she never existed. We were together for over thirty years. You can't just wipe that out. But…' he sighed again, '… life goes on.' He glanced over at Gill and smiled. 'You've been married too.'

Gill didn't know if it was a question. She thought everyone knew about her and Max. 'Yes, I still am.'

'I'm sorry. I didn't know…'

'It's okay. It's not something I talk about. Only a few friends are privy to the fact that while I can arrange divorces for others, I can't seem to get my own settled.'

'I didn't mean to intrude.'

'It's okay.' Gill realised it was. While she was normally at pains to keep her personal life to herself, she didn't mind Joe knowing. He'd have to find out anyway if they were to become friends, she thought, suddenly struck by the realisation it might be nice to have Joe Harris as a friend. He was proving to be good company.

*

When they walked into the hotel, Gill was immediately struck by how spacious the foyer was. The large open area held a few comfortable-looking sofas and low tables, with a reception desk to one side. This evening, it was filled with groups of well-dressed people, all of whom seemed to know each other. Gill was glad she'd chosen the black dress. It was an unusual experience for her to find herself in a room full of strangers.

Joe ushered her towards a group of people standing in one corner. On the way, they paused to allow her to pick up a glass of champagne from one of the waiters moving through the crowd, while Joe chose a beer.

'This is Will Rankin, and Cleo,' Joe said when they reached the group. 'Will's mayor here in Bellbird Bay. Meet Gill Dickson,' he said to them.

Gill smiled at Cleo and shook Will's outstretched hand. He seemed an odd choice for mayor, looking more like the surfer Joe had said he used to be. His faded blond hair was tied back in a bun, and he seemed uncomfortable in the dinner suit and bow tie. Gill was sure he'd be more at home in board shorts and a tee-shirt.

Will turned to introduce the other couple in the group and Gill's eyes widened in surprise to see Ali Wells.

'I know this lady,' Ali said. 'Lovely to meet you again, Gill. This is my husband, Neil. He owns the local bookshop,' she said clearly seeing Gill's puzzled expression.

'And lovely to see Joe with a partner,' Cleo said. 'He's been on his own too long.'

'Oh, we're not...' Gill began, but her attempt at an explanation was lost as another couple joined the group and were introduced as Leo and Greta Carlson. Gill recognised Greta from her forays down to Bellbird Bay to visit Greta's boutique, *Birds of a Feather*, and from when Greta judged *Fashions of the Field* at the previous year's Melbourne Cup Luncheon in Pelican Crossing. It appeared she knew some people here, after all.

At the sound of a bell, people began to move towards a door leading to the restaurant where Gill discovered she and Joe were seated at a table with the six people to whom they'd been chatting. She was seated between Joe and Ali, giving her the opportunity to renew her friendship with the other woman and apologise for not having been in touch.

As Joe had predicted, the meal was delicious, bowls of vichyssoise, followed by steak which melted in the mouth and was served with tiny potatoes, broccolini and baby carrots. The dessert was a decadent crème brûlée.

When coffee was served, Will Rankin rose and made his way to a podium. He welcomed everyone with a few jokes, then said, 'It's my pleasure tonight to introduce our guest speaker. Several of you will already be familiar with Joe Harris, mayor of neighbouring Pelican Crossing. Like *The Bellbird Bugle*, his town's local newspaper was a casualty of the regional consortium's decision to go digital and close down our local newspapers. Unlike Bellbird Bay, Pelican Crossing, led by their mayor, fought back and succeeded in funding the birth of a new paper which has risen like a phoenix from the ashes. He's here tonight to tell us how he did it, and hopefully explain how we can learn from his example.'

Everyone cheered and banged on their tables as Joe rose to take Will's place at the podium.

Gill was stunned. Joe hadn't said anything about being the guest speaker. Confused, she missed the beginning of his speech, only tuning in to hear him praise Finn Hunter, editor of both *The Crossing Courier* and now *The Crossing Echo*, and former editor of *The Bellbird Bugle*. She listened avidly as he described how the town had come together to raise the funds required to establish the new paper and encouraged Bellbird Bay to follow their example. He resumed his seat to an enthusiastic round of applause.

'Well done,' she whispered when he took his place beside her again, gulping down a full glass of water. This was an aspect of Joe she wasn't familiar with. She was impressed. 'You didn't tell me.'

Joe shrugged. 'Nothing to tell, really. I'm glad it's over.'

Now the evening was almost at an end, a wave of chatter erupted in the room. At their table, both Will and Leo were eager to question Joe about the details of the funding drive, but he batted away their questions, referring them to Finn who he said was in a better position to answer them than he was. 'It's him you should have here tonight,' he said, 'not me.'

Although not completely *au fait* with the funding process, Gill thought Joe was being too modest. From what she'd heard, Joe had been the driving force behind it.

Suddenly, it seemed, people began to leave. As Gill and Joe walked to the door with Will and Cleo, Cleo said, 'I hope we see you again soon, Gill. It would be good to see a friendly face at these boring regional mayoral gatherings Will and I have to attend.'

'Oh, I don't think...' But, yet again, her response was drowned out by Leo and Greta joining them to make their farewells.

Gill was embarrassed when she got into the car with Joe.

Neither spoke till they had left Bellbird Bay behind, then Joe said, 'I'm sorry. I didn't think... Will and Cleo didn't know Barb. They've only ever seen me on my own. It didn't occur to me they'd draw the wrong conclusion... I could see you were embarrassed.'

'Thanks. It's okay.' So why did Gill feel worse hearing Joe's stumbling apology? 'They seem like a nice group of people.'

'They are. I hadn't met the other two couples before, but you know Ali?'

'And Greta. I've patronised Greta's boutique. And I visited the women's centre where Ali is director. They do such good work, I wanted to see it firsthand... and to invite her to speak to the Pelican Crossing Zonta group. Seeing her again reminded me I still have to set a date.'

'Of course, you belong to all these organisations, don't you?'

Gill felt a tinge of irritation. What was he suggesting?

As if sensing her annoyance, he said, 'I didn't mean to disparage you... or the groups you belong to. I expect that, like me, you need to be seen to be taking an active role in such things.'

'Exactly.' The word came out more strongly than Gill intended. 'Tell me about Bellbird Bay,' she said, to soften the atmosphere which was in danger of becoming fraught. 'I've only been there to replenish my wardrobe at *Birds of a Feather*. The women's centre is on the outskirts of the town.'

'It's much like Pelican Crossing,' Joe said. 'A tad smaller. It's more of a surfing town than ours, with a thriving surf club and surf culture. Will still runs his surf school, and his son designs and makes surfboards. He's a surfing champion too, a chip off the old block.'

'And Ali's husband owns the local bookshop? I think I've seen it when I came down to shop.'

'It belonged to his father, but the old man's not up to it these days. I've only heard about it from Finn Hunter. He was the editor of the Bellbird Bay local paper before moving to Pelican Crossing.'

'You said.' Gill remembered Joe's speech. 'That was a wonderful talk you gave,' she said. 'I hope it bears fruit and they can revive their local paper too.'

'I hope so. It won't be easy. We were able to resurrect ours before it died completely. They'd have to start from scratch.'

'Mmm.'

'Tell me a bit about yourself,' Joe said, changing the subject. 'What made you decide to specialise in divorce and family law?'

For the rest of the trip, Gill gave Joe a potted version of her law career, making him laugh with some of her more amusing anecdotes.

'And it hasn't put you off men?' he asked with a chuckle when she had finished.

'Actually, it has.' Gill hesitated before adding, 'Tonight is the first evening I've spent with a man since my husband left.'

'I feel honoured,' Joe said.

Gill felt rather than saw him glance at her. 'Not really,' she said. 'You'd been kind to me. It would have been churlish to decline. We all need friends.'

'Thank you. And I'm sorry again you felt embarrassed. Friends?'

'Friends,' she agreed, pleased he didn't want anything more intimate. He was a nice man, but she wasn't ready to let down the barriers she'd constructed around her emotions.

Eighteen

It was late when Joe got home from dropping Gill off, and Erica was already in bed. He poured himself a glass of the Highland Park malt he'd received for Christmas from the council, which he kept for special occasions, and took it out onto the deck. Coco, who had awakened when she heard him come in, padded after him and lay down at his feet when he dropped into the old wicker chair he should probably have thrown out years ago. Barb had always nagged him about it, but it was comfortable, and he liked to sit there and think.

Tonight, as he gazed up at the stars, his thoughts were about the woman he'd spent the evening with. Gill Dickson was a strange one, a bag of contradictions. On the one hand she was attractive, intelligent, interesting and good company, on the other she was quick to take offence, easily embarrassed, and as tightly wound as the spring of the old grandfather clock which had belonged to his parents and sat in his hallway. Joe had felt her almost physical withdrawal when Cleo assumed they were a couple. He wondered what had happened in her marriage to make her this way, or if it was the result of seeing so many other marriages fall apart. He knew he and Barb had been lucky to have had over thirty happy years together. But he was a firm believer you made your own luck, and that marriage was something to work at. He and Barb had hugged a lot, had said they loved each other every day, and had rarely disagreed.

When the car had stopped outside her apartment block, she'd thanked Joe for inviting her, said she'd enjoyed the evening, and he'd thanked her for coming and said he'd enjoyed it too. He'd meant what he said, but had she been honest with him, or was she only being polite? He got the impression she was good at that, at hiding her feelings under a layer of politeness. He supposed it came with the job.

Joe sighed and took a sip of the Scotch, savouring the peaty flavour on his tongue. 'What do you think, Coco?' he asked the dog, whose ears shot up at the sound of her name. 'Should I invite Gill Dickson out again, or leave her alone?'

*

Erica was sitting on the deck with Coco at her feet when Joe emerged next morning. 'How was the dinner?' she asked, one hand ruffling Coco's ears. 'I didn't hear you come in.'

'I was late, then Coco and I sat outside for a bit. The dinner was good.'

'And…?'

'There's no "and". It was the usual sort of do, good food, good company. They seemed to like what I had to say.'

'And Gill?'

'She said she enjoyed it too. Turned out she knew a couple of the women. One who owns a dress shop and one who's the director of the women's centre.'

'I've heard of it. There's a women's refuge too. It's the sort of place I might have ended up in, if I didn't have such a kind big brother.' Erica attempted a laugh but didn't quite succeed. Joe could see she meant it.

'Just as well you did, then. And it being Sunday, why doesn't your kind brother take you out to breakfast?'

'You don't have to.'

'I'd like to. Cam is always telling me I should go to *The Blue Dolphin Café* for Sunday breakfast. He and Poppy have been going there for years, since Poppy's kids were little, and they're all grown now.'

'Okay, you've twisted my arm. But I expect you to tell me more about how you and my solicitor got on last night,' she chuckled.

'Nothing to tell. We enjoyed each other's company and decided we could both do with a new friend.'

'Hmm.' Erica didn't pursue it, but Joe felt he wasn't off the hook, that she'd come back to it later. He hoped when she did, he'd be able to fend her off again.

As soon as they were in sight of the café, Joe could see Cam and Poppy. They were seated at one of the outside tables in a patch of sunlight.

'Hey there. Isn't it a glorious morning. Why don't you join us?' Poppy said, when they reached them.

'Good to see you again,' Poppy said to Erica when they had all hugged. 'I hope you took my advice.'

'I did. Gill was very helpful.' She seemed about to say more when to Joe's relief, the waitress arrived to take their orders.

The next few minutes were taken up with Poppy recommending the eggs benedict, and Cam the big breakfast, the couple laughing as they revealed it was what they'd eaten for Sunday breakfast for years. Erica decided to follow Poppy's recommendation, while Joe accepted Cam's. Joe ordered a macchiato, and Erica a peppermint tea.

By the time they'd placed their orders, there had been no further mention of Gill. Joe and Cam started to discuss an issue which had cropped up at the marina, while he could hear Erica and Poppy chatting about Poppy's grandchildren. Joe wondered if the talk about grandchildren might be upsetting for Erica, given her estrangement from her son and daughter-in-law, but there was nothing he could do about it.

Erica was very quiet on the drive home. Glancing across at her, Joe said, 'I'm sorry Poppy chose to rattle on about her grandchildren. Being a grandmother is a pretty new experience for her and she does tend to want to talk about it. It must have struck a chord.'

'She couldn't have known,' Erica said. 'When I spoke with Gill, I suggested contacting Kieren and Briony, but she advised me against it.' She sighed. 'She's right, of course. Kieren would tell Geoff, and...' She fell silent again.

Joe shot her another glance, wondering how long it would be before Geoff worked out where Erica was, and how long it would take him to follow her to Pelican Crossing.

Erica must have been thinking the same thing. 'I should go ahead with organising the AVO Gill recommended,' she said, 'in case...'

'Good idea,' Joe said, unsure how he would cope if his brother-in-law appeared at his door.

Back home, they were greeted by Coco, who was excited at their return and eager for a walk.

'Want to join us?' Joe asked, worried at how quiet Erica had become on the drive home.

'Not this time,' Erica said. 'I'm okay,' she added, clearly seeing Joe's concerned expression. 'I want to check out what I need to do if I go ahead with an AVO. You take Coco on your walk. I'll be fine. I'll have lunch waiting for you.'

Joe was about to protest, the big breakfast he'd eaten still weighing heavy on him. But he knew she was just trying to be helpful.

'You sure you won't come?' Joe was loath to leave her.

'I'm sure.'

'Okay. Here, Coco,' he said to the dog who was waiting patiently by the door.

He and Coco headed to the beach where he unfastened the dog's leash to allow her to run. She immediately raced off to join a couple of other dogs which were diving into the waves. Nearby, walking in the shallows, were old Agnes, the pelican lady, and a small boy Joe recognised as Finn's grandson.

'Joe!'

Turning, Joe saw Finn coming towards him. 'Hey, Finn. Doing grandfather duty today?'

'Liz and Adele are busy cooking lunch, and I've been banished from the kitchen,' he said. 'What about you?'

'I left Erica resting, but she's promised to have lunch ready too. Young Sandy looks happy.' He gestured to where the boy was laughing with Agnes.

'He's a different child from what he was. Having the pup has helped, along with Agnes's encouragement. We were beginning to think he'd never go near the ocean again, but I reckon we'll have him swimming by summer.'

'I'm glad.' Joe knew how seeing his father drown had been traumatic for the little boy, resulting in him being afraid of the water. He knew Olivia had helped his recovery too, and hoped the counsellor she'd recommended could do the same for Erica. He hated to see his sister so unhappy and cursed his brother-in-law for how he'd treated her. She had her interview at the hospital next week. Hopefully, if she was offered a nursing position, it would help her make a fresh start.

He chatted to Finn, while they watched Sandy and the dogs, then his friend checked his watch. 'Time to go,' he said, and called to his grandson who raced back with his dog. Coco joined them, making Joe realise that perhaps it was time for him to go home too.

On his way home, Joe reflected how his friend had changed in the past few months… ever since he'd got together with Liz. It was amazing what the companionship of a good woman could do, he thought, wondering if he would ever enjoy that again himself. His thoughts turned to the woman he'd spent the previous evening with. Gill Dickson was a bit of an enigma. It had been a good evening. They'd got along well. He'd begun to wonder if maybe he was ready for another relationship. Then she'd seemed to withdraw, and they'd agreed to be friends. Well, he consoled himself, friendship was a good start.

Nineteen

When Gill awoke, she was aware of a sense of dread. It only took a few moments for her to remember. It was today she was to have the biopsy. By this time tomorrow, she'd know the worst.

She showered and dressed in a daze, then headed to the kitchen. She didn't feel hungry but forced herself to choke down a slice of toast, liberally spread with the ginger, lemon and lime jam which had been recommended to her by Barb Harris before she became ill and which had become a favourite of Gill's too. This morning it tasted like cardboard, but she knew she needed to eat. There was no telling when she'd be able to eat solid food again. The results of her internet searches all agreed she would be restricted to liquids and soft foods for several days after the procedure. She washed the toast down with a cup of camomile tea which failed to have its usual calming effect.

Gill sent her morning text to Freya, wishing she could tell her about the procedure she was about to undergo, did a quick check of the news without really taking anything in, then it was time to leave.

The clinic where the biopsy was to take place was situated some way up the coast, so Gill loaded up one of the series of podcasts she had listened to on the way to Bellbird Bay. This time, it was an interview with Sam Mostyn on *women breaking through in business, sport and equal opportunity*, most appropriate as Sam had been named as Australia's next Governor General. But this morning even that failed to hold her attention. All she could think of was what if her bump proved to be malignant? What if she required surgery, chemotherapy? How would she cope?

What she did know was that, immediately after the procedure her mouth would be numb, and she'd need to avoid talking or eating till the numbness wore off. She was glad the appointment was on a Friday which should give her the weekend to recover.

Gill arrived at her destination before she was emotionally prepared. Taking a deep breath and trying to subdue the nauseous feeling in her stomach, she got out of the car, walked to the long grey building and pushed open the door.

A short time later, she was lying in a dental chair, and the oral pathologist, a man of similar age to herself with a kind face and floppy blond hair, was putting her at her ease by explaining the procedure to her in words which, even in her nervous state, she could understand. To her relief, he told her that at first glance, the bump didn't look cancerous.

Then he proceeded to inject her tongue with an anaesthetic. It was just like being at the dentist, she thought. as the anaesthetic began to take effect.

The procedure was painless. The pathologist held her tongue, a piece of gauze on his fingers, while he scraped away the bump which was to be sent off to be tested – a routine process only, he assured her, and not urgent. Then it was over, the wound was packed with more gauze, and she was handed more pieces of gauze and given instructions to repack it if necessary. The entire process had only taken around fifteen minutes.

While the initial information from the pathologist had indicated a follow up appointment, he told Gill he was so sure it was benign that no further appointment would be necessary. Instead, he'd phone her with the result.

Gill felt as if the worry which had been weighing on her had suddenly disappeared. It wasn't cancer. Her mouth was numb and when she tried to arrange a time for the follow-up call with the receptionist, she found herself unable to speak and forced to use sign language. She was glad she didn't need to see anyone else that day.

Back home, and feeling tired, Gill was glad to drop into bed and close her eyes.

*

Awaking a few hours later, Gill was aware the numbness had worn off and the part of her tongue which had been scraped was now very painful. Since leaving the clinic, her teeth had been tightly clenched to hold the gauze in place, but now she needed to take some painkillers and wasn't sure how she would manage it.

With difficulty, she swallowed two Panadol and washed them down with a couple of mouthfuls of water, then went out to stand on her balcony, seeing the familiar scene through a different light from before. It was as if everything had a new glow about it. Suddenly all of her worries about Max and her divorce seemed insignificant. So what if he wanted half her earnings, half of the value of this apartment. She didn't have cancer. She wasn't sick. She wasn't going to die. For the first time Gill acknowledged what had been her worst fear. She knew she still had to receive the result of the biopsy, but she believed the pathologist, and he'd been sure it was benign.

As the pain receded, Gill began to feel the pangs of hunger, reminding her she'd had scarcely any breakfast. She was glad she'd thought to stock up on cans of soup, yoghurt, and almond milk and bananas to make smoothies, but it was too soon. She checked the packing on her tongue removing the blooded gauze and replacing it, then she lay down again, this time choosing to listen to the book for her next book club till her eyes began to close.

Next time Gill opened her eyes, it was almost dark. She was pain free. Cautiously, she checked the gauze to discover the healing process had begun, and a blood clot had formed in the wound. She took out the blender. Into it she fed a cup of almond milk, a chopped-up banana and a dash of vanilla essence. She could do this. She might even manage to lose weight if she kept to a liquid diet for the next few days till her tongue healed sufficiently for her to be able to eat scrambled eggs and mashed potatoes – maybe even one of the frozen cottage pies in the freezer.

The smoothie tasted delicious, making Gill wonder why she'd never made one before. She took it out to the balcony and gazed up at the sky. In her heightened sense of well-being, the stars seemed brighter than ever before. She gave thanks for her health, suddenly aware her happiness wasn't dependent on possessions. She thought of the last missive from her solicitor, of Max's latest demands, and realised they didn't matter. Nothing mattered apart from the fact she was healthy; she had the rest of her life to look forward to.

There was nothing she could do today; it was too late. But she promised herself that on Monday she would contact her solicitor and instruct her to finalise her divorce, to agree to Max's demands. Life was too short to continue to battle over the divorce settlement. She'd been granted a future. It was more than Barb Harris had had. The thought of the woman who'd lost her battle with cancer turned Gill's thoughts to Joe, to Barb's husband, the man who'd recently entered her life, their decision to be friends. She remembered the list she'd made, the changes she wanted to make in her life. One of these related to friends, to become more sociable, less isolated. Maybe she could start by developing her friendship with Joe.

Twenty

Joe hugged Erica and wished her luck when he dropped her off at the hospital for her job interview. He had been delighted to see her excitement at breakfast this morning, hoping it was a sign she was beginning to put Geoff and his abuse behind her and make a fresh start.

'You're looking great,' he'd said, when she appeared in the kitchen wearing the navy suit she'd bought on a shopping expedition with Poppy. After they'd met at breakfast, and when she learned about the interview, the other woman had taken Erica in hand, insisting she needed at least one smart outfit. It had taken all of Joe's persuasion before she agreed to accept money from him, and only on the condition he regarded it as a loan which she'd repay as soon as she could.

Joe watched his sister's tall figure disappear through the entrance to the hospital. He wished there was more he could do for her, but he was doing all he could. He was confident she'd be offered a position on the nursing staff; he knew how short-staffed they were. And she had her first appointment with the counsellor Olivia had recommended later in the day. Hopefully she could work her magic too.

On the way to his office, Joe stopped to pick up a copy of *The Echo*, thrilled to see a photo of the group of dog owners on the front page with the headline *Man's Best Friend*.

'You're certainly my best friend,' he said to Coco, who was seated beside him as usual.

He chuckled and threw the paper on the back seat to read later.

Making himself a cup of coffee from the machine he'd installed in the office, Joe settled at his desk to read the article Finn had written. In the editor's usual fashion, he'd managed to present a balanced view, leaning ever so slightly in favour of the dog owners and suggesting dogs deserved to enjoy the beaches too. It was well done. Joe picked up the phone to congratulate his friend, just as Debbie popped her head through his office door.

'You have visitors,' she said in a worried voice.

Joe heaved a sigh. He knew who it would be, though he hadn't expected them quite so soon. Alan Coatts and Bert Small must have been up at the crack of dawn to buy the papers as soon as they arrived at the newsagency. Now they'd be on the warpath… again. His call to Finn would have to wait. 'Show them in,' he said, 'but come and interrupt us in ten minutes. Good girl, Coco. Best you keep quiet,' he said to the dog who, as usual, was lying under his desk.

Debbie gave him a knowing grin and left, and a moment later, the two councillors stormed into his office. Alan was waving a copy of *The Echo*.

'Have you seen this trash?' he yelled. 'I thought it was a good thing for the town when you managed to save our newspaper, and then Hunter prints things like this.'

Joe groaned inwardly at the reference to him saving the paper yet again. 'Why don't you both take a seat and tell me what it is in the article that upsets you,' he said quietly, pleased to note Bert didn't appear as angry as his companion. 'Coffee?'

'No,' Alan replied for both of them. 'You're not going to get around us with a cup of coffee.'

Bert looked uncomfortable as they both took a seat.

'Well?' Joe asked, very conscious of Coco moving restlessly at his feet. He hoped his pet would behave and not choose this time to emit one of her low growls as she sensed the men's antagonism towards him.

'It's this!' Alan waved the paper in Joe's face again. 'This article. And you're in the photograph, you and that dog of yours.' He glanced around the office as if searching for signs of Coco.

Joe held his breath, as Coco moved again, then settled down.

'There are a number of us in the photograph,' Joe said mildly. 'Are dog owners a problem for you?'

'You know what I mean. Don't try to pull the wool over our eyes. How did the editor know we had an issue with the dog beach. Someone must have told him.' He glanced at Joe.

'I would imagine a lot of folk knew, if you go around complaining about it. I thought it was a very balanced article.'

'Balanced? Have you read it?' He suddenly seemed to notice the copy of *The Echo* on Joe's desk. 'That last comment… "dogs deserve to enjoy the beaches too". What does that say about his views? Dogs need to be controlled. Look at what's happening on Fraser Island…'

'K'gari,' his companion reminded him, referring to the new name for the island.

'Whatever.' Alan brushed his comment away. 'What about it, then?'

'The issue on K'gari is dingos, wild animals who people have treated inappropriately. What we're talking about here are domestic pets, walking on a beach with their owners. I don't think you can make a comparison.'

'Well, I think I have a valid point and I want it on the agenda for next week's council meeting, I…'

The door opened and Debbie peeked in. 'Your next appointment is here, Joe,' she said, her eyes widening at the sight of Alan's face, red with anger.

'Thanks, Debbie,' Joe said. 'If that's all, gentlemen. I'll be happy to include your item on the agenda, Alan. As you know, I'm always open to a genuine discussion on issues concerning our community.'

'Hmph.' But Alan rose to go, Bert joining him.

'Thanks, Deb,' Joe said, heaving a sigh of relief. Under the desk, Coco seemed to sigh too. Joe leant down to pat her. 'You didn't like them either, did you, Coco?' he said. Then he realised Debbie was still there. 'Something else?'

'You do have someone here to see you,' she said, moments before Finn walked in.

'Hey, good to see you. I was about to call to congratulate you when…'

'I passed two irate looking guys on the way in. Your disgruntled councillors?'

'Yeah. Your article ruffled their feathers more than a bit. We're to discuss it at next week's council meeting.'

'Oh!'

'You did a great job. Front page too!'

'Thanks.' Finn grinned. 'We should get some interesting responses. There are a lot of dog lovers in Pelican Crossing. You got Coco here today?' He glanced around the office, much as Alan had done, but in a more positive way.

Hearing the sound of her name, Coco stretched and came out from under the desk to greet Finn, pushing a wet nose into his hand.

'Hello, Coco,' Finn said, ruffling the dog's ears. 'I might have to attend your meeting, Joe. I guess it'll be a lively discussion. Remember, we always publish the agenda.'

'Of course.' Joe had forgotten. Finn was right. Alan's item would bring along a host of people who otherwise would never attend a council meeting. *What had he started?* 'So, what brings you here?'

'Oh, Liz asked me to come. I told her about your sister coming back to Pelican Crossing and she wanted to meet her. She doesn't remember her from school. Suggested the two of you come to dinner so she could make her acquaintance.'

'That's kind of her. I don't know…' Joe pulled on one ear. First Cam and Poppy, now this. His social life was certainly improving with Erica's arrival in town. But how would Erica feel about it? 'Can I check with her and get back to you?'

'No worries. I told Liz she might not be up for it, but you know Liz…'

Joe didn't, not well. But from what he did know, he could imagine how Liz might want to meet Erica and maybe take a hand in helping her settle back into her hometown. People were kind that way, though some might call it interfering. Liz was one of Poppy's friends, one of the group of women Joe knew met on a regular basis, had done for years. It would be good for Erica to be accepted by them. And she already knew Poppy. He had a notion Gill was part of the group too. His mind went back to the woman whose image had crept into his dreams, and he wondered when their paths would cross again.

Twenty-one

By Sunday morning, Gill was feeling a lot better. She'd be fine to go back to work on Monday as planned. She hadn't told anyone about the biopsy, reasoning her health issues were none of their business, and now she was fine, there was nothing to arouse their sympathy, something she'd have hated.

About to make one more banana smoothie, Gill realised she had finished the last container of almond milk the previous evening. For a few moments she stood undecided with the pantry door open, then made up her mind. She'd make a quick dash to the shops for two more, and she'd stock up on more frozen meals while she was there. She hadn't progressed from smoothies, yoghurt and soups yet, but would do soon.

Running her fingers through her hair and pulling on a jacket, Gill slid her feet into a pair of canvas shoes and headed out. She looked a mess but wouldn't meet anyone she knew this early on a Sunday morning.

She was browsing the freezer compartment in the store, debating whether to choose the macaroni cheese or another cottage pie when a voice behind her made her turn.

'I can highly recommend the chicken stir fry.'

'Oh!' Gill flinched. Of all people to see her looking like this. Joe Harris had caught her at a disadvantage again. 'Thanks,' she said, picking up two frozen meals of macaroni cheese and one of cottage pie, and hoping he'd leave and get on with his own shopping. But it wasn't to be.

'Seems we have the same taste in food,' he said. 'Until Erica joined me, I lived on frozen meals. They're handy when you're on your own and can't cook. Though I don't imagine it applies to you… the not cooking part.'

'I can cook, but I agree, these do come in handy,' Gill said, wondering if her voice sounded as strange to him as it did to her. This was the first time she'd spoken to anyone since the biopsy.

It must have, because Joe said, 'Are you all right, Gill, you sound…'

'… odd,' she finished for him. 'I had… some dental work.' It wasn't really a lie. As far as the medical services were concerned anything in the mouth was classified as dental.

Joe gave her a strange look.

Gill flinched, remembering her vow to make friendship with him a priority. But she hadn't expected to meet him here like this. 'I…' she began.

'Why don't you join me for coffee?' he asked. 'We can put these,' he gestured to the frozen meals which were now in her basket, 'in an esky I have in the car. Unless you have something else planned…'

'No… yes… I mean…' What did she mean? He'd caught her looking like a tramp in the store on a Sunday morning when most residents of Pelican Crossing were either at church or eating breakfast. 'Your sister…' she said lamely.

'Erica's having breakfast with Olivia. I don't have to be anywhere.' He paused. 'I'd like it if you would join me for coffee… and you can tell me about your dental procedure.' He smiled.

All of a sudden, looking into the brown eyes filled with a concern she recognised from their first meeting, Gill felt herself relax, knowing she could share what she'd been through with Joe. 'Thanks,' she said.

*

A short time later, having stashed her shopping into the esky in Joe's car, Gill was seated opposite him in *Books and Coffee* with a mug of hot chocolate. 'No dog today?' she asked.

'I left Coco at home this morning. She's not allowed in the shops and hates being left in the car. I'll take her for a walk when I get back.

Now, are you going to tell me what's up, why you are taking tiny sips of your chocolate, and your voice sounds strange? It wasn't only a dental procedure, was it? Don't think I'm being intrusive. but sometimes it helps to talk about these things.'

Gill wrapped both hands around her mug. For a few moments she didn't speak, then she began… 'I had a scare. I thought it was cancer.' She saw Joe flinch at the word and regretted she'd spoken it. But she'd started now. There was no going back.

'So, that's why I sound a bit odd,' she said, when she had finished. 'I was lucky, not like Barb. I'm sorry.'

'Don't be. It's not your fault. Sounds like you had quite a scare. I'm glad you got a clean bill of health. But you're right. It does tend to put things into perspective.' He placed his hand over hers, which was now lying on the table, then removed it, as if he'd been burned. 'What do you say we have dinner together once you're able to eat properly again?'

Gill was surprised to find herself smiling. 'Sounds lovely,' she said, liking the idea of getting to know Joe better. It was time she broadened her circle of friends, she told herself, ignoring the flash of a long-forgotten yearning she had felt when his hand covered hers. *Had he felt it too?*

'Have you seen Friday's copy of *The Echo*?' Joe asked, changing the subject as if he'd read her mind.

'No.' Gill shook her head, 'I was otherwise engaged on Friday.'

'Of course. Sorry.'

'What did I miss?'

'Coco and me, along with other dog owners made the front page.'

'Oh!' Gill had a vague recollection of Poppy and Rachel mentioning something about photos of dog owners on the beach, something about… She tried to remember. 'I think Poppy may have mentioned it last time we had lunch.'

'She was there, along with a number of others. Finn did us proud with the covering article. But…' his forehead creased, '… not everyone was pleased. A couple of the councillors are waging a campaign to ban all off-leash dogs on beaches.'

'Surely not?' Now Gill remembered the discussion and her own comment. She repeated it now. 'They don't do any harm. I don't remember ever hearing of anyone being bitten or attacked on our beaches. It's not like K'gari and the dingoes.'

'Exactly!' Joe seemed pleased. 'But that's their argument.'

'I think I need to come along to the meeting.' Poppy would no doubt be there, Rachel, too, and with Finn's connection, probably Liz.

'I hope a lot of people will feel that way. Our four-legged friends need all the support they can get.'

'They won't be at the meeting?' Gill asked trying to keep a straight face.

Joe stared at her for a moment, his eyes wide, then he seemed to realise she was joking. 'Probably not,' he said, chuckling.

A few minutes later, they both rose to leave. When Gill picked up her shopping from Joe's car, she thanked him for the hot chocolate and for listening. It had helped to share her fears and subsequent relief with someone who understood. They parted without making any plans to see each other again, but Gill was confident their paths would cross again and there was the promised dinner to look forward to, though right now, Gill couldn't imagine when she might feel like eating normally again.

Back home, she smiled as she packed her shopping away, and set about making herself another banana smoothie. She had just taken a seat on the balcony and was about to sip it when her phone rang. She gazed at the screen in amazement, seeing Freya's name.

Twenty-two

Gill stared at her daughter's name, too stunned to answer. Her first thought was that something had happened to Freya, and this was a friend or medico calling to tell her. Her stomach lurched as she pressed to accept the call, her hand suddenly slick with sweat.

'Hello?'

'Is that you, Mum? You sound strange.'

Gill's heartbeat returned to normal at the sound of her daughter's familiar voice. 'I'm fine, just a dental procedure,' she lied again. 'It's so good to hear your voice. What...' But before she could say anymore, Freya was speaking again.

'Have you heard what Dad's done now?' she said.

Gill flinched. Freya had been incommunicado for years and now, in her first phone call, she wanted to talk about Max. To which of his many offences was she referring?

Freya didn't give her time to wonder. 'He's taken up with a woman who's no older than me... and she's pregnant.'

If Freya hadn't sounded so outraged, Gill would have laughed. Max hadn't been much help first time around, when Freya was a baby, preferring to leave all the hard work to Gill. How was he going to cope with an infant in his fifties? But it was news to her. Maybe this was the reason he'd become more demanding. A younger partner and the prospect of a child would certainly stretch his finances.

'What about me?' Freya wailed.

Gill suddenly understood her daughter's fury. She'd always been her dad's little girl, his favourite. With another child on the horizon, she'd be forced to share his love and attention.

'Mum? Why don't you say something?' Freya demanded.

'What do you want me to say? I'm the last person to defend your dad after all we've been through… are still going through.' Gill thought of her decision to give in to his demands. Maybe she'd been too hasty. He'd kept very quiet about this new relationship, the pregnancy.

'You're still married?'

'We are, but not for much longer.' *Hopefully.*

'Can I come home, Mum?'

Gill's heart leapt. This was the last thing she'd expected. It was years since Freya had left Australia to take up a place in a doctoral program at a university in California, promising to come home regularly. Then Max had left, Freya had accepted a teaching position in the university, and any communication with Gill had dried up.

'With Dad doing this… it's made me realise that perhaps I've been unfair to you. I thought… I thought it was all your fault. Dad said… Anyway, I want to see you. My contract here is up soon. I can take a break, find something else, maybe in Australia.'

Gill swallowed. She'd wanted this to happen for so long, but not in this way, not because Freya was upset with Max. But she'd take what she could get if it meant seeing her daughter again. 'I'd love to see you, sweetheart,' she said, tears coming to her eyes at the thought of having Freya back home.

'And I can't wait to see you, Mum. I'll let you know when I've booked my flight.'

'Wonderful. I love you, darling.'

'I love you too, Mum… and I'm sorry.' Freya ended the call.

Gill didn't need to ask what Freya was sorry for. Remembering all the unanswered calls and texts, she knew. But it didn't matter. Her daughter was coming home.

*

Gill clutched the silent phone wondering if she'd imagined the conversation. She'd dreamt about it so often. Now it had actually happened. She should have predicted Max's choices would eventually catch up with him and alienate their daughter. Freya had always put Max on a pedestal, assumed she'd always be his blue-eyed girl. Gill could understand how the thought she'd have to share him would anger her. Although she didn't endorse Freya's need to be her dad's number one, she did empathise with the girl who had always been the apple of her dad's eye.

She gazed around the apartment. Freya had never lived here, in the apartment she and Max had bought when Freya left for university and which they'd furnished in an austere Scandinavian style. It had suited them, and Gill still loved its clean lines. It always made her feel good when she returned home from a busy day at the office, or when she received yet another demand from Max via her solicitor. Freya had only spent the odd weekend there, preferring to remain in the city or go off somewhere with her university friends on the holidays. Then she'd accepted the position in the States, and she'd been lost to Gill... until now.

Well, it was an ill wind, as Gill's mother would have said. And this one, Max's unthinking new relationship and the prospect of him becoming a father again, had resulted in Freya reaching out to her mother. For a brief moment, Gill wondered how he felt about this pregnancy, then the thought passed. It was none of her business. Her heart hardened reversing her earlier decision about Max. She certainly didn't intend to be forced to sell her apartment to fund his new family.

Meanwhile, she had Freya's arrival to look forward to. She couldn't wait. Maybe she could arrange her diary to enable her to spend quality time with her daughter.

She thought back to their conversation. There had been something in Freya's voice, something more than the anger with her dad. Gill had the impression something else had happened to unsettle her daughter, something completely unrelated to Max and his relationship. And she intended to find out what it was.

Twenty-three

Joe gazed around the room, surprised to see how many members of the community had chosen to attend the council meeting. Normally, there were only a few, usually retired individuals looking for a way to pass the time. But Finn's front-page article, followed by the notice of the meeting agenda, had brought out all the local dog owners and animal lovers. The council chamber was filled, and many, unable to find seats, were standing at the back of the room. As a result of Joe's bid for transparency of council proceedings, the meetings were also livestreamed, and there was no way of knowing how many others were watching and listening.

The first part of the meeting covered apologies, confirmation of minutes of the previous meeting and reports from the various committees. During these routine matters, Joe was conscious of many of their audience becoming restive. This wasn't why they were here. Then the main item of business was announced, and Alan Coatts rose to move the motion that the dog beach be discontinued and dogs be restrained on all Pelican Crossing beaches.

He had barely finished speaking, when a loud muttering broke out among the audience, forcing Joe to call for silence. Then various councillors were invited to speak for and against the motion, the only other speaker in favour being Coatts' mate, Bert Small, who reiterated his ally's view that loose dogs were a danger to beachgoers.

Given it was such a contentious issue, Joe had decided to dispense with normal procedure and open the topic up to questions from the audience, and the questions came thick and fast. It was clear Alan and Bert were practically alone in wanting to change the status quo. Joe was about to call for a vote on the motion when one member of the audience rose to her feet.

'We're supposed to be a nation of dog lovers,' Agnes said. 'It appears two of our councillors have forgotten that dogs are man's best friend… woman's too.'

Everyone chuckled. But Agnes hadn't finished.

'I'd like to suggest councillors Coatts and Small consider how they'd like to have their freedom curtailed when they visit the beach on the weekend. Perhaps we can arrange for it to happen.'

There was more laughter, and both Alan and Bert's faces turned red, whether from anger or embarrassment, Joe wasn't sure. 'I don't think that will be necessary,' he said, trying to hide his amusement. Old Agnes had done it again, just as she had at the meeting about the development. 'It's time for a vote on the motion.' He read the motion again and called for a show of hands. Only two councillors voted in favour.

'I think we can all agree the motion lost. Our dog beach is safe.'

There was loud applause as the meeting came to a close.

It was some time before Joe managed to get away, but when he left the council chambers, there were still groups of people standing around chatting. He saw Cam and Poppy with Finn and Liz. With them was Gill, looking much better than she had last time he saw her. He'd been intending to call to make good his promise to invite her to dinner but work and Erica had got in the way. As he'd predicted, his sister had been offered a position at the hospital, and had checked out the procedure for applying for an AVO, afraid Geoff might follow her to Pelican Crossing. It would also prevent him from contacting her by phone or text, though she had kept her phone turned off in case of that eventuality, sad that it meant Kieren was also unable to get in touch with her. She had mentioned she would need to see Gill again to have the application signed by her. She could go to a justice of the peace, but had said she felt more comfortable arranging to see Gill again. She'd also mentioned Gill hadn't been swimming for the past week. Joe hadn't told her about Gill's procedure.

He was disappointed to see Gill leave the group just as he

approached. He wanted to follow her, but Cam had already seen him and called out, 'Hey, Joe. Good result. Well done.'

'I didn't do anything,' he said. 'But I agree it went well. I only hope that's an end to it, and those two can accept the council – and the community – decision.'

'Wasn't Agnes wonderful again,' Poppy said. 'Every community needs someone like her who's not afraid to speak their mind.'

They all chuckled.

Joe noticed Liz nudging Finn.

'Oh, yeah,' Finn said. 'Now you're here. As I think I told you, Liz has been bugging me to invite you and Erica to dinner. What are you doing on Saturday?'

'I'm free, but I'll have to check with Erica. Now she's working, it'll depend what shift she's on. Can I let you know?' Joe realised he'd forgotten to tell Erica about Finn's earlier invitation.

'Sure. We should be going now. Big day tomorrow. I intend to do a full report on the meeting for *The Echo*.'

'I'll look forward to it.' Joe hoped Finn wouldn't make too much of his part. He had only chaired the meeting. The decision about the dog beach wasn't his responsibility, even though he was delighted about it. He grinned, knowing Coco would be too.

Erica was still awake when Joe arrived home and, after checking her roster, agreed to dinner with Finn and Liz on Saturday. 'She didn't grow up here, did she?' she asked. 'I don't think I remember her.'

'She came to Pelican Crossing and started at the high school in year ten, over thirty years ago,' Joe said. 'But some people would still regard her as an incomer. Finn only arrived in town just over a year ago to join his daughter. You wouldn't know him either.'

'Over thirty years and she's still regarded as an incomer?'

'You know Pelican Crossing,' Joe replied. 'She wasn't born here. Whereas despite having lived in Western Australia for so long, you'll always be native to Pelican Crossing.' He chuckled. 'It's just how things are. I think you'll like both Finn and Liz.'

'I hope so. I'm looking forward to meeting them. Now, I'm heading to bed. I was just about to do so when you came in.'

It wouldn't be long before Joe would be hitting the sack himself, but first, he thought, bending to rub Coco's neck, a celebratory drink was in order.

Out on the deck with a tumbler of Highland Park in his hand and Coco lying at his side, Joe took a long sip and savoured not just the taste, but life itself. He enjoyed his job, his friends, and most of all his gorgeous dog, but his last thought as he drained the glass, was of Gill Dickson, the enigma in a scruffy old jacket with messy hair, buying frozen meals. The woman who he'd promised to take to dinner.

'Life's good, old girl,' he said, reaching down to pat Coco's head.

*

Saturday arrived without Joe making contact with Gill again, though Erica had met with her and was feeling more secure, having submitted the important AVO. She'd reported that a copy of her application would be forwarded to her husband who would be required to appear in court to answer it. Joe was glad of the distance separating them.

He was looking forward to the evening, to seeing Finn with Liz Phillips, with whom Joe had merely a passing acquaintance. He only knew her as a friend of Poppy's… and Gill's, reminding him of his promise to call her. He didn't know why he hadn't done so yet, putting it down to his concern she might still be recovering. But he knew it was more than that. He was trying to come to terms with the attraction he felt for her – an attraction he'd never expected to experience again – and the knowledge she was clearly only interested in him as a friend.

When they reached the door of Liz's apartment, where Finn was now living, Joe was surprised to hear the sound of voices, more than would be made by two people. Finn hadn't said anything about other guests.

Erica gave him a worried look.

Joe squeezed her hand. 'It'll be fine,' he said, 'probably people you know.'

He was right. When Finn opened the door, Joe recognised Poppy's laugh – he would know it anywhere. He relaxed. It was only Cam and Poppy. It was good of Liz – he was sure it had been her idea – to think of inviting the couple Erica already knew. But when he and Erica joined the others, where they were enjoying wine on a wide deck almost covered with greenery, he was shocked to see Gill there too. It should have occurred to him. The three women were part of a group who lunched together on a regular basis; Poppy's husband, Jack, used to call them the *gang of four*. Joe had an idea they'd all met when their children were babies, though those children were now all grown women.

'You know Gill, don't you?' Finn said, once he had introduced Erica to Liz and had poured wine for Joe and his sister.

Joe nodded, while Erica smiled and said, 'Good to see you again, Gill.' He thought Gill looked a little uncomfortable. Was it seeing him here? Hadn't she known he and Erica had been invited?

The conversation was all about the council meeting which, apart from Erica, they had all attended, and Poppy, as a dog owner, was full of praise for the council decision.

'But it's all down to you, Finn,' she said. 'Your article was amazing.'

Liz, clearly seeing Finn's embarrassment, announced dinner was ready, and they all made their way inside.

During the meal of poached salmon with steamed vegetables, Joe frequently glanced across the table to where Gill was sitting. He had been pleased to hear her voice was back to normal, but noticed she was eating slowly and cutting her food into tiny pieces. He realised that although she was improving, she was still not completely recovered. He experienced an unexpected urge to give her a hug to comfort her.

When the meal was over and they had moved back onto the deck with coffee, Joe was pleased to note Erica seemed relaxed, asking Liz about the profusion of plants.

'You must enjoy gardening,' she said.

'I missed my garden when I moved here,' Liz replied. 'Then I read a book called *The Edible Balcony*, about building a garden on a balcony. The deck is north-facing, so it's perfect. Are you a gardener?'

'I used to be.' The colour drained from Erica's face, then she seemed to recover. 'And I will be again,' she said, her voice firm. 'Joe's garden needs some TLC.'

Joe winced. The garden had been Barb's province; he hadn't been able to bring himself to do much other than keep the grass down since she passed. Maybe it would be a good project for Erica.

As the group reformed, he found himself seated next to Gill. 'You feeling better?' he asked in a low voice, so no one else could hear. He didn't know if she'd shared her condition with the others.

'Yes, thanks,' she whispered. 'Thanks for asking. It'll take me a bit longer to get back to how I was, but I'm getting there.'

'Well enough to have dinner with a friend?'

'Perhaps.' Gill smiled at him, and Joe felt his stomach lurch. As the conversation flowed around them, it was as if the pair were encased in their own little bubble. When it came time to leave, he had arranged for them to have dinner together the following Friday, though he sensed a hint of reticence behind Gill's agreement.

Twenty-four

Gill awoke on Sunday morning feeling happier than she had for some time. It took her a few moments to remember the call from Freya, then her agreement to have dinner with Joe. She had almost refused Liz's invitation, unsure how she'd cope with eating food she hadn't prepared herself. But it had been okay, though she'd felt uncomfortable when she caught Joe glancing at her from time to time during the meal.

It was early and, for the first time since the biopsy, she felt ready to go swimming again. Rising, she pulled on her swimsuit, shorts and tee-shirt, glugged down a glass of water and set off.

It was a smaller group than usual who made the effort to join the wild swimmers on a Sunday morning, many choosing to stay in bed, or to have plans for family breakfast. Gill shivered in the slight breeze when she got out of the car. She ran down to join the others on the beach, pleased to see Olivia among those standing there. Then they were off, striding into the ocean to dive through the waves and strike out across the bay.

As Gill once again experienced the exhilaration of being at one with nature she struck out, forgetting everything in the pleasure of being back in the environment she loved. She'd missed this. She turned to float on her back and gazed up at the changing colours of the sky, glad to be alive.

She was still in high spirits when she emerged to grab her towel from where she'd left it on the beach.

'Hey, Gill. Haven't seen you for a few days. Is everything okay?' Olivia asked.

'It is now.' Gill hoped Olivia wouldn't ask anything further.

She didn't, but did say, 'It's been a while. Why don't we have breakfast together… unless you have other plans?'

'Sounds good, but I need to go home and change first.' Gill looked down at the old shorts and tee-shirt she'd pulled on earlier.

'Me too. How about we meet in *The Blue Dolphin* at eight-thirty?'

'See you there.'

Gill arrived at *The Blue Dolphin Café* just before eight-thirty. She looked around. There was no sign of Olivia, but she could see Poppy and Cam with a young couple she recognised as Poppy's daughter, Scarlett, and Cam's son, Lachlan. They were accompanied by a small child who Gill knew must be their son, Poppy and Cam's grandson.

She smiled, waved to her friends and took a seat at a vacant table. Now she was in touch with Freya again, seeing her friend with her daughter and grandson didn't hurt as much. Thinking of her daughter, Gill took out her phone, her heart leaping at the sight of a new text. It must be mid-afternoon in California, she calculated. She read it quickly, conscious Olivia could arrive any time.

Flight booked. Arriving next Sat. Will make my own way to Pelican Crossing. Be home for lunch. Fxx

Gill beamed, her heart pounding with excitement, then seeing Olivia walk into the café, replied with a thumbs up emoji. She would send a proper reply later when she was alone.

'Hey!' Olivia took a seat. 'You're looking very pleased with yourself.'

Gill couldn't keep her news to herself. 'Freya's coming home,' she said, grinning.

'Freya? But I thought…'

'It's complicated, but we're back in touch.' Gill had no intention of sharing the story of Max's situation with Olivia. She may have decided to be more sociable, but she preferred to keep some things to herself. She glanced across to where Poppy was laughing down at her grandson. Freya would be back in Pelican Crossing by the time their next lunch meeting came around, and her three close friends would want the details. She'd have to figure out how to tell them before then. Then she thought about Joe. Did he deserve to know? All this deciding to be more open with people was full of pitfalls. After being reserved for so long, it was going to be difficult to change.

'I'm glad for you, and I understand if you don't want to share the details,' Olivia said.

Gill relaxed. Even though Olivia had supported her through Max leaving and Freya's rejection, and Gill knew that as a counsellor, her friend was accustomed to keeping confidences, she was still hesitant to share this latest news with her… maybe later when everything had been resolved… if that ever happened. But somehow, Gill was feeling more positive about her situation and the divorce. Perhaps it was the knowledge that Freya had shunned Max, that he'd finally done something to alienate their daughter and brought her back to Gill, perhaps it was the positive result from the biopsy, perhaps it was the prospect of dinner with Joe. She stifled that last thought before it could take root. He was a friend, nothing more. But whatever the reason, Gill was feeling more positive about the future than she had in a long time.

'Shall we order?' Olivia picked up a menu. 'I don't know about you, but I'm starving.'

'Let's.'

The two women studied the menus before each deciding to order the savoury mince with poached egg served on Turkish bread, accompanied by skimmed milk cappuccinos.

'So,' Olivia said, when their orders had been placed, 'what's been happening with you?' She leant forward as if anticipating some sort of revelation or explanation of Gill's absence from their early morning swims.

'I've been busy,' Gill said, determined to keep news of the biopsy to herself. 'But it was good to get back this morning. How are you enjoying *The Wild Coast*?' she asked, moving on to the book chosen for their next month's book club meeting. 'I've been listening to the audiobook and love the Scottish narrator's voice. It reminds me of my grandmother.'

'I didn't realise you had Scottish ancestry,' Olivia said. 'I haven't got very far yet. You may have the right idea, listening instead of reading. I'm finding the concept of wild camping interesting. Very different from wild swimming.'

'And a lot more dangerous… according to Lin Anderson.' Gill shivered at the memory of the missing girls in the story she'd been listening to. 'But it was good to be reminded of the trip I took to Scotland between school and uni. I visited several of the locations in the book, and it brought back happy memories.'

'Scotland's on my bucket list,' Olivia said. 'I hope to get there one day.'

'Don't hope. Make a plan.'

'Listen to you. Are you sure it's only about Freya coming home? You sound different.'

'I guess I've come to the realisation we should make the most of what we have. We never know what's in store, how much time we have left.'

'Wow! That's pretty heavy for a Sunday morning,' Olivia said, just as their coffee and breakfasts arrived.

While they ate, Olivia regaled Gill with the latest news from her daughter who was finding this pregnancy more difficult than her earlier ones, and how she wished they didn't live so far away – a common complaint of Olivia's.

'Why don't you go over to visit, combine it with a trip to Scotland. Didn't you say she wanted you to go?' Gill asked, taking a gulp of coffee. 'You could be there for the birth.'

Olivia didn't immediately reply, then said, 'Do you know, I think I will. I have some leave owing. The baby's not due till early next year. It would give me time to arrange a locum. Thanks, Gill.' She smiled.

'No problem, Livvy. I know how much I'd want to be there if it was Freya.' But first Freya would have to find a partner, and she had made no mention of one in any of the emails they'd exchanged since her first call. But now she was coming back to Australia, who knew what might happen?

When they left the café, Gill hugged Olivia. 'See you tomorrow,' she said. 'Thanks for suggesting breakfast.'

'Thanks for coming.'

As Gill hurried off, it occurred to her for the first time that perhaps Olivia was lonely too. Since Max left, she'd been so wrapped up in her own problems, she'd been blind to what might be happening in the lives of those around her. Well, that was about to change. And now she had things to look forward to – Freya's arrival, her dinner with Joe, and Ali Wells coming to speak with the Zonta group which she'd finally managed to organise. Life is good right now, she told herself, and she was going to make the most of it.

Twenty-five

'Are you sure you want to go to this?' Joe asked, seeing Erica dressed and ready to leave. When she told him Gill had invited her to attend the Zonta meeting at which Ali Wells was to speak, he'd tried to dissuade her. He didn't have anything against Zonta – they did good work in supporting and promoting women – but he wondered if it would bring it all back to Erica and hinder her recovery. He'd checked out Ali Wells after meeting her in Bellbird Bay and was aware of her views on abuse of women, which he assumed would be the topic of her talk.

'I'm sure. Don't worry about me, Joe. It's time I did something for myself... and if I can find a way to help other women who've suffered as I have, I mean to take it.'

'Okay.' Joe sighed. Growing up, Erica had always had a mind of her own. It had only been since she met and married Geoff that he'd noticed how she'd changed, become more passive, more subservient. And while he was glad to see the old Erica reasserting herself, he worried it might be too much for her.

'I want to contact Briony, too. She's having my grandchild, and I need to know how she's doing.'

'I'm not sure it's a good idea,' Joe said, his stomach clenching at the thought of Geoff finding out where she was. 'Geoff...'

'It's okay. I plan to get a new phone. She won't know where I'm calling from, and I can withhold the number. I want to know about Kieren, too. He's my son, and we've never been out of contact for so long before. You can't change my mind,' she said, as Joe opened his mouth to speak. 'I've decided. Now, I'm off. I won't be late. Gill said the meeting will only last for an hour, then there'll be tea and cakes and a chance to chat.'

Joe managed a smile. 'You have fun,' he said.

After Erica left, Joe poured himself a Scotch and took it into his study, Coco padding loyally behind him to settle at his feet before gratefully crunching on the offered gravy bone. He fired up his laptop intending to make some inroads on a speech he had promised to give to the local Rotary group on the challenges of local government. But ten minutes later he was still staring at a blank screen.

'It's just not happening, Coco,' he said to his pet whose ears pricked up at the sound of her name. He was worried about Erica. While she might think she was safe contacting her daughter-in-law from a withheld number on a new phone, Joe was afraid Geoff would discover she'd been in touch and that would make him even more determined.

He hadn't told Erica about the call he'd received from Geoff demanding Joe tell him where his wife was hiding. Joe had pleaded surprise and ignorance, mentioning an old schoolfriend of hers living in Cairns and hoped he'd managed to convince him.

From what he knew of his obdurate brother-in-law, the man would move heaven and earth to find his wife and bring her home. Joe doubted any love was involved. From what Erica had revealed, that had gone out the window years ago. But to men like Geoff, their wife was a possession, one they didn't give up readily – or rationally – and not without a nasty fight. He dreaded to think what might happen if Geoff worked out Erica had sought refuge with him in Pelican Crossing, sure the presence of an AVO would do nothing to prevent him from banging on the door.

Deciding he wasn't going to get anything done on his speech, Joe closed down the laptop and, Coco following, made for the door, pausing only to pull on a jacket and take Coco's leash from its hook. What he needed was some fresh air to clear his head.

He headed towards the marina. It was beautiful at this time of night, the lights from those boats which were occupied mirrored in the water, the clear sky filled with stars, the moon almost full. As Coco padded along at his side, stopping to sniff every few seconds, Joe's mind went to the woman who was never far from his thoughts. Although he'd tried to dissuade Erica from going to the Zonta meeting, it was good of Gill to invite her, to take an interest in what was, for her, only another client. Though he did wonder if the fact Erica was his sister might have something to do with it. Whatever the reason, Erica seemed to enjoy speaking with Gill both as her client and as the friend she was becoming. Joe wasn't sure how he felt about that. His feelings for Gill were so new, so unexpected. The fact she was also becoming friends with his sister felt a bit odd. And from what he knew of Gill, it was unusual for her to befriend a client. She seemed a very private person, not one given to making friends easily. The entangling enigma that was Gill Dickson appeared to be growing by the day.

Which left him wondering why she'd agreed to have dinner with him.

*

Gill was pleased to see Erica stepping into the room where the Zonta meeting was to be held. Ali had already arrived, and Gill and she were chatting when the other woman made her tentative entrance.

'Excuse me,' she said to Ali before going across to where Erica was standing just inside the door.

'Hi, Erica. I'm glad you could make it,' she said. 'Let me introduce you to Ali.' She led Erica across to meet her.

The room began to fill, and the women took their seats around an oval table. It wasn't a large group, and Gill was pleased to see Erica being welcomed and shown to a seat.

The meeting began with her introducing Ali and giving an overview of her background finishing with, 'Ali is now director of *Bellbird Women's Centre* and has kindly agreed to come here tonight to tell us about the services it offers. I hope by learning of the good work of the centre, we can work out a way in which we can help.' Gill sat down, and Ali took her place.

At first, Gill listened closely as Ali outlined the goals of the centre and the various sections. Then her mind wandered as Ali began to repeat much of which Gill had learned on her visit to the centre. She could see Erica listening intently and wondered not for the first time, where she might have ended up if she hadn't had Joe to rescue her. Would she had stayed with her abusive husband, or gone to a women's refuge similar to the one attached to the women's centre? As she watched the woman who looked so like her brother it was almost as if he was there, Gill saw the colour drain from Erica's face. *Had she made a mistake in inviting her?*

Then Ali's presentation was over, and she was replying to a barrage of questions. To Gill's delight, the group were keen to offer their support to the centre both in terms of funding and, in some instances, as volunteers. She was surprised to hear Erica offer to visit and talk to the women about how it had taken her so long to recognise that the control her husband had exerted over her was a form of abuse, and how his behaviour had escalated. It was a huge step forward for her to acknowledge this publicly.

When a couple of the women disappeared to reappear a few minutes later with tea and cakes, the group moved from the table to enjoy the refreshments and chat. Gill took the opportunity first to thank Ali informally – she'd given a more formal vote of thanks earlier and presented her with a basket of goodies – then to join Erica.

'That was very brave of you… your offer to speak to the women at the centre,' she said.

'Brave? I don't think so. I wish I'd had someone to tell me earlier. As Ali said, many women don't recognise their husband's behaviour as abuse. I found it interesting that the centre doesn't only cater for woman like me who've made the decision to leave. If I can help just one person in my position…' She gave a tight smile, and Gill could see Joe's determination in her expression. It was the sort of determination that had helped the town outwit a developer, save a newspaper and protect the dog beach.

Joe Harris was a good man. He was her friend. And they were having dinner together in two days' time. Gill's stomach fluttered as it had a couple of times before… when she thought of Joe, she realised. For the first time, Gill began to wonder if she and Joe could become more than friends, if, for him, she could forget her vow, let down the barriers she'd erected around her emotions and allow herself to feel something for another man.

Twenty-six

Joe had noticed a difference in Erica on the morning after she'd attended the Zonta meeting. It was as if she was lit up from the inside. But when he asked her how it was, she'd only said, 'Good' before heading off to work.

Now it was Friday evening, and he was getting ready to go to the yacht club, but before he left, he wanted to have a word with his sister. He found her in the kitchen heating up some leftovers. Coco was standing beside her in the hope of receiving something to eat, even though Joe had already fed her.

'How are you managing getting to and from work?' he asked. He was feeling guilty he hadn't pursued the idea of finding her a car.

'It's fine,' she said. 'It's not too far to walk and it's good to get some fresh air after being inside all day.'

'What about when you're on night shift?' Joe had checked the roster Erica had posted on the fridge and had noted it would be in a week's time.

'I expect I'll manage.'

'We talked about getting you a car. How about we check out the used car yard tomorrow. You're off, aren't you?'

'Yes, but…'

'No excuses. I don't want to think of you walking to work and home in the dark. As I said before you can pay me back, or we can treat it as an early birthday present.'

'Oh Joe. You're too good to me.' Erica threw her arms around Joe and gave him a hug. 'You won't regret it.'

Joe blushed. It was the least he could do. 'Okay. If you're in bed when I get back, I'll see you in the morning. Maybe we can have lunch or dinner at *Crossings*.' He was aware he had yet to make good his promise to take her to Poppy's restaurant.

'Sounds wonderful,' she said, adding to Joe's guilt. He should have taken her there before now. But better late than never, and maybe she would open up to him about what had happened at the Zonta meeting to give her that inner glow.

Joe headed to the yacht club where he'd arranged to meet Gill. She'd said she preferred to meet there rather than being picked up at home, and that she could walk there. He thought perhaps it was a way of her retaining the privacy which he felt was very important to her, and hoped that one day, she might feel comfortable enough with him to allow him to see her home.

As he approached the club, Joe saw Gill walking towards him. Hearing a loud squawking overhead, he glanced up to see a flock of black cockatoos flying over.

'Aren't they magnificent,' Gill said, joining him and gazing up too, as the birds disappeared in the distance.

'But noisy... and they make a mess of the banksia in my front yard,' he said, remembering the heap of debris he'd had to sweep up after a pair of the birds had feasted on it. 'Ready to go in?' he asked. 'You're looking lovely tonight.' Joe couldn't take his eyes off the picture she made. In a pair of black pants and a bright pink jacket, she looked so different to what she had on the previous occasions they'd met.

Gill blushed. 'Thanks,' she said. 'Let's go in.'

Tempted to take her hand, Joe restrained himself, worried she'd pull hers away. It wouldn't be a good start to the evening.

The restaurant was busy, making Joe glad he'd had the foresight to book. Apart from Erica, Gill was the first woman he'd brought here since Barb, and it brought back memories – good ones. He wondered if the place had memories for Gill too, and whether hers were as good as his. He presumed some of her married life had been happy. Hadn't he heard something about a daughter? He had a lot to discover about this woman who liked to keep her personal life close. But she had opened up about her medical procedure, so perhaps she'd be willing to disclose more about herself.

'Hello, Gill,' the waitress greeted Gill, who reddened.

'Mandy,' she said. 'I didn't expect to see you tonight.'

'I don't usually do weekends,' the waitress said as she handed them menus and listed the evening's specials.

'She's Liz's daughter,' Gill explained when she left. 'Now everyone will know we had dinner together.'

'Is it a problem for you?' Joe knew Gill liked to be private, but it was difficult to keep things secret in a town like Pelican Crossing. Maybe he should have taken her to somewhere out of town.

'I guess not.' But she sighed. 'I've lived in a bubble for so long. It seems odd to be out with you like this.'

'Not too odd, I hope.' Joe smiled.

'Not too odd,' Gill agreed, returning his smile.

When they placed their orders – a pasta dish for Gill and barramundi and chips for Joe – Mandy told them there might be a delay as the kitchen was busy.

'We're in no hurry,' Joe said, 'but if we could have the wine.' He'd also ordered a bottle of a Clare Valley pinot gris.

'Certainly.'

A few moments later Mandy brought the wine and poured two glasses.

'This is lovely.' Gill sipped her wine and gazed out at the twinkling lights of the marina.

'Mmm.' Joe was unsure if she was talking about the wine, the restaurant, the view or the company. Probably the restaurant. It was pleasant sitting here, drinking wine.

'Thanks for suggesting this. It's been a while since I came out like this. I can't remember when it was.'

'No problem. Thanks for agreeing to join me. Barb and I used to come here a lot, but since…' He sighed. 'Erica and I came here not so long ago, and I realised I'd missed it.'

'Me too. We used to bring Freya here on birthdays.'

'Your daughter?'

Gill smiled. She seemed to relax. 'Yes. She's coming home tomorrow.'

'She's been away?'

'California. She left soon after Max did. We lost touch.'

Joe wondered how you could lose touch with your daughter. If he and Barb had been lucky enough to have a family, he knew he'd have made sure they kept close. He glanced at Gill to see tears in her eyes. 'Want to talk about it?'

She took a tissue from her pocket. 'Sorry,' she said, pressing the tissue to her eyes.

Joe's heart went out to her. He wanted to reach out, hug her tight.

'It's all right,' Joe said, 'you've nothing to be sorry for. It must have been hard for you.'

She took a sip of wine. 'Everything was fine till Max left – or I thought it was. I guess it started to go wrong when I was made partner around the same time he was turned down for the position of principal. But life went on, Freya left for university, we bought the apartment. It was only later the arguments started. Max complained I spent more time at work than at home, cared more for my clients than I did for him and Freya.' She took a deep breath and another sip of wine. 'What I didn't know was that he had been seeing other women. He must have infected Freya with his views too, because soon after he left, she accepted a teaching position at a university in Santa Barbara, where she'd completed her doctorate. Since then… until just over a week ago… I hadn't heard from her.'

'Not at all?' Joe couldn't hide his shock. For him, family was paramount. He couldn't imagine a scenario such as Gill described.

Gill shook her head.

'So why now?'

'It seems Max has finally managed to do something she can't accept. He's in a relationship with a younger woman – around Freya's age – and she's pregnant.'

'Wow!'

Their meals arrived, and Joe refilled their glasses.

'So, tomorrow,' he said. 'You must be excited.'

'I can't wait, but…' Gill bit her lip, '… it's been so long, I hope… I hope I don't disappoint her. Now she's finally seen Max's true colours, I can't help thinking she might find fault with me again too.'

'I'm sure that won't happen.' But how could he be? He'd never met Gill's daughter who must be in her late twenties by his reckoning.

'She's thirty,' Gill said, as if reading his thoughts, 'the same age as Poppy, Liz and Rachel's eldest. They all grew up together. It was when they were all babies that the four of us got together. It was so long ago.' Her eyes misted again.

Suddenly Joe understood. He knew her friends' daughters all lived in Pelican Crossing, were married, and he had a vague idea at least one of them had children. Gill must feel her daughter's absence even more when they all met. He wished there was something he could say or do to comfort her, the urge to hug her so strong.

'Sorry,' she said again, patting her eyes with the tissue. 'I didn't intend to dump all this on you.'

'It's not a problem. I'm glad you felt you could share it with me.' He had the impression she hadn't shared it with many others – perhaps only with her closest friends?

'Thanks for listening.'

Greatly daring, Joe reached across the table to cover Gill's hand with his. 'I'm happy to listen any time. Barb always told me I was a good listener.'

'She was right.' Gill gave him a teary smile. 'Now I guess we shouldn't let this lovely food get cold,' she said, gesturing to their meals which had been served while they were talking.

By the time they left the yacht club, a stiff breeze had blown up, tempting Joe to put a protective arm around Gill's shoulders, but he managed to restrain himself, aware it might not be welcome. He was still trying to come to terms with the complicated woman he'd had dinner with. He'd seen different aspects of her, from fiercely independent to endearingly vulnerable, and wasn't sure how to respond.

Thanks again, Joe. It was a lovely evening,' Gill said with a smile. 'Good night.'

And all Joe could do was smile back as she turned and walked away.

'Good night,' he called after her, unable to take his eyes off the dark-haired enigma in pink until her jacket had faded into the darkness.

Gill was right, it had been a lovely evening. He'd learnt a little of the real Gill Dickson, and he was sure now that he wanted to learn a lot more

Twenty-seven

Gill couldn't stop thinking about the dinner at the yacht club and the way she'd opened up to Joe. It was completely out of character for her to have shared such personal issues with someone who was practically a stranger – even if she had known who he was for years.

But Freya was arriving today, and Gill wanted everything to be perfect for her. So, she put her concerns about Joe to the back of her mind and concentrated on making up the bed in the spare room and cooking a lasagne for lunch. It was Freya's favourite meal – or had been. It was so long since Gill had seen her daughter, her tastes could have changed. She planned to serve it with a salad and had bought a bottle of prosecco to celebrate Freya's return home.

Gill was on edge as she waited for Freya's arrival, unsure how to greet the daughter she hadn't seen for almost six years. It felt like a lifetime. In that time, all three of Freya's best friends had married, Jess, Rachel's daughter, had three children, and Amber, Poppy's eldest, had recently given birth to twins. Liz's daughter, Tara, seemed to be more focussed on her career than having children.

At first, when Max left, there had been no talk of divorce, then, as he began to enjoy his freedom, the letter from his solicitor had arrived. Gill should have anticipated it. She knew how these things worked. But she'd been shocked to realise her life was following the pattern of that of her clients. That had been three years ago, and still nothing was settled.

Gill was putting the final touches to the table on the balcony when there was a knock at the door. With her heart suddenly racing, she hurried to answer it.

The figure standing on the doorstep looked like a stranger. The curvy, young woman with the shoulder-length, chestnut curls who had left Australia full of hope and excitement at the prospect of entering a doctoral program in an American university had gone, replaced by this lean woman with a cap of short blonde hair and a network of lines around her eyes and mouth.

Then she smiled tremulously, and it was the Freya Gill remembered, the little girl who had followed her around, who had sat on her knee listening to bedtime stories, whose skinned knees she had kissed better. Without thinking, Gill pulled Freya into her arms. 'Welcome home, darling.'

'Mum!' Freya hugged her back.

It was so good to feel her daughter in her arms again, but she was so thin. What had been happening to her?

When they separated, both women were in tears.

'It's so good to see you, Freya. I…' Gill bit her lip. Now wasn't the time. 'You must be hungry,' she said. 'I hope you still like lasagne.'

'You remembered.' Freya wiped her eyes with one hand. 'Can I just…?' She gestured to the bathroom.

'Of course. When you're ready.'

When Freya disappeared, Gill wiped her own eyes and carried Freya's case into the hall. It was heavy. She must have brought almost everything she owned. Gill wondered if she'd been sincere when she said she might find work in Australia. She hoped so. She went into the kitchen, took the lasagne out of the oven and carried it out to the balcony, along with the salad. The wine was already there, sitting in a cooler.

By the time Freya joined her, they had both recovered from their tears.

'Sorry,' Freya said. 'It was seeing you again. You still look exactly the same, Mum.'

'A few more wrinkles,' Gill said, grimacing. 'But you've changed.'

'The Californian experience,' Freya said, putting one hand up to her hair. 'I've had it like this for some time. Maybe now I'm back, it's time to go natural again. What do you think?'

'I think I could get used to this look, but you had lovely hair.'

'Hmm.' Freya gazed into space. It was as if she was remembering something. Then she shrugged. 'I suppose so.'

During their meal, Freya gave little away about her life in California, and Gill managed to steer clear of asking too many questions.

When they had finished eating, Freya yawned, stretched her hands above her head and said, 'I'm bushed. I need to lie down. Is that okay?'

'Of course. I thought we might go to *Crossings* for dinner if you feel up to it. You won't recognise the place. Poppy...' Gill paused. 'You do know about Jack?' Poppy's husband had died in a freak sailing accident around the same time Freya had left for the States.

'Yes, I heard. I've kept in touch with Amber from time to time.'

Gill hadn't known. It had never occurred to her to ask any of her friends if their daughters had been in communication with Freya. Maybe they didn't know. 'You know she has twins?'

Freya's eyes widened. 'No. I haven't heard from her for ages. I got busy. I lost touch with Tara and Jess too. Are they still living in Pelican Crossing?'

'They are. It'll be good for you all to catch up.'

'Mmm.' Freya didn't sound enthusiastic about seeing the women who had been her best friends. Gill decided to leave it.

'About *Crossings*... sounds good. I'd like to see what Aunt Poppy has done with the place. Thanks, Mum.'

When Freya had disappeared into her bedroom, Gill cleared up the dishes and made herself a coffee. Taking it out to the balcony, she stared out at the distant ocean, wondering what had happened to her daughter to put that sad expression into her eyes.

*

'This is amazing, Mum.' Freya gazed around the restaurant in surprise. 'Aunt Poppy did all this? It looks completely different.'

'It is. She and Jack completely remodelled it. The renovation had only just been completed when... It happened on the day *Crossings* was scheduled to have its grand opening.'

'I think Amber said. It must have been awful for her. I can't imagine… And she continued with all this?' She gestured around the room, at the tables filled with couples and family groups, the waiters and waitresses darting between them and the kitchen.

'Not only continued. *Crossings* has won several awards, been featured in various magazines and even on television, on *Weekender*.'

'Wow!'

Gill was pleased Freya seemed refreshed from her nap and appeared more cheerful than she had during lunch. Had she imagined her daughter's sadness? Had it only been the exhaustion of the long plane trip?

They had placed their order, deciding to share a seafood platter – with Freya saying how much she had missed their locally caught fish – and were enjoying glasses of a chardonnay recommended by the waiter, when Gill recognised a couple entering the restaurant.

Her heart began to pound at the sight of Joe and Erica being shown to a nearby table.

'Mum?' Freya's eyes followed Gill's to where the couple were seated and where Joe was looking across at Gill with a smile. 'You know them?'

'Joe Harris. He's our mayor. And his sister, Erica, is a client of mine. We both go swimming in the mornings too.'

'Swimming?' To Gill's relief, Freya made no comment about Joe, though why should she?

She was more comfortable talking about the swimming. 'I belong to a group of wild swimmers. We meet at the beach before the sun is up. I didn't go this morning because you were on your way here, and it was your first morning back home.'

'Wild swimming… sounds awesome. I may join you.'

'Sure. I'd like that.' Gill stared at her daughter. She couldn't get used to seeing her and had to pinch herself to make sure she wasn't dreaming. She had dreamt of this moment so often. But in her dreams, it was the old Freya. This blonde, harder version of her daughter took some getting used to.

They had finished their platter and were drinking coffee, when Joe came over.

'Hi, Gill,' he said easily, 'this must be your daughter.' He stood waiting to be introduced.

Embarrassed, Gill said, 'Yes, this is Freya, Joe. Freya, Joe Harris, our local mayor…' she felt Joe staring at her, '… and a friend of mine.'

'Delighted to meet you, Freya,' Joe said, holding out his hand. 'Your mum has talked about you.'

Freya shook his hand.

'I'll leave you to your coffee. Hope to see you soon, Gill.' Joe walked off.

When he had gone, Freya stared wide-eyed at Gill. 'Hope to see you soon, Gill,' she repeated. 'Just how good a friend is our local mayor?'

Twenty-eight

Joe had sensed Gill's embarrassment when he went across to speak with her. Had he done the wrong thing? But he couldn't ignore her, though her blush and the expression on her daughter's face made him wish he had. He'd never get a handle on dealing with women. It was one of the reasons he'd never made any women friends since Barb died… not until now. But there was something about Gill that made him want to wrap her up and carry her off to a place where no one could hurt her – figuratively, of course. Unlike most people who, he was sure, only saw the hard outer shell, the successful divorce and family law solicitor, he sensed the vulnerable woman inside and wanted to comfort her.

'Everything all right? Who is the young woman with Gill?' Erica asked, when he returned to their table.

'Fine. It's her daughter.'

'Oh… they look alike, apart from the hair.'

Joe glanced across again to where the two women were sitting. Neither was looking in his direction. He hadn't noticed at the time – he'd been too busy looking at Gill and wondering if she was upset with him. But now he considered it, they did look alike. He could imagine Gill looking exactly like Freya at thirty – apart from the hair, as Erica said. 'You're right,' he said, taking a sip of wine to hide his confusion and embarrassment, as Freya glanced over at their table, clearly asking Gill about him. What was she saying? He wished he could hear.

'You are going to see her again, aren't you?' Erica asked. 'It's about time you moved on, and Gill's perfect for you. Barb would like her,' she added when he didn't respond.

Joe knew Erica was right – on both counts – but it wasn't so easy. Gill was a hard nut to crack and if he made a false step, it could so easily go wrong.

When he still didn't respond, Erica said, 'Sorry, Joe. I'm probably not the best person to give relationship advice.' She looked down at her empty plate, then took a sip of wine.

'I'm sorry. Of course you can offer advice. Isn't it what sisters do? What happened between you and Geoff wasn't your fault. But regarding Gill… best leave it up to me.' Though he hadn't done too well so far. Maybe he did need Erica's advice. Women understood other women, didn't they?

*

'Well?' Freya asked, glancing across to where Joe sat with Erica. She had the mischievous twinkle in her eyes Gill remembered from when she was a teenager.

'We're just friends.' Gill felt herself redden. 'I was his plus one at a business do, and we've had dinner together.' As soon as she spoke, Gill knew it had been a mistake. Freya seized on her words.

'His plus one? And dinner? Sounds serious.'

'It wasn't.' But Gill remembered the misconceptions of his friends in Bellbird Bay. 'A Chamber of Commerce thing down the coast. A bit of a bore, to be honest, though I did manage to chat with the director of the women's centre I'd visited earlier. Ali gave a talk to our local Zonta group last week. She's an interesting lady.'

If Gill hoped she'd manage to distract Freya, she'd forgotten her daughter's ability to get the bit between her teeth once she thought she was on to something.

'He's pretty hot for someone his age,' she said, glancing over again. 'I bet Dad hasn't aged so well. It must take a lot out of him trying to keep up with Mercedes,' she said more bitterly than Gill might have expected.

Mercedes, so that was the name of Max's pregnant girlfriend. It conjured up the image of some exotic creature as unlike Gill as could be. 'Have you spoken to your dad recently?' she asked.

'No way. Not since he told me about her. Can you imagine? She'd be like my sister and she's with my dad. I'm guessing you're not in touch?'

'Only through our solicitors.'

'I thought you'd be divorced by now.'

So did I! 'There have been a few challenges.' Gill had no intention of going into their disagreements with Freya, or of bad-mouthing Max to their daughter. He was still her dad, after all, even if he was currently on her blacklist.

'Ready to leave?' Gill asked, seeing Freya had finished her coffee. She was keen to change the subject.

'Okay.'

Freya was silent on the drive back to the apartment, giving Gill the impression she was caught up in her thoughts. Was she thinking about Max and his new girlfriend, or was it something else entirely? Why did Gill have the impression Freya had some other reason for coming home, and Max was only the catalyst?

Twenty-nine

Next morning, both Gill and Freya were up before sunrise, Freya making good her agreement to join Gill and the other wild swimmers. As was typical on Sundays, the group was smaller than usual, but Olivia was there and welcomed Freya to the group. Gill saw Erica too, but they didn't speak.

'That was amazing, Mum,' Freya said when they were back on the beach, 'so exhilarating. It almost made me forget…' She stopped, as if realising what she'd been about to say.

'What?' Gill asked.

'It's nothing.'

But Gill noticed how her daughter's lips tightened and determined to get to the bottom of what was upsetting her. She was sure it was more than Max.

Freya was quiet again on the way home.

'Why don't we go out to breakfast?' Gill asked, when they were back in the apartment, remembering how much she'd enjoyed her breakfast with Olivia at *The Blue Dolphin Café*.

'Okay. I need to shower and change first.' Freya disappeared into her bedroom, and Gill headed for the shower in her ensuite.

When they met again in the kitchen, Freya was wearing a pair of jeans with a University of California sweatshirt, which made her look younger.

'Ready?' Gill asked, picking up her bag.

'Ready.'

As they walked down to the café, Freya commented on the pelicans sitting around the harbour. 'I've missed the pelicans,' she said. 'It's good to be home.'

'It's so good to have you here.' Gill gave her daughter a hug, and linked arms with her. Freya hadn't given any indication of how long she intended to stay, and Gill was afraid to ask.

When they reached the café, Gill saw Poppy and Cam at their usual table. This morning, they were accompanied by Poppy's oldest daughter, Amber, and her husband. Beside the table was a double stroller containing two tiny babies.

'I heard your babies had arrived,' Gill said, stopping to greet her friend and peeping into the pram. 'Aren't they just perfect. Two boys?' she asked Amber who was looking tired but beaming.

'Jack and Andrew,' Amber said proudly. 'Jack for Dad, and Andrew for Chris's dad.'

'You must be so pleased,' Gill said, knowing the difficulties Amber had experienced in becoming pregnant. 'These two will keep you busy.'

Amber nodded. 'I'm glad Mum's here to help out, though she's had her hands full with Megan and Scarlett's little ones as well.'

Seeing the way Poppy was beaming too, Gill knew her friend didn't mind.

'Good to see you back,' Poppy said to Freya. 'Will we be seeing more of you?'

Freya didn't answer, but Gill could see how moved she was at the sight of Amber's babies.

'We must catch up, Freya,' Amber said. 'Call me.'

Freya nodded.

'Wasn't it lovely to see Poppy and Amber and the twins?' Gill said once she and Freya were settled at a table inside the café, and some distance from the others. 'It's my first glimpse of them.'

When her daughter didn't immediately reply, Gill peered at her. 'What's up?' It wasn't like Freya to be so withdrawn.

'It's all these babies,' Freya said at last. 'Amber, Dad…'

Gill thought she was about to say another name, but she buttoned her lips. 'And…? Is there something you're not telling me?' *Was Freya pregnant? Was this what it was about?*

'Oh, Mum!' Freya's eyes moistened. 'I thought he loved me, wanted me to have his babies.'

'What happened?' Gill asked gently, relieved her daughter was at last going to confide in her.

'Hugh… he was another professor. We taught together. I thought…' She wiped her eyes and sniffed. 'I thought he loved me,' she repeated, 'then he told me he'd got one of his students pregnant. How could he? It was just after that, that Dad told me about him and Mercedes. Men!' she said bitterly. 'They can't be trusted. It's when I decided to come home. I couldn't face seeing Hugh with her next semester.'

'Oh, my darling!' Gill reached over to squeeze Freya's hand. She wanted to hug her again but didn't want to embarrass her by doing it in the café.

'I'm fine, really.' Freya said. 'It was just seeing Amber… and her babies. It brought it all back. But…' she gave a wry grin, '… I'm not going to fall apart every time I see a baby. I promise. But I can't go back to the university. It's why I'm going to look for a position back here.' She straightened her shoulders. 'Now, what about breakfast?' She wiped her eyes again.

Gill sighed inwardly. She should have known there was a man involved. She wondered how long Freya had been with him… long enough for her to consider it to be a serious relationship, obviously. No wonder she was bitter about Max. His timing couldn't have been worse as far as Freya was concerned.

They ordered breakfast, cappuccinos and eggs benedict, but Gill didn't enjoy hers and she was sure Freya didn't either.

'I will call Amber,' Freya said, when they left the café, 'but I'll leave it for a bit.'

Gill gave her daughter the warm hug she'd wanted to give her in the café. 'It gets easier,' she said. 'I know you don't think so now, but believe me, it does. At least you weren't married to the bastard.'

'I'm sorry, Mum. I didn't realise what it must have been like for you when Dad…'

Gill couldn't speak. She hadn't known Freya was aware of Max's other women, even when they were still married. 'It's okay, honey,' she said, hugging Freya again as if she was still a little girl. How she wished she could do more to help. But this wasn't another skinned knee she could kiss better.

*

When they returned from breakfast, Freya decided to go for a walk along the beach, shrugging off Gill's offer to accompany her.

Feeling at a loss, Gill made herself a cup of lemon and ginger tea and carried it out to the balcony with her iPad, intending to finish her book before Wednesday's book club. Wednesday was also the monthly lunch with her friends, though she wondered if she should attend either now Freya was home. She turned on the audiobook, but soon had to turn it off again when she realised she hadn't been paying attention and had lost track of the story.

Her poor daughter. Gill knew what it felt like to be betrayed by a loved one and she'd have walked over hot coals if she thought she could have prevented Freya from experiencing the hurt she had. But there was nothing she could have done, could do. It was something Freya would have to cope with. The one bright spot in all this was it had brought her home to Australia, to Pelican Crossing, and with luck, one day she'd meet someone else, someone more worthy of her love.

Thirty

Ever since he'd seen Gill with her daughter at *Crossings* the previous evening, Joe hadn't been able to stop thinking about her. They looked so alike, mother and daughter, it had made him feel the lack of a child of his own more strongly than ever. But he'd noticed a sadness in the eyes of the younger woman and wondered what had caused it. He also wondered what they'd said about him when he returned to join Erica.

He'd heard Erica leave early this morning in the second-hand Mazda they'd purchased yesterday at a local caryard, despite Erica's protests. It being Sunday, he'd turned over and gone back to sleep. Now he wakened again to the smell of bacon cooking. Checking the time, he saw it was almost eight o'clock. Erica must have been back for ages and got tired waiting for him to wake up. Coco would be wanting her breakfast too.

He rose, took a quick shower and dressed.

'There you are,' Erica said, as he entered the kitchen to see Coco standing over her food bowl.

'Thanks for feeding Coco,' he said. 'Something smells good.'

'I thought the scent of bacon might get you up,' Erica chuckled. 'I saw Gill and her daughter at the beach this morning but didn't speak to them. Olivia did.'

So, Gill's daughter was joining the wild swimmers too. He wondered how she and Gill were getting on. It must be strange for them both… after so many years apart, and with no communication, on her daughter's part at least. He'd call her after breakfast, he decided.

He wanted to see her again, but perhaps she'd be too busy with Freya to spend time with him. Maybe he should ask Erica's advice. She'd been eager to give it to him last night.

His plan to call Gill after breakfast was thwarted by Coco who, now her master was awake, was ready for a walk. 'Okay, Coco,' he said, incapable of disappointing the dog, who had been his sole companion for so long.

Joe wandered along the beach, throwing a stick into the waves for Coco, who loved diving in to fetch it then dropping it at Joe's feet and standing there panting and waiting for him to throw it again. Joe always tired of the game faster than Coco. He greeted several other dog owners as he and Coco made their way along the beach, only stopping to speak with Agnes who was there with Lady.

He was on his way back when he spotted Gill's daughter. She was sitting hunched up on a patch of grass at the edge of the beach, and looked as if she was crying.

Deciding to avoid her, he called to Coco who was padding along at the edge of the water, stopping from time to time to sniff at something Joe couldn't see. But when the dog raised her head, instead of coming to Joe's side, she bounded up to the woman huddled into a ball, pushing her wet nose into her lap. With a sigh, Joe followed her.

'Sorry my dog's bothering you,' he said. 'Come, Coco,' he called. But to his annoyance Coco refused to move.

'It's okay. I like dogs,' she said, fondling Coco's ears and causing the dog to emit a low-pitched moan of pleasure. 'You're Mum's friend. You spoke to us in the restaurant last night.'

'Joe. You're Gill's daughter, Freya. You're on your own?' It was a stupid thing to say, but he couldn't think of anything else. He wondered where Gill was, why Freya was on the beach all alone, and why she'd been crying.

'I needed to get away,' she said, dislodging Coco and getting up. She brushed the sand from her jeans, 'but I should be getting back now. Mum'll be worrying.'

'Can we walk back with you?' he asked, as Coco seemed reluctant to leave her new friend.

'Sure.' She fell into step with him, and Coco padded alongside.

'How are you finding being back in Pelican Crossing?' he asked. 'Your mum mentioned you'd been gone for some time.'

'Too long. It's good to be back.' She didn't volunteer any more information, and Joe didn't feel game to ask. But he was glad to see she seemed more cheerful than when he'd first seen her. Something had clearly upset her. He hoped she and Gill hadn't argued. He knew how much she had been looking forward to her daughter's return.

'I'm this way,' she said when they reached the end of the dog beach. 'Thanks for sharing your dog with me.'

'No problem. Coco seems to have found a new friend.'

'Coco. I like it. It suits her.'

Suddenly, Joe felt the need to say something before she disappeared. 'Your mum loves you,' he said.

'Thanks, I know but I don't deserve it. I love her too.' And she was off, running across the road in the direction of Gill's apartment block.

Joe shook his head as he attached Coco's leash and continued on his way. Freya wasn't a child, but she was clearly a confused young woman. Seeing her, talking to her, made him all the more eager to speak to her mother, but it might be better to wait till later, to give the pair time to sort out whatever was bothering Freya.

*

Gill was still sitting on the balcony gazing into space and trying to work up the energy to do some housework, when Freya returned.

'I met your *friend* on the beach,' Freya said.

Initially puzzled by Freya's emphasis on *friend*, Gill blushed. Did she mean Joe?

'The mayor. He was on the beach with his dog, a chocolate labrador called Coco.'

'You spoke to him?'

'I was sitting on a patch of grass, and the dog came up to me. She's very friendly. He followed her and we had a chat. He seems nice.'

Although curious what Freya and Joe might have found to talk about, Gill waited, hoping for more information. But she was disappointed.

'What are we doing for lunch? The fresh air has made me hungry.'

Checking the time, Gill was surprised to discover how late it was.

She'd been sitting there, lost in her thoughts for a couple of hours. She tried to remember what was in the pantry and the fridge. She'd done a big shop in preparation for Freya's arrival, intending to get back to cooking. This wasn't a good start. 'How about I heat up a pizza?' she said. 'I'll cook us a proper meal tonight.'

'Works for me. No need to go to a lot of trouble. I've lived on takeaway a lot for the past few years.'

'I'd like to. I'll enjoy having someone to cook for again. This morning... time got away from me. I don't know what happened.'

'No worries. I'll just freshen up, then I can set the table. Shall we eat out here?'

'If you like. Thanks, Freya.'

After lunch, during which Gill didn't learn anything further about her daughter's conversation with Joe, Freya disappeared into her bedroom, saying she was still suffering from jetlag.

Left alone, Gill reverted to her usual way of filling her time, opening her laptop to catch up on work. She was busy checking out information for a new client when her phone rang. Seeing Joe's number, she felt the flutter in her stomach his calls now triggered, whether of excitement or apprehension, she wasn't sure.

'Hello.'

'Gill. Joe here. I promised to call.'

'You did.' She didn't know why she couldn't be more welcoming. 'Freya tells me you met on the beach,' she said, trying to sound friendlier.

'How is she? I could see she'd been crying. I tried to comfort her.'

Gill was suffused with guilt. She should have been the one to comfort her daughter, but she'd allowed her to go off on her own. 'She's gone through a difficult time... relationship wise... and with her dad.' What was it about this man, she wondered, that encouraged her confidences. He'd soon know more about her and Freya than anyone else in Pelican Crossing. But there was something about him, something that invited confidences in the knowledge they'd go no further. She remembered him telling her how Barb said he was a good listener. But it was more than that. He'd have made a good dad, better than Max had. It was a pity he and Barb had never had any children. 'She's having a rest,' she said. 'I'm not a great comfort, I'm afraid. Too many sharp corners.' She gave a sigh. She hadn't been a great mother either, but maybe it wasn't too late to change. There was that word again.

'I'm sure that's not true. You help a lot of women, you've helped Erica. I'm sure she'd never have gone down the track of seeking an AVO against Geoff without your help.'

'Maybe.' But that was work. She'd always been good at her job. It was in her personal life she was lacking in empathy.

Seeming to read her mind, Joe said, 'And I haven't noticed too many sharp edges.'

Gill gave a short laugh. 'You don't know me very well.'

Joe cleared his throat. 'Which brings me to the purpose of my call. I'd like to get to know you better.'

Gill's stomach fluttered again. *Definitely not apprehension, maybe anticipation?*

'I'd like to see you again,' he continued, 'have dinner again, though perhaps this time we should go farther afield. I've heard the food at *Addisons* is pretty good,' he said, naming a restaurant situated in the hinterland.

Gill remembered Poppy mentioning it… and hadn't Liz gone there too… with Finn?

Joe was speaking again, 'I was thinking maybe Wednesday, or will you be too tied up with Freya?'

'Freya? I'm not sure what her plans are. I do know she wants to catch up with old friends. But I'm afraid Wednesday's no good. It's my book club.'

'Of course. I should have remembered. It was always on our calendar when Barb…' He was silent for a few moments, then, 'What evening would suit? You will come?'

Gill realised she hadn't actually accepted his invitation. Did she want to have dinner with him again, go on another date with the town mayor, risk getting involved with him? Because, no matter what she might tell him, even tell herself, about only regarding him as a friend, she knew that the flutter she kept experiencing meant some part of her wanted more than friendship.

'Gill?' Joe prompted.

'Yes,' she said before she could decline. 'Dinner will be lovely.'

Thirty-one

It was three days since Freya had opened up to Gill, but since then, she hadn't revealed anything more about her relationship. Gill couldn't understand how she could manage to uncover the source of her clients' problems, but when it came to her daughter, all her skills deserted her.

'What are you doing today?' she asked. 'It's my monthly lunch with the gang, but I could stay home.'

'You're still doing those lunches?' How long has it been?'

'Since you were a baby.' Gill remembered how inadequate she'd felt when she brought Freya home. Neither she nor Max had known what to do with this tiny person. The Mums and Bubs group had been a godsend, and from it, her friendship with Poppy, Liz and Rachel, a friendship which had endured.

'Wow! Well, I guess you all stayed around. No need to stay home for me. I thought I might call Amber, see if I can drop in. I can't avoid babies for ever, much as I'd like to, and it'd be good to chat with her again, Jess and Tara, too. I need to check how to contact them.'

'Tara is a high-flying career woman these days. She's in recruitment. I'm not sure what Jess does, but I do know she has three little ones.' Gill realised she often blanked out when the topic of children and grandchildren came up in the group. 'It will be nice for you to catch up with your old friends again.' The four girls had been inseparable all through school… until Freya left to attend university. Then the other three had married and Freya had gone overseas.

Freya took a sip of the coffee with which she liked to begin each day. 'I had a text from Dad.'

Gill's heart plummeted. 'What did he want?'

'For me to meet Mercedes. Honestly, who calls their daughter Mercedes? It sounds like a car.'

Gill couldn't keep the smile off her face, glad Freya's opinion matched hers. 'So, will you?'

'No way. But…' she twisted her fingers, '… he's talking about bringing her here.'

'What?' Gill's voice was shrill.

'Oh, I don't think he meant it. It was just his way of trying to force me to visit him… them. I can't see him coming back here.'

But the image of him appearing in Pelican Crossing, walking along Main Street, entering *Books and Coffee* where they used to go together, was the stuff of Gill's nightmares. 'I hope not,' she said, annoyed Max could disturb her, even from a distance.

Gill cleared the breakfast dishes while Freya went off to call Amber, but the thought Max might decide to come to Pelican Crossing refused to leave her. She wished she was going to the office today, where she could spend her time helping other women with their problem marriages and forget about her own. Having the day to herself, lunching with her old friends, would give her too much time to worry about what Max might do next, if Freya continued to refuse to visit him.

*

Gill was last to arrive at Liz's apartment, and when she walked into the kitchen, the others were already drinking wine. Today, the apartment felt different than it had on her previous visits, and at first she couldn't work it out. It was only when the others started teasing Liz about Finn moving in, that Gill realised what it was.

Until now, the place had had a very feminine atmosphere, the home of a woman who lived alone, not as spartan as Gill's but with a distinct character. Now there were signs of a male presence. They were subtle, but they were there – the sweater thrown across the back of a chair, the pair of dark-rimmed glasses lying on the coffee table alongside a bundle of newspapers, the pair of running shoes she'd noticed lying in the hallway. It made Gill think of Max again and remember how he used to scatter his belongings around their apartment.

'Thanks,' she said, as Liz handed her a glass of wine, and she banished the memories into the past where they belonged.

Lunch was delightful as usual. Liz served roasted pumpkin soup with homemade bread and a variety of cheeses, perfect for the cool day. It was followed by a *tarte tatin* which she claimed to have made from a Donna Hay recipe book her newly discovered daughter had given her.

The conversation over lunch was general, allowing Gill to relax somewhat, until Liz said, 'Mandy tells me you had dinner with our mayor, Gill.'

Gill blushed. She could feel three pairs of eyes on her. 'He was being friendly. I'm advising his sister.' It was too much information. She knew that as soon as the words were out of her mouth. Client information was sacrosanct, not to be divulged to anyone. 'I mean...' she stammered.

'We'll pretend we didn't hear that,' Rachel said, always the one to smooth things over. 'Did I hear Freya's home?'

'You did. She arrived on Saturday. She's actually hoping to see your Amber today,' Gill said to Poppy.

'Is she back home for good?' Poppy asked. 'I saw her with Gill on Sunday,' she told the others. 'I thought she was looking well.'

'I don't know.' Gill sighed, more comfortable now they were talking about Freya, not her, but it was still a minefield. 'Once they're grown, they have minds of their own. I'm just enjoying her company while I can. She's been coming swimming with me in the mornings.'

'I don't know how you do it. A few days was enough for me,' Liz said, referring to her own attempt at wild swimming the previous year. 'But we all know what you mean about minds of their own.' She gave an exaggerated sigh, and the others nodded.

'It's good she's back,' Poppy said. 'Amber was looking forward to catching up. It'll be good for her to have company. I think she's finding the twins hard work.'

'Twice the work, but twice the love and twice the fun,' Rachel said, familiar with her own twin granddaughters. 'How's Mandy going?' she asked Liz, whose daughter was pregnant.

As the conversation about grandchildren and pregnancies continued, Gill relaxed, heaved a sigh of relief and let their talk flow over her, but as soon as she did, the memory of Freya's text from Max forced itself into her mind again. He wouldn't come here, would he? And then there was Joe. What had possessed her to agree to have dinner with him again? Though she had to admit a small part of her was looking forward to it.

*

It was a few days since Joe had met Freya on the beach and arranged to have dinner with Gill. Suggesting *Addisons* had been inspired. It had been Finn who'd given him the heads up on the restaurant, telling Joe it was a good idea to head out of town. He didn't know why Gill had seemed so hesitant about agreeing to see him again, but at least she hadn't declined.

She'd said tonight was her book club. He wondered what they were reading this month. He missed sharing Barb's monthly book club reads. Now he had to choose his own reading matter from the library, he stuck to the Australian crime authors he was familiar with, but he sometimes yearned for the eclectic mix he'd read in the past. Maybe Olivia would persuade Erica to join the book club, and he could widen his choice of books again.

Coco stirred under Joe's desk, reminding him it was time for her walk. He shut down his computer and picked up the dog's leash. 'Off for a walk,' he said to Debbie as he passed her desk. 'Back in half an hour.'

As always, it was good to get out into the fresh air. Coco wasn't the only one to feel claustrophobic shut up in the office. Sometimes he longed for the days before he became mayor, when he was a land surveyor and spent his days outside. It had been Barb who'd encouraged him to go into local government telling him he was a born leader. He sighed, as he always did at the memory of his wife. Maybe if she'd lived, he wouldn't mind his enforced office life.

He was heading for the marina, planning to catch up with Cam, see if he had time to join him for a quick beer, when someone calling his name caused him to pause and turn towards the harbour. Coco started pulling on her leash, excited at the sight of two pelicans perched on bollards at the edge of the water.

'Joe,' Jamie called again. 'I thought it was you.'

'Jamie, how are you?' Jamie Whittaker was another of Joe's old mates. He had taken over his father's fishing boat, then had sold up and now ran fishing charters for tourists, very successfully, Joe had heard.

'I'm good. I've been wanting to speak with you. I heard Erica's back in town.'

'Erica, yes.' For a moment Joe was puzzled, then he remembered. When they were all teenagers, hadn't Erica and Jamie had a thing? Back then, he hadn't paid much attention to his younger sister's boyfriends, but Jamie had been one of his own group of friends, and he seemed to recall him being upset when Erica left to study nursing in Sydney. Joe had already been dating Barb by then and had other things on his mind.

'How is she? Husband not here?'

Joe stared at his old mate, sure Erica wouldn't want her marital problems broadcast. But Jamie was a mate. 'She's here on her own.'

'Well, if there's anything I can do, if she wants someone to talk to…' Jamie's voice trailed off as he clearly saw Joe's shuttered expression.

Surely Jamie wasn't interested in Erica after all this time? But he'd been divorced for a number of years, and Joe knew how lonely it could be when you'd been accustomed to being part of a couple.

He didn't reply. It was all too complicated.

Thirty-two

'Where did you say you were going?' Freya asked.

Gill was peering into the mirror, applying the minimal makeup she favoured, when her daughter popped her head in. '*Addisons*, it's a relatively new restaurant in the hinterland. It's had good reviews.'

'And is well away from the curious glances of the residents of Pelican Crossing. I expect that's why the mayor chose it.' Freya winked.

'Don't call him that. His name's Joe.'

'But he *is* the mayor.'

'Hmm.' Gill studied her image in the full-length mirror. *Did the calf-length, blue, wool dress look as if she was making too much of an effort? Should she have chosen her usual black pants with a coloured top?*

'You look lovely, Mum,' Freya said as if sensing her concern. 'You'll blow him away.'

'That's not my intention. We're only friends. We're not…'

'Well, you should be. It's about time you found someone, someone who'd treat you better than Dad did. I'm sorry I didn't realise what a jerk he was. He had me fooled. Not anymore. The mayor… sorry, Joe, seems like one of the good guys. There aren't many of them around.'

Gill turned to see Freya was almost in tears.' Oh, my darling.' She pulled her daughter into a warm hug. 'Would you prefer me to stay home tonight? It's not too late for me to cancel.' *And it might not be a bad idea*, Gill thought, trying to calm the butterflies in her stomach that seemed to have a life of their own.

'Of course not. I'll be fine. I want to check out a few of the Australian university websites. There may be some positions available for next year. Amber thought I could find some tutoring in the meantime.'

'Oh.' Gill had been very careful to avoid asking Freya about her plans. It seemed she had been more forthcoming with Amber than she had with her mother. But it wasn't too much of a surprise. The two had always been close. 'What sort of tutoring?'

'She says there are a few high school kids who are having challenges with their studies and may be open to private tuition.'

'Would you like that?'

'If it was short term, just until something permanent comes up. In the States, around half the university positions are on a one-year contract, so it's always a bit of a challenge not knowing what's going to happen from one year to the next. It's almost impossible to get tenure. I've heard it's different here.'

Gill's heart lifted. It sounded as if Freya had decided to stay, to make a future right here in Australia. And even if it meant she might have to travel interstate, it was better than her being on the other side of the world.

By the time Gill heard Joe's knock at the door, she'd convinced herself of a future in which Freya lived within travelling distance and would continue to be part of her life. Now, if only her daughter could find someone to love her too…

Joe looked very handsome tonight, in a pair of khaki chinos and white shirt, a brown sweater which matched his eyes knotted casually around his shoulders. Gill's heart gave a flip.

'You're looking very nice,' he said. 'Colour suits you.'

Gill blushed, realising her outfit probably matched her eyes too. *Was that why she'd chosen it? Had she subconsciously wanted Joe's admiration?* 'Thanks, you do too.' She blushed again. *What had possessed her to say that?*

Once they were in the car, Gill began to relax as Joe recounted some of Coco's antics.

Then he said, 'I'm worried about Erica. She seems determined to contact Briony. Her daughter-in-law,' he added, clearly seeing Gill's puzzled expression. 'She's pregnant, and Erica wants to check up on her. She wants to know how Kieren is too. She says she'll get a new phone, withhold the number, but I'm afraid Geoff will find out. What do you think?'

'She shouldn't. Of course she shouldn't. But I can understand why she wants to.' Gill thought about how she would feel if Freya was pregnant, and she wasn't able to contact her. It had been one of her greatest fears. 'We can only hope he doesn't find out. He should be facing court soon. Let's hope it makes him see sense.' But she could hear the doubt in her voice.

'They don't always, do they? Abusive husbands. I'm guessing you've seen it happen a lot. You read about it every day, see it on the news. Wives killed by their husbands, by the one person who promised to love them.'

'You don't think…' Gill was horrified. Erica had told her Geoff had hit her. It hadn't occurred to her he could be an actual danger to her. She remembered some of the horror stories Ali had told her.

'I don't know. I've never liked the guy. I've seen her bruises, but I doubt he'd go that far. I just hope he stays in Western Australia.'

'Me too. Erica tells me she's nursing again.'

'She loves it, always has. I hate how he forced her to give it up. He called me, you know, trying to find out where she was. Put on the spot, I gave him the name of an old school friend of Erica's, living in Cairns, hoping to send him on a wild goose chase. I haven't told Erica about his call.'

By this time, they had reached their destination. The long, low building was situated on top of a cliff with distant ocean views, which must be amazing in daylight. Tonight, there was a full moon shining on the water, and Gill could easily imagine what it would be like as the sun went down.

'It must be quite something at sunset and sunrise,' Joe said, echoing her thoughts.

Gill turned towards him and smiled. This man continued to surprise her.

'Shall we go in?' Joe said.

The restaurant was almost full, but Gill didn't recognise any of the other diners. *Had Freya been right?*

Once they were seated, Joe's next words confirmed it. 'No familiar faces to speculate on our being together,' he said. 'Unlike the yacht club.'

'Is it why you chose to come here?'

'Partly. I'd also heard the food was really good. Finn Hunter told me about it.'

'I believe he brought Liz here.'

Joe didn't reply then said, 'I'm glad we've become friends. It's too easy to stop making new friends as we grow older. I enjoy your company, Gill. I hope we can see more of each other. I'd like to know what makes Gill Dickson tick, who the woman behind the divorce and family law solicitor really is. So far, I've only seen glimpses of her, and I like what I've seen. You don't find it easy to drop the barriers, do you?'

Dazed by Joe's sudden abruptness, Gill took a sip of wine before replying. She didn't remember Joe ordering it. But it tasted good and gave her time to consider what to say. No one had ever spoken to her like this before. She placed the glass carefully on the table. 'You're right,' she said. 'I'm often not aware the barriers are there. I've become so accustomed to them. It surprises me how you've managed to make your way through them. I've made a vow to change, to become more like other people, but I don't always succeed. I hate to feel vulnerable and without the barriers…' She grimaced and took another sip of wine.

'There's no need. You're the least vulnerable person I know. Opening up to others isn't a sign of weakness. It can be a sign of strength.'

'Hmm.'

'Anyway, enough of the introspection. We're here to have dinner and an enjoyable evening.' Joe picked up a menu, and Gill did the same.

The rest of the evening passed pleasantly. Both were pleased with their choice of half-shell scallops followed by barbecued quail. Gill was about to shake her head when the waiter produced the dessert menu, only to change her mind when he listed the specials. The dark chocolate mousse with hazelnut crumb and wattle seed ice cream sounded too good to refuse. They agreed to share a serving and Joe ordered coffee to accompany it.

'I won't need to eat for a week,' Gill said, as they piled back into the car. 'The meal was delicious. Thanks for bringing me here. I know Liz raved about it, but she didn't do it justice. It compares very favourably with *Crossings*.'

The whole evening had been delightful – the restaurant, the food, the company. Gill couldn't remember when she had last enjoyed herself so much. She stole a glance at the man in the driver's seat. Freya was right. Joe was one of the good guys. The problem was… Gill didn't need another man in her life. She was still trying to free herself from Max, and it wasn't fair to let Joe believe there could be a future for them. But how could she say it, how could she tell him without embarrassing herself? What if she was wrong? What if he had no intention of being anything but a good friend? Maybe she was making his friendship into something it wasn't. Maybe it was the influence of the full moon putting ideas into her head, ideas which had no bearing on reality.

You're right,' Joe said. '… about it comparing favourably to *Crossings*,' he added when she didn't reply. 'We should definitely come again.'

'Of course,' she said, unable to stop herself.

Thirty-three

Joe was glad it was the weekend. He'd promised to help Erica get the garden into shape and, to his surprise, was looking forward to it. He regretted letting it go after Barb's passing but hadn't had the inclination to do it without her. She'd been the one to take the lead, the gardener in the family. He had just been her willing assistant. Now he'd be Erica's.

It was time, he decided, time to move on, not only to get the garden into shape, but maybe time for him to move on in his life too. As he drank his morning coffee, Coco waiting impatiently for him to finish, Joe thought about the previous evening. Dinner had been good, Gill's company even better. But she was still a bit of an enigma. During the meal, he'd thought he was getting through to her when she admitted to putting up barriers, and to him managing to get through them. Then, later, she'd closed up again. It was as if the shutters had come down.

He was aware she was still married, going through a difficult divorce. He understood how she might find it challenging to become involved in another relationship. And while for the present he was content to remain friends, he hoped things might change. From time to time, he caught a hint she might have feelings for him, then the barriers went up again. He saw it with Erica too, how everything was going well, then suddenly things changed.

Coco nudged Joe's leg again, reminding him it was time for her walk.

'Okay, Coco,' he said, then turning to Erica. 'I'll take Coco for her walk then I'm all yours.'

'I thought we could go to the garden centre first,' Erica said. 'You've let a lot of plants die. We need to replace them, maybe with something hardier you won't be able to kill off,' she chuckled.

This was the first indication she'd given that she might not stay with Joe. He gave her a puzzled look.

'I won't be here for ever,' she said. 'Once things are settled with Geoff…' Her voice trailed off at the possible realisation it could take some time and might never happen. 'Well, whenever.'

'You can stay here as long as you want. You know that.' Joe hugged her.

'I know what you said, but this is your home, not mine. I can't stay here for ever. I need my own place, Joe. But I'm grateful to be here.' She hugged him back. 'Now off you go on your walk, and I'll make a list of what we need to buy.'

Once away from the house, Joe set off in the direction of the beach. It was one of his favourite spots, and Coco loved it too. He was so glad of the council decision to retain the area for dogs to run free. The two councillors who were against it were still unhappy but there wasn't much more they could do after the vote had gone against them. Though it didn't stop them from complaining loudly whenever they were in Joe's presence.

This morning, the beach was a hive of activity. Joe had forgotten it was the Pelican Crossing kitesurfing championships, and the beach was filled with onlookers. For a few moments, Joe watched as the brightly coloured kites billowed in the breeze, pulling the surfers along, before saying, 'Not for us today, Coco.' He was about to turn around when he caught sight of Gill and Freya. Coco spied his new friends too and pulled on his leash.

Gill was busy watching the surfers and their kites, but Freya must have noticed them. 'Look, Mum,' he heard her say. 'It's the mayor.'

Gill turned quickly and a blush rose on her cheeks.

Heartened, he said, 'Hey Gill, Freya. Good to see you. I'd completely forgotten about all this.' He gestured to where the crowd was now cheering.

'Freya insisted on coming,' Gill said, as if embarrassed to have been caught there.

'I did a bit of kitesurfing in the States,' Freya said. 'They didn't have this in Pelican Crossing before I left.'

'It only started up a few years ago,' Joe said. 'It's the brainchild of Gary Whittaker. You may remember him and his brother, Rory? Rory works at *Pelican Marine*, and their dad runs a fishing charter.'

'I remember Rory,' Freya said. 'He's still here? He always said he couldn't wait to leave, didn't want to end up like his dad. Oh, look!' she said, as one of the surfers came a cropper.

'Thanks for last night,' Gill whispered while her daughter was otherwise occupied. 'I enjoyed it. I may not have said so at the time.'

'I enjoyed it too. Sorry If I came on a bit strong.'

'No, you were right. I sometimes…'

'Did you see that?' Freya interrupted them. 'Oh, I'd love to get involved again. How do I contact Gary Whittaker?' she asked Joe.

'He runs things out of a shed next to his dad's charter business. It's by the marina, close to *Pelican Marine*.'

'And Cam Mitchell owns and manages it,' Gill said. 'A lot's changed since you left.'

'So it seems. I need to get caught up.'

Joe was about to ask the pair if they'd join him for coffee, when he remembered Erica would be waiting for his return. 'I should get back,' he said. 'I promised Erica, but…' he thought quickly, '… if the two of you are free this afternoon, how about you join me for coffee?'

'Sorry, I'm catching up with some old friends, but Mum's free,' Freya said with a twinkle in her eyes.

'Gill?' Joe asked, his heart leaping at the prospect of spending more time alone with Gill, although he sensed her embarrassment.

'Mum?' Freya prompted.

'I guess so.'

It wasn't the enthusiastic response Joe might have hoped for, but it wasn't a refusal.

'Great. How about we meet in *Books and Coffee* around three? You don't mind if I bring Coco, do you?' he asked, feeling the dog nudge him.

'Of course not. She's a sweetie.' Gill bent down to ruffle Coco's ears. The dog gave a whine of pleasure.

'She really likes you too,' Joe said. *And so do I*, he thought.

*

As soon as Joe left, Gill turned to Freya. 'Why did you say that?' she asked. 'You made it impossible for me to refuse.'

'Did you want to? I saw you blush. You enjoyed your dinner last night, didn't you?'

Gill glared at her daughter. When did she become so annoying? 'Last night was one thing, but... it's too soon.' Despite her denial, she experienced that flutter in her stomach again at the prospect of spending more time with Joe.

'It's only coffee,' Freya said, 'and it'll get you out of the house. Don't think I haven't noticed how you gravitate to your study and become engrossed in work.'

'I'm sorry. I should be spending more time with you.' Gill was overcome with guilt. She had meant to reduce the time she spent working while at home, but old habits die hard.

'I don't mind really, but I hate to think it's how you spend your time. You need to get a life, Mum. Dad has, and while I may not like what he's doing, it's heaps better than burying himself in his work.'

Gill almost laughed at the idea of Max burying himself in his work. If he had, he might have been offered the principal's position he'd been so eager for. He'd always preferred the easy life. It had been what attracted her to him in the first place. But she'd soon tired of his lackadaisical attitude, wishing he shared her ambition. What Max had never understood was that life didn't hand you success. You had to work for it. And she had, still did. But had she become too work focussed?

'Your dad...' she began.

'Okay, Dad was a bad example. But take the mayor. He doesn't seem to spend all his time worrying about council business. He takes time out, time with his sister, his dog... you, if you'd allow him.'

'I wish you wouldn't call him the mayor.' But Gill knew she was ignoring Freya's point. Her daughter was right. For years, she'd allowed work to take over her life. Spending time on the problems of her clients had blinded her to her own, to the failings in her own marriage. Was Freya right about Joe? Should she give in to the fluttering she experienced in his presence, when she heard his voice on the phone?

Should she let her guard down and damn the consequences? It was a scary thought.

When Freya had left to meet her friends for a girls' afternoon at Tara's – Amber and Jess's husbands had agreed to take care of the children – Gill made herself a cup of calming camomile tea and stared out at the ocean. The competition was over, but there were still a few kitesurfers out there, swooping and circling over the sea like giant multicoloured birds. She hadn't known Freya had gone kitesurfing in California. There was a lot about her daughter's life there Gill didn't know. Maybe now she was back, Gill would be able to grow close to her daughter again, fill in the gaps in her life and recapture the close relationship they'd once enjoyed.

Checking the time, Gill realised she needed to leave if she was to meet Joe at three as arranged. She dragged a comb through her hair, renewed her lipstick and grimaced at herself in the mirror. Was this how Joe saw her – a middle-aged woman with grey-streaked hair who had wrinkles around her eyes and mouth? Today, the loose top she wore over her jeans hid the spare tyre which had appeared in recent years, but she had managed to keep reasonably trim with her early morning swims. *Not too bad for someone who'd never see fifty again*, she thought.

By the time Gill reached *Books and Coffee*, she'd decided this was a good idea. Joe was already there, seated at one of the outside tables, Coco lying at his feet. When she walked up, the Labrador rose to greet her, pushing her wet nose into Gill's hand.

'Hello to you too,' she said, bending down to pat the dog, before raising her eyes to meet Joe's. 'Hello,' she said, suddenly shy.

'I'm glad you made it,' he said with a smile, half rising to greet her.

'Of course.'

'Coffee?'

'Thanks. Cappuccino.'

Joe disappeared inside to order, leaving Gill with Coco. 'I wish I knew what your master is thinking,' she said, but Coco only settled herself more comfortably. Gill sighed and gazed at Joe's back as he stood at the counter to place his order.

'What's Erica doing today?' Gill asked, when Joe returned. She wanted to keep the conversation away from the sort of personal issues they'd touched on the previous evening.

'Gardening.' Joe sighed. 'We bought up half the garden centre this morning, and I helped her for a bit, but I'm no gardener. I suspect I was more of a hindrance than a help. The garden was always Barb's province. I'm afraid I let it go after… She'd be pleased Erica is taking it in hand.'

'I've never been much of a gardener, either,' Gill confessed, wondering if her focus on work had prevented her from becoming involved in many of the pursuits which other women enjoyed. She thought of Liz with her deck full of plants, and Rachel's luxuriant garden.

'It takes all sorts,' Joe said. 'I'm sure you have other attributes.'

'I'm not sure I do,' she said ruefully. 'My work seems to have taken over my life.'

'Well, we'll have to see if we can do something about that,' Joe said, as Denny appeared with their coffees and a plate containing two delicious looking raspberry and white chocolate muffins.

'Thanks, Denny,' Joe said, in reply to Denny's 'Enjoy!'

'Wow, these look good,' Gill said, her mouth-watering at the sight of the muffins. 'Ron's muffins are the best.'

'He said they were just out of the oven, and I couldn't resist them. They're still warm.'

'Yum.' Gill bit into the muffin, then took a sip of her coffee. This was fun. She wondered why she'd had doubts about coming. It was lovely sitting here in a patch of sunlight with a companion who… if she was being honest with herself… she was becoming increasingly fond of.

'To get back to what we were talking about earlier,' Joe said, when they'd demolished the muffins, and Coco had enjoyed a treat.

'What was that?'

'Doing something about your life. It sounds as if you need to get out of your comfort zone, try something new, have an adventure.'

Gill stared at him in amazement. Was this the conservative mayor of Pelican Crossing talking? Then she remembered Barb and he had travelled around Australia in an old caravan, how Barb had recounted their experiences to the book club. Maybe he wasn't so conservative after all. 'What do you have in mind?' she asked.

'I've got into a bit of a rut too. After the business with the developer, and saving the newspaper, I was at a bit of a loss till Erica arrived. But I can't rely on my sister to solve my problems. So…' he took a deep breath, '… how about we try a few things together? I suspect you're as lonely as I am. I resorted to spending all hours in the office, to fill in the emptiness in my life and…'

How did he know? It was only recently that Gill had admitted to herself she was lonely… then Freya had come home.

'I have Freya home,' she said. But she knew her daughter wasn't the answer to her loneliness. Freya would want a life of her own, one that didn't necessarily include her mother. It was what she wanted for her daughter, wasn't it?

'Like I have Erica. But they'll eventually want their own lives,' he said echoing Gill's thoughts. 'Why don't we live a little? Pelican Crossing offers all sorts of activities for the adventurous tourist. We may not be tourists, but we can still enjoy hot air ballooning, paragliding, kitesurfing, scuba diving. The list goes on. What's your preference?'

Gill gulped. She'd never considered any of those, assuming they were designed for younger people. Then she remembered that Liz had gone hot air ballooning, and Poppy learned to scuba dive, so maybe… 'You choose,' she said, her heart racing.

Thirty-four

The afternoon with Joe at *Books and Coffee* had been the beginning.

In the past few weeks, Gill had joined Joe in a variety of activities in which she'd never have imagined herself participating. They'd taken a hot air balloon ride, which she'd enjoyed more than she'd anticipated, booked into one of Jamie Whittaker's fishing charters on which, to her surprise, she managed to actually catch a fish, and taken scuba diving lessons from Jamie's son, Gary. She'd drawn the line at kitesurfing, deciding to leave that to Freya who had already booked several sessions, also with Gary, though Gill suspected his brother, Rory, might be part of the attraction. She was keeping her fingers crossed and carefully avoiding any mention of him to Freya.

Erica had joined them on the fishing trip, and Gill had found it heartwarming to see her come out of her shell. She was pretty when she managed to overcome her fear of her husband, and Gill had seen a reflection of her attractiveness in Jamie's eyes.

Today, Gill was to have her first experience of scuba diving in the ocean – before they started lessons Joe had admitted to having gone scuba diving before, but not for a long time, he'd added. When she'd heard about Gill taking lessons, Poppy had insisted on her and Cam joining Gill and Joe for this first trip, and Gill was looking forward to her support.

'Ready for another adventure?' Joe asked, when she opened the door to him.

'I think so.' Freya had already asked her this before heading off to go kitesurfing. 'I guess I can't back out now.'

'You'll be fine,' Joe assured her. 'You did okay last week.'

'Hmm.' The previous week had been in the rock pool at the edge of the harbour. The open ocean was something else entirely.

Poppy and Cam were already there when Gill and Joe arrived at the harbour. Gill joined Poppy in the change room in Gary's dive shed to pull a wet suit on over the bikini she'd worn under her clothes. Glancing across at Poppy, she thought they must both look like creatures from another planet in the black stretch neoprene outfits which covered them from their necks to their wrists and ankles, leaving only their feet, hands and heads exposed. Then they joined the others to board the dive boat.

Gill had an empty feeling in the pit of her stomach as they headed out to sea, her hand tightly clasped in Joe's. It was strange, she thought, how she'd come to depend on him, though there had been no hint of anything more than friendship between them, despite Freya's comments, and Poppy's curious looks. Her friend knew better than to make any comment, regardless of what she might be thinking.

Once out of the harbour, Gill's excitement began to build. *Is this how Poppy had felt on* her *first dive?* She glanced at her friend, but only saw her grinning at Cam whose arm was around her shoulders. For an instant, she wondered how it would feel to have Joe's arm around *her*, then dismissed the thought. They were only friends.

While Gill had been musing, imagining Joe's arm around her, the boat had stopped. This was it. First Cam, then Poppy, slipped over the edge of the boat, then it was her turn. When she hesitated, Joe said, 'I'll be right behind you, and I'll keep close. Gary's with you too. You'll be right.'

Gill felt scared, but it was too late to back out now. Carefully, she slid into the water to join her friends, Joe following. At first, Gill felt claustrophobic, with the mask covering her face and she was acutely aware of how loud her bubbles and the other sounds around her were. But she remembered this from her experience in the rock pool and after a few moments she became used to it and began to experience a sense of relaxation, not unlike she felt in the ocean each morning when she turned to float on her back. The difference this time was… she was underneath the water.

As she became more aware of her surroundings, Gill realised Joe was nearby, Gary close beside her, and Poppy and Cam not far off. As she moved through the water, she experienced a feeling of freedom, unlike anything she had ever encountered before. *Was this what it was like to be in space?* A sense of exhilaration filled Gill as she watched tiny fish swim by, fronds of soft coral swaying with the movement of the water and a turtle make its way past the group of divers. All too soon, it seemed, Gary indicated it was time to surface again, and they all made their way back.

'How was it?' Gary asked, when they were back on board the dive boat, and Gill had removed her face mask, regulator and fins, and unstrapped the tank.

'Amazing! I can't believe how wonderful it felt. I want to do it again.'

'I knew you'd like it,' Joe said, coming over and, to her surprise, throwing his arms around her. 'Well done! You're a natural. Certification next.'

'I'm not so sure,' Gill said, aware of Poppy and Cam staring at them and smiling. 'But at least I didn't make a fool of myself.' She laughed, partly to disperse the rush of desire she'd felt at Joe's embrace. He was only congratulating her as any friend would.

On the trip back, the conversation was all about the dive. To Gill's surprise, Gary held the same opinion as Joe. 'A few more sessions and we'll see you get your certification,' he said. 'Then you won't need me.' She'd also been surprised to learn Joe had been a certified diver since he was in his teens. He'd been modest when telling her he'd dived before.

Back on land, Gill struggled out of her wet suit and back into the jeans and skivvy she'd been wearing when she arrived, then she and Poppy went out to join the men who were standing by the harbour wall drinking beer and chatting.

Cam gave Poppy a warm hug and Joe nodded to Gill. She had a weird impulse to hug him, but quickly suppressed it. *What would he think?*

'Why don't you and Joe join us for dinner?' Poppy asked. 'Were having my usual table at *Crossings* and I can guarantee a good meal.'

Gill shot a glance at Joe, but his expression gave nothing away. 'It sounds lovely,' she said, 'but Freya…'

'Your daughter? Don't worry about her,' Gary said. 'She and Rory are coming to the yacht club with Mandy and me tonight.'

'Oh!' Freya hadn't mentioned anything about meeting Rory Whittaker again. Had Gill been right about him? She remembered Freya's surprise he was still living in Pelican Crossing. Perhaps her daughter wasn't quite as negative about men as she pretended… or did she consider Rory to be safe since they'd grown up together? Maybe they were just friends too. Not all relationships were about sex, as she well knew. Although… she glanced at Joe who was looking out to sea and felt her stomach flutter again.

Thirty-five

Joe was feeling cheerful as he prepared to go to dinner at *Crossings*. The diving expedition had gone well, bringing back memories of his youth. He had given up diving after meeting Barb. She hadn't been keen, and they found plenty of other things to do together. He was delighted to be able to pick it up again with Gill. He smiled at the memory of her grin when she'd removed her mask. She'd been like a child with a new toy.

She'd looked so happy, he had embraced her without thinking… and she hadn't pulled away. Of course, she'd still been wearing her wet suit, so it wasn't as if there had been any skin contact, but… it was a start… and maybe… But he wouldn't think of that now. It was enough they were to have dinner together again, albeit with Poppy and Cam. For once, the thought of spending the evening seeing his friends being affectionate with each other didn't upset him.

'Seeing Gill again?' Erica asked, when he told her – and Coco – of his plans. The dog merely sighed and curled up in her bed. 'How many times is it this week?'

'I haven't been counting,' he said, even though he had been counting and wondering how he could move their relationship forward from friendship to something more intimate. Gill was proving a difficult woman to get to know, but he felt he was gradually managing to break down the barriers she'd erected around her emotions. Perhaps tonight would be a turning point.

'You're looking very smart. She's a lucky lady.'

'Hmm.' Joe glanced down at the blue sweater, the collar of the blue and white striped shirt peeking out of the neckline, and the navy pants. *Would Gill think it was over the top?* He missed having Barb advise him what to wear. *What did other men do?* Everyday was easy, but he was out of practice at this dating business. 'Thanks, Erica,' he said. 'And thanks for keeping Coco company.'

'She and I will have a lovely time together. Won't we, Coco?' she said to the dog, whose ears pricked up at the sound of her name. 'We had a good walk this afternoon while you were on your dive. I presume it went well?'

'Very well. You should try it sometime.'

'Maybe I will.'

Joe felt guilty. *Had he been so busy finding things to do with Gill, he'd forgotten to consider Erica?*

'But not yet,' she said. 'I have a few things to work out before I start trying anything new. You've no need to worry about me.'

'But I do,' Joe said, suddenly serious. 'I want to see you happy again.'

'It's what I want too,' Erica sighed. Then she smiled. 'Now, off you go, and enjoy your evening. Don't waken Coco and me when you come in,' she chuckled.

'I won't be late.'

Erica laughed as if she knew something he didn't.

*

It had been agreed they would all meet at the restaurant, and when Joe arrived the other three were already there, seated at the table reserved for Poppy, close to the kitchen. He had barely greeted his companions – Cam with a handshake and the women with a kiss on the cheek – when a waiter arrived with a bottle of white wine.

'I hope you don't mind, I already ordered the wine,' Poppy said.

'Not at all,' Joe said, still reeling from the touch of his lips on Gill's cheek. It was a first for him with Gill. He always greeted Poppy this way, and it had seemed natural to greet Gill in a similar manner. He'd noticed her blush at the contact, whether from embarrassment or some other emotion, he wasn't sure.

After Poppy insisting she order, given it was her restaurant and her kitchen, they were served the house special of the day which was a sashimi plate followed by coral trout served with potatoes, leek and fennel. They were enjoying chocolate pavlova for dessert, having spent the meal talking diving and the various sailing expeditions Poppy and Cam had undertaken, when Poppy fixed Joe and Gill with her gaze and said, 'What about you two?'

Joe flinched, but Gill, seemingly more accustomed to Poppy, said, 'What about us? Not everyone is in the market for the sort of relationship you and Cam have, Poppy.'

Joe's heart sank. This wasn't what he wanted to hear. He'd had a relationship like Poppy and Cam's and would love to have one again, if only… He noticed the two spots of colour on Gill's cheeks, and wondered if she really meant what she'd said, or if it was her way of protecting herself and her emotions.

But before he could speak, Cam said, 'Leave it, Poppy. Gill's right. We've had a good day together and a lovely evening. There's no need to spoil it.'

'I'm sorry. I didn't intend to spoil things,' Poppy said. 'I suppose it's because I'm so happy myself, I want the same for my friends… and you two have been doing a few things together. You're both single, and…'

'Leave it,' Cam repeated.

This time Joe did find his voice. 'Gill and I are friends, Poppy, and friends do enjoy spending time together. I'm happy for you and Cam, pleased you've been lucky enough to find happiness a second time around. But not everyone can be as lucky as you. Life's not like that. Some of us have to be satisfied with what we have.'

'I'm sorry,' Poppy said again. 'Forgive me. I won't try to force my opinions on you again.'

'You're forgiven, Poppy,' Joe said. No one could remain annoyed with Poppy for long.

Gill nodded, but Joe knew Poppy's words had disturbed her.

'You two should come sailing with us some time,' Cam said in an obvious attempt to clear the air, and discussion followed on where the best spots were for fishing and the prime bays for picnicking. No firm arrangements were made, but it was agreed Cam would sort something out with Joe. Joe was pleased to see Gill looking relieved the focus had shifted from her and Joe's relationship.

They rose to leave, and after a short wrangling between Cam and Joe as to who was to pay, they all left the restaurant together. Poppy and Cam went off arm-in-arm, leaving Joe and Gill standing together. It was very dark, clouds hiding the stars. 'Why don't I walk you home?' Joe asked. He assumed Gill would have walked to the restaurant.

'There's no need,' she said.

'I'd like to.' He fell into step with her, and they headed off in the direction of her apartment.

They walked in silence, then as they approached their destination, Gill said, 'Thanks for what you said earlier. I don't know what Poppy was thinking.'

'I expect she was thinking about her and Cam, about how they started off as friends.'

'Mmm. But her marriage to Jack was happy, and she was free. It's not like…'

Joe sensed her tense up, the way she always did when she started thinking about her husband. 'Not all men are like the one you married,' he said.

'I know, but…' She gazed up at Joe, and he caught sight of something in her expression, something he hadn't seen there before. It gave him hope.

Before he could stop himself, Joe leaned in. His lips brushed hers. It was the merest touch, but the contact sent his heart racing.

Thirty-six

Gill trembled when Joe's lips brushed hers. It had been the merest touch, but with it, it was as if her world shifted on its axis.

'I'm sorry,' Joe said, 'but you looked so...' He touched her cheek gently with his finger.

Gill trembled again, feeling the same rush of desire as when Joe's arms had wrapped around her on the dive boat. She quickly stifled it and pulled away. She wasn't ready for this, whatever *this* was.

'I'm sorry,' he said again. 'If you don't want me to...'

'It's not...' How was she to explain to this lovely man about the vow she'd made to herself never to become involved with a man again? But there was also her decision to change, a small voice reminded her.

'It's late. You've had a big day,' Joe said, filling the silence. Why don't we talk about this some other time? Can we meet for breakfast tomorrow?'

Gill swallowed. *Would anything be different tomorrow?* But it would give her breathing space, and things might look different in the light of day. Her mother had always told her to sleep on a problem, that things always looked better in the morning. So, that's what she'd do. 'Breakfast sounds good,' she said, her voice shaking.

'*The Blue Dolphin* at eight? Will that give you time for your swim?'

Gill nodded, unwilling to trust her voice again. She couldn't imagine she'd feel like swimming tomorrow with breakfast with Joe to look forward to.

'Poppy and Cam will be there. They always are on Sundays, but we don't need to join them.'

Gill nodded again. 'Okay,' was all she could say. She gave Joe a tight smile, and pushed open the door to the apartment building, relieved to be inside.

The apartment was silent when she went in. Freya must still be out. Gill hoped she was having fun. She deserved something good to happen to her, to help her to forget the man in California, to believe in the future again.

As she undressed, and slipped into bed, Gill wondered if she could do that too, believe in a future… with Joe?

Gill lay awake, thoughts whirling around in her head till she heard the door open and close. Freya was home. She fell into an uneasy sleep, tormented by visions of a demanding Max, whilst running from the charms of gentleman Joe.

*

Gill awoke tired and disgruntled; she was no further forward in her thinking. It was dark outside, so she decided to go for her usual swim to help clear her mind.

There was no sign of Freya, and when Gill peeped into her daughter's room, she saw she was still sound asleep, the clothes she had been wearing the previous evening scattered on the floor. Gill didn't know what time her daughter had come home last night, but it had been late. She closed the door quietly.

Once at the beach, Gill felt the customary lift in her mood as the sky began to lighten. After greeting the other swimmers, she ran into the ocean and swam strongly out into the bay.

This morning, when she turned on her back to float, she thought again about what had happened with Joe… his kiss, her reaction. Had she been too quick to dismiss the emotions which surfaced at his touch? Could she… should she… allow herself to feel again? She had kept her emotions in check for so long, it would be like pulling off a band aid. The sky changed colour, the sun hinted at its arrival, and Gill experienced the sensation of lightness she always did at the emergence of a new day.

Back on the beach, she responded to the greetings of the others, towelled herself dry and pulled on her shorts and tee-shirt. She was about to leave, when Olivia joined her.

'No Freya today?' she asked.

'She had a late night and was still asleep when I left. It's good to see her having some fun.'

'You too.'

Gill stared at her friend, unsure what she meant. *She couldn't know about Joe, could she?*

As if reading Gill's uncertainty, Olivia said, 'You need some fun in your life too. I know things are difficult for you at the moment, have been for some time. But you can't live your life in Max's shadow for ever. He's moved on. It's time you did too.'

Gill stared at her again. In the past Olivia had skated around the issue of what Gill should do with her life. This was the first time she'd spoken so bluntly.

'How about breakfast?' Olivia said, when Gill didn't reply.

Gill shivered, suddenly remembering her promise of breakfast with Joe. 'I'm sorry. I've already made plans for breakfast. Maybe next week.'

'Okay.'

As Olivia picked up her towel and left, Gill hoped her friend didn't intend to have breakfast at *The Blue Dolphin* this morning. How would she feel if Olivia saw her there with Joe? Suddenly, she decided she didn't care. She shrugged and headed to her car.

When Gill arrived home, the aroma of coffee beans greeted her. A bleary-eyed Freya was seated at the kitchen table, her hands wrapped around a mug of coffee.

'Good morning, sweetheart.' Gill went across to give her daughter a hug. 'You were asleep when I left. Late night?'

'Mmm. There's plenty of eggs if you'd like them.' She gestured to the pan of scrambled eggs. A plate containing a slice of toast and a portion of egg looked untouched. 'I'm not very hungry.'

'Did you have a nice time?'

'Hmm. We had dinner at the yacht club, then went back to Gary and Mandy's for drinks. They're going sailing today.'

Gill waited. Was Freya joining them?

'I said I might go but…' she yawned, '… I think I might go back to bed.' She yawned again.

'It's a lovely day. It would be awesome out on the bay.'

'Hmm. What about you? You went out with the mayor, didn't you?' Freya suddenly seemed to revive.

'With Joe, and Poppy and Cam. We had a lovely meal at *Crossings*, then I came home.'

'Are you going to have breakfast?' Freya pushed her plate away.

'I'm going out for breakfast.'

'With the mayor?' Freya asked, clearly not expecting Gill's answer to be in the affirmative.

'With Joe. Yes.'

Freya's eyes, which had been half-closed, suddenly became wide open. 'Wow!' she said.

'You should eat something,' Gill said. 'I'm going to have a shower and get dressed. Don't spend the whole day in bed.'

'Yes, Mum,' Freya said in a mocking tone, as Gill left the room.

Gill thought she heard a phone ring when she was in the shower, and by the time she emerged, dressed in a pair of jeans and a bright pink shirt over a long-sleeved, white tee-shirt, she could hear the shower running in the main bathroom.

Before leaving, she popped her head into the bathroom. 'I'm off now,' she said. 'Did I hear the phone?'

Freya stuck her head out of the shower recess. 'Rory called. I'm meeting them at the marina.'

Gill smiled. It hadn't taken much for Freya to forget her tiredness. She was glad her daughter seemed to be putting what had happened to her in California behind her and was enjoying herself. Maybe she should take a page out of Freya's book.

Joe was waiting for her outside the café. He looked relieved when she joined him, greeting her with a hug and kiss on the cheek, sending her stomach fluttering again. 'Good morning. Sleep well?' he asked.

'Not great,' she admitted, 'but I went swimming this morning and it helped me wake up.'

'Good.'

She expected him to say more, but instead, he led her inside. On the way they said good morning to Poppy and Cam who looked surprised to see them. They were on their own this morning.

When they were seated, Joe asked, 'Coffee?'

'Yes, please.' Gill had missed her morning herbal tea and hadn't taken time to have coffee with Freya. *Perhaps she should have*, she thought as a wave of guilt engulfed her. She picked up a menu.

They ordered breakfast, savoury mince with a poached egg on Turkish bread for Gill, and eggs benedict with smoked salmon for Joe. Their coffees arrived. Gill took a sip, feeling better as the caffeine entered her system.

'About last night,' Joe said. 'I'm sorry if I overstepped the mark. I didn't intend to upset you.'

'You didn't. It's me.' Gill picked up her cup again, then put it down. She ran a finger around the rim. 'Since Max left, I've bottled up my emotions, vowed never to let my guard down with a man again, decided I couldn't trust any of them.' She gazed across the table into the brown eyes regarding her with such concern. 'I guess the clients I deal with every day didn't help, either. When all you see, all day, every day, is broken marriages, unhappy women, it tends to rub off. In my case, it only served to confirm my viewpoint.'

'I'm sorry.'

'I am too, sorry for the way I reacted last night. You'd done nothing to deserve it, quite the reverse. You're the kindest, gentlest man I know. Can we start again? This time, I promise I won't act like an idiot.'

'You didn't… act like an idiot, more like someone who was confused.'

He was right. She had been confused. She thought about what Freya had said, Olivia too. She deserved to have some fun, to live a little, to move on from all the stuff which had been holding her back, keeping her tied to a past which she couldn't change. But *she* could.

'I was, but not anymore. I *would* like to get to know you better, and I promise not to pull away next time…' She glanced at Joe with a tentative smile. It would serve her right if he had changed his mind about her. But he was here, wasn't he? 'But I'm not sure if I'm ready for…' She paused. How could she say she wasn't ready to have sex with him? He hadn't suggested it, might not even be thinking about it. Maybe it was a fallacy that it was all men thought about.

Their meals arrived. Joe waited till the waitress had left, then said, 'Sounds good to me. Let's take it slowly, see how we're travelling, and take it from there. Deal?'

'Deal,' Gill said in relief.

Thirty-seven

Joe heaved a sigh of relief. After last night, he'd been afraid either Gill would fail to show up for breakfast, or would arrive, only to tell him she didn't want to see him again. Her agreeing to his suggestion they move their relationship on but take it slowly, was a very welcome reprieve.

All smiles, they stopped to chat with Poppy and Cam on their way out, Joe feeling oddly as if they had suddenly become a couple as their friends talked about going sailing. He chastised himself, told himself to take it easy as they said goodbye to Poppy and Cam.

'It's a lovely morning,' Joe said. 'Fancy a walk along the beach?'

With another smile, Gill agreed, and, greatly daring, Joe took her hand as they walked across towards the marina.

'Oh, look!' Gill said. 'It's Freya with her friends. She was late home and didn't make it to swimming this morning.'

'She looks pretty wide awake now,' Joe said, observing the lively group of young people Freya was part of. 'Isn't that the two Whittaker boys she's with?'

'Rory and Gary. The girl's Liz's daughter, Mandy. You remember her from the yacht club? She and Gary are a couple, and Freya…' Gill's voice trailed off as Rory helped Freya onto the boat, seeming to hold her hand for a few moments longer than was necessary. 'It seems she's getting over the man who hurt her so much in California. Oh, not physically,' she added, seeing Joe frown. 'But men hurt women in lots of different ways.' She bit her lip, making Joe remember she was still battling with the man she'd been married to.

'Looks like they're having fun,' he said. 'What are your thoughts about going sailing with Cam and Poppy?'

'It might be fun,' Gill said cautiously.

'They mentioned next weekend. It looks as if you're going to have no need to worry about your daughter.'

'You're right.' Gill's eyes followed the yacht making its way out of the harbour. She sighed. 'I wish *my* troubles could be resolved so easily.'

'What would it take?' he asked.

'To satisfy Max? More than I'm prepared to hand over. But let's not talk about him today.'

By this time, they had reached the way down to the beach which, given the good weather, was filled with people determined to soak up the sun and enjoy the ocean. Today, there was no sign of any kitesurfers, but the surfers were out in force taking advantage of the large waves. Finn was there with Liz and his small grandson, Sandy, building a sandcastle which Sandy's dog was destroying almost as soon as they built it.

'Hi there,' Finn said, as Joe and Gill approached.

Joe noticed a gleam in Liz's eyes as she gazed at him and Gill. He felt Gill tense and tightened his grip on her hand. This was going to be a test of her resolve.

'Good to see you, Gill,' Liz said.

Gill nodded to her friend, and the four chatted for a few minutes before Finn said, 'Sorry, guys, we have a castle to build,' as Sandy pulled on his arm.

'That wasn't too difficult, was it?' Joe asked Gill, when they moved off.

'I'm not sure,' she said. 'I'll be the topic of conversation at our next lunch. First, Poppy, now Liz. All it needs is for us to meet Rachel too, then all three will know.'

'Is that a bad thing?'

'I'm not sure,' Gill repeated. 'I've been so outspoken about my feelings about men, it'll be difficult to admit I might have changed my opinion, but…' she smiled up at him, '… I do enjoy your company, and you're not like any other men I've met.'

'I'll take that as a compliment.' Joe chuckled. Barb used to tell him he was a one-off. He'd thought she was exaggerating… maybe not.

As they reached a less populated part of the beach, they took off their shoes and walked along in the shallow water at the edge of the sea. It was beautiful here with the sun on their faces, Gill's hand in his. Joe wished their walk could last for ever.

The mood was broken by the arrival of a spaniel with her mistress. 'Nice to see you two together,' Agnes said. 'It's taken you long enough. I knew you'd make a good couple.'

Joe saw Gill open her mouth and, worried she was going to deny they were a couple, quickly said, 'You always were a good judge, Agnes,' squeezing Gill's hand tightly to prevent her from speaking.

'Why did you do that?' Gill asked, when they were out of earshot of the older woman.

'It was a natural thing for her to say when she saw us together holding hands. It's not the end of the world if people know we are in a relationship. We are, aren't we?' Joe held his breath.

For a few moments, Gill didn't speak, then, 'I suppose we are. It's just so new to me, and…' she shook her head, '… I don't know how to react when people make those sort of remarks.'

'You're doing fine so far.'

They stopped and Joe, after checking they were alone on this stretch of beach, pulled Gill into his arms. As their lips met, he was conscious of her initial resistance before she melted into his embrace.

*

After Joe kissed her on the beach, Gill felt more confused than ever. Not about the kiss. It had been a good kiss. And not about Joe. He hadn't forced his attentions on her. It was her own emotions that led to her feeling awkward. But she hadn't pulled away. It had felt good. Was that the problem, she wondered, or was she worrying too much, instead of just enjoying the moment?

Now she was home, she wished she'd invited Joe back for coffee. But they'd already spent several hours together, and she needed space, time to herself to think. Changing into an old, comfortable pair of tracksuit pants and an oversized tee-shirt, she went into her home office to study the latest missive from her solicitor. It quickly brought her back down to earth and banished all thoughts of Joe and his kiss. Her rage intensified at the thought of Max with his new partner, at the prospect of him becoming a father again… and expecting her to fund his new lifestyle. How dare he!

When Gill had dashed off her response, she felt a lot better and turned to the client files needing her attention.

She was still engrossed in them when Freya returned.

'What are you doing stuck in here?' her daughter asked. 'I thought you'd still be with the mayor. How was breakfast?'

'Good. And you went sailing after all. We saw you set off. I didn't expect you home yet.'

'It's after five,' Freya said to Gill's surprise. She'd become so absorbed in her work, she hadn't noticed the time, hadn't even stopped for lunch. 'Don't worry about dinner for me. I'm going out again. There's music at *The Grand* tonight, and Rory knows one of the group playing.'

'Rory again.' Gill grinned to see Freya blush.

'We're just friends, Mum. Everyone else around is married or part of a couple. And he's fun to be with.'

'I don't have a problem with you seeing Rory Whittaker. It's your life. He's a nice boy and I doubt he'd hurt you the way the guy in California did.'

'It's not like that, Mum, and he's hardly a boy.'

'Whatever.' Gill smiled, hearing her own denials in her daughter's voice.

Freya spoke again. 'I had another call from Dad.'

'You spoke with him?'

'No way.'

'You should, darling. Whatever he's done, he is your dad, and I'd hate to think of you cutting him out of your life completely.'

'He should have thought of that,' Freya said. But Gill hoped she'd reconsider. While she was delighted to have Freya with her again, to have regained her affection, she knew what it was like to feel isolated from her daughter. She wouldn't wish that on her worst enemy, not even on Max.

Once Freya had departed on a wave of perfume with promises not to be late and not to waken Gill when she did – seemingly unaware of the absurdity of her comments – Gill stared at the computer screen.

She was a sad case, spending most of her Sunday working. But it was what she did, what she'd done for years. Her mind went back to Joe, to that kiss, to what she'd been trying to forget ever since she got back.

Now, she allowed herself the luxury of contemplating what it might be like to have a relationship with Joe Harris, a proper relationship, one which everyone knew about, what it would be like to feel his lips on hers, not in a brief kiss but in something deeper, more sensuous, to lie in his arms, to… She shivered. It had been so long since she'd been with a man, not since Max left. What if she'd forgotten how?

Thirty-eight

The week had been busy, giving Joe little opportunity to do much other than council work. He had called Gill a couple of times, feeling the need to hear her voice, but she had been busy too, and it hadn't been possible for them to meet, though she had agreed to going out on the bay with Cam and Poppy. He had managed to squeeze in lunch with Cam at *The Grand* one day and, after being the butt of his friend's teasing, had arranged for the four of them to meet at the marina on Sunday morning to spend the day on the water. Joe was looking forward to it, not only to seeing Gill again, but to getting out on the bay with Cam, something he hadn't done for some time – apart from the time they went scuba diving. Since Cam had linked up with Poppy, he hadn't had much time for his old friends.

Now it was Sunday and Joe couldn't wait. He had risen early, but not early enough to beat Erica who was still enjoying her early morning swims.

She was already eating breakfast when he walked into the kitchen to be greeted by the aroma of fresh coffee and the enticing scent of bacon. 'Hey, sleepy head,' she said. 'Aren't you going sailing today?'

'I am.' Joe rubbed his chin and checked the time. It was only seven o'clock, and he was due to meet the others at the marina at eight. 'Time for a quick bite before I go,' he said, helping himself to coffee and dropping a slice of bread into the toaster and another strip of bacon into the pan.

'You and Gill,' Erica said. 'Is it serious? I love you and I like her. I'd hate to see either of you get hurt.'

'Difficult to tell at this stage.' As the toast popped up, Joe topped it with the piece of bacon and took it and his coffee to the table. He sat down and took a sip of coffee. 'Gill is the first woman I've been interested in since Barb. I never thought I'd feel this way again, Erica, but Gill has got under my skin.' As he spoke, Joe remembered their kiss on the beach, remembered the sweetness of Gill's lips, the way her body had melted into his. It had been all he could do to stop himself from taking it further. But it was broad daylight… on a public beach, so common sense and his innate sense of decency prevailed. However, Gill's unexpected response had given him more than hope.

The others were already there when Joe arrived at the marina. He'd left Coco at home with Erica who was happy to have her company. She said the dog made her feel safe, which worried Joe. *Did she think Geoff was going to turn up looking for her?* Now wasn't the time to worry about his brother-in-law, he decided, seeing Gill standing there.

She was wearing a pair of white shorts with a blue and white striped tee-shirt which looked very nautical. The sight of her sent Joe's heart racing. He felt somewhat overdressed in his jeans and white, short-sleeved shirt, but seeing Cam similarly dressed made him feel better. Poppy had donned a pair of khaki, three-quarter pants with a pink shirt tied at the waist.

They made their way to Cam's boat, Cam carrying an esky, and Poppy a picnic basket which she said the kitchen at *Crossings* had prepared. When they were all on board, and the food had been stowed in the cabin, Cam cast off, and they were on their way.

It was glorious to be out on the water, with just enough swell to make things interesting, and the sun beating down on them. When Joe put his arm around Gill's shoulders, he felt her tense for a moment before she relaxed against him, turning to smile into his eyes. He felt as if all his Christmases had come at once and knew Barb would approve.

As they sailed along, a pair of dolphins joined them, delighting them with their antics before they swam off again. The water was so clear, they were able to spot a few turtles and several varieties of fish. They were even lucky enough to see a whale breeching in the distance.

By the time Cam dropped anchor in a quiet bay, they were all ready for lunch, but first Poppy suggested a swim.

Joe was glad he'd had the foresight to wear a pair of board shorts under his jeans, just in case. He'd had the suspicion swimming might be part of the day's activities, and he couldn't wait to see Gill in a swimsuit again. He remembered the brief glimpse he'd had of her on that first morning when he'd driven Erica to the beach. On that occasion, she'd quickly waded into the water. She wouldn't be able to do that today.

The women disappeared into the cabin, while Joe and Cam stripped down to their shorts. When Gill reappeared, Joe found it difficult to keep his eyes off her. She looked amazing in a turquoise and black swimsuit which revealed her perfect figure. She was hugging her arms around her body as if ashamed of it, but she had nothing to be ashamed of. Joe wanted to hug her again, to tell her how beautiful she looked, but something in her expression told him a hug wouldn't be welcome. This was different from seeing her in a wetsuit, and Joe knew he needed to tread warily.

Once in the water, Gill seemed to be in her element, swimming off, then turning to float on her back. Joe wondered if this was what she did each morning and wished he had the courage to join the women, as Erica had. He swam over to join her. They floated side-by-side for a few moments, then Gill said, 'I love floating like this, looking up at the sky, It helps me to forget everything going on in my life, and I feel as if I could stay like this for ever.'

'Is it why you swim every morning?'

'Partly. I do enjoy swimming, and there's nothing quite like being out on the ocean watching the sky change colour as the sun comes up, a new dawn. It's magical. You should join us.'

'I thought it was only women who were part of the group.'

'It mostly is, but sometimes the odd man joins us. I'm not suggesting you're odd,' she said, laughing. 'Not too odd, anyway.'

'Thanks.' Joe chuckled, intrigued by the idea he might join the wild swimmers. Now they'd swum together here, it wouldn't seem such a challenge, such a test of their friendship. 'I might take you up on that. Erica is certainly enjoying it.'

'I'm glad. It's been hard on her, leaving Perth, coming here, and with her daughter-in-law pregnant...'

'Hopefully, it'll all sort itself out.'

'If she can just stick it out for the requisite twelve months, then apply for a divorce.'

'Yeah.'

'Hey, you two,' Cam called. 'Time for lunch.'

Joe waved, and he and Gill swam back to the boat where Cam and Poppy were already drying off. When they climbed aboard, Poppy produced towelling robes for each of them.

'I thought this would be better than climbing back into our clothes,' she said. 'We may want to take another swim later.'

Dressed in the thigh-length robe, Joe felt as if he was lounging around in a resort instead of sitting on the deck of Cam's yacht. Cam brought the esky and picnic basket out of the cabin, and they laid the food on a table on the deck.

Soon they were drinking champagne from plastic glasses and enjoying the selection of tiny quiches, sausage rolls and sandwiches the *Crossings* chef had prepared, along with fresh bread and a variety of cheeses, with strawberries and grapes to finish. When he was unable to eat another morsel, Joe leant back against the side of the boat. Gill fell back against him.

'That was delicious,' she said. 'All I want to do now is have a nap.'

'Why don't you close your eyes? We're not going anywhere right now. I thought I'd do a bit of fishing,' Cam said, 'and Poppy…?'

'I might have a nap too,' Poppy said.

'Joe? Fancy a spot of fishing?'

Joe was happy to stay exactly where he was, with Gill lying against him. 'I'm fine here,' he said, feeling her snuggle into him.

*

It was late afternoon when they returned to the marina, feeling tired after their day in the fresh air. They'd had a second swim after their nap – and Cam's unsuccessful attempt at fishing.

'Thanks for a great day,' Joe said, giving Poppy a kiss on the cheek and slapping Cam on the shoulder. 'I'll have to figure out how to return the hospitality. I assume another council meeting is out of the question?' he chuckled.

'You're right there,' Cam said with a grin.

'Guess I'll have to think of something else.'

'No need. We enjoyed it too. It's not often we have the opportunity to go sailing with good friends.'

'Thanks so much. I had a lovely time,' Gill said, kissing both Poppy and Cam on the cheek. 'Sailing, swimming, good food, good company, what more could I ask for.' She grinned and looked directly at Joe.

As their eyes met, Joe's heart skipped a beat. *Did she mean* his *company?*

'Bye, guys.' Cam and Poppy headed off, leaving Joe and Gill standing alone.

'Well,' Joe said. He wasn't ready to leave Gill but hesitated to suggest anything. It was late afternoon on a Sunday in Pelican Crossing. People were leaving the beach, preparing for the evening. Owners of boats on the marina were gearing up for the evening too. What he wanted was to spend the evening with Gill.

'I need a shower. You probably do too,' Gill said. 'Why don't you come back with me? We can freshen up and have a bite to eat. It won't be a gourmet meal. I'm not much of a cook, and I don't know about you, but I'm not very hungry after the lunch Poppy and Cam provided.'

'Thanks, I'd love to.' Joe couldn't believe his ears. It was as if Gill had read his mind.

'You'll have to put up with Freya's company too, I'm afraid,' she added.

'No problem.' He liked what he'd seen of Gill's daughter and had the impression she liked him too. Her company could be a bonus, even if it did mean he wouldn't have Gill to himself.

*

Gill's heart was thudding as she opened the door to her apartment. Was it a mistake to have invited Joe back here? She had been careful to keep her home to herself. Apart from her and Freya, the only people who had been here since Max left, had been the group of friends she lunched with. She took a deep breath as she walked in, very conscious of Joe's presence behind her. 'Freya!' she called. There was no reply.

The silence of the apartment wrapped around them as she and Joe went through the hall and into the kitchen.

'This is different,' Joe said, glancing around at the stark white kitchen with its bare, white surfaces. 'Very... functional.'

'I guess so.' For the first time, Gill was aware of how her home must look to a stranger, how the Scandinavian style she had sought to emulate might seem odd to someone more accustomed to the normal clutter of the average home. 'It's easy to maintain.'

'Hmm. You mentioned a shower?'

'Of course.' Gill directed Joe to the main bathroom, while she headed to the ensuite, checking Freya's room on the way, but it was empty too. Where was her daughter? When she'd invited Joe back, she hadn't expected them to be alone. *Would she have made the same decision if she'd known Freya wouldn't be here?*

Hearing the shower running in the bathroom along the hall, Gill hurried into the bedroom and into her own shower. The rush of hot water, both washed away the salt and restored her confidence. She'd been alone with Joe before. He was an honourable man. She could handle this.

Dressed again, this time in a pair of jeans and a white linen shirt, Gill emerged from her bedroom, just in time to see Joe, his hair wet from the shower, step into the hallway. Her breath caught. Even though she had seen him half-naked already earlier, the sight of him here in her apartment, knowing he'd recently been naked in her shower, sent her stomach into freefall.

'Hey,' he said. 'You changed. You look good.'

'Thanks,' Gill said, suddenly shy and aware they were completely alone.

'Your daughter?'

'She's not here,' she said, then realising she was stating the obvious, added, 'I thought she would be.' As if by magic, her phone pinged. Gill took it out of her pocket to see a text. She scanned it quickly. 'It's from Freya. She's gone to Tara's for dinner. Seems it's just us.' She looked up to see Joe grinning at her.

'Sounds good to me.' He moved forward, his arms outstretched, and without thinking, Gill moved towards him, into his arms, into a kiss that seemed to go on for ever.

'I've been wanting to do that all day,' he said, when they finally parted.

Gill was too breathless to reply, stunned by the realisation it was what she'd been wanting too, ever since she'd seen Joe standing on the marina. But now they were alone in her apartment, she wasn't sure how to react. She pulled herself out of his arms and headed to the kitchen, Joe following. 'I promised you something to eat,' she said. 'Wine?' She needed a drink to calm the trembling in her legs after that kiss.

When Joe nodded, clearly as stunned as she was by the torrent of emotion their kiss had unleashed, Gill opened the fridge to remove a bottle of semillon blanc. She poured two glasses, handed one to Joe and took a gulp from the other. Then she fossicked in the freezer, before taking out a pizza. 'Pizza?' she asked, holding it up.

'Fine by me.'

While they waited for the pizza to cook, Gill and Joe went out to the balcony where he admired the view. The lights on the marina and on the boats were being turned on, and tiny figures were visible moving about on the decks. Gill could imagine them drinking wine too, and probably cooking something more exotic than pizza.

By the time the timer on the oven went off, the temperature was dropping, so Gill and Joe were glad to go inside to eat. They were more relaxed with each other now and were able to chat comfortably while they demolished the pizza. After helping Gill load the dirty plates in the dishwasher, Joe held up the half-empty wine bottle. 'Shall we finish this?'

'Let's,' Gill said, trying to still the butterflies in her stomach.

They carried their refilled glasses into the living room and sat together on the sofa. It was becoming dark, but neither of them turned on the lights, content with the glimmer from outside which filtered through the windows from the balcony.

'Thanks for today,' Gill said.

'I didn't do anything. It was Cam and Poppy's thing.'

'You were there, and I would never have gone on my own. I doubt if they'd have invited me.' Poppy never had before.

Joe reached an arm around Gill's shoulders and to her surprise, she found herself leaning into him, her head falling on his shoulder. It was comfortable there, his warm body close to hers. She inhaled the scent of the soap from his shower and another aroma that was his alone and felt a peace she hadn't experienced for as long as she could remember. They finished the wine, but didn't speak, content to be together.

As time passed, despite her attempts to stifle it, Gill was aware of a rush of desire. She could sense Joe's rising passion too. She turned towards him, his face a pale glow in the darkness, when there was the sound of a door opening, a light was turned on, and she was almost blinded. She and Joe leapt apart.

'What are you doing sitting here in the dark?' Freya asked.

Thirty-nine

'Sorry if I spoiled things for you last night,' Freya said at breakfast next morning. She'd skipped the morning swim again, and Gill was beginning to wonder if, now her daughter had reconnected with old friends, she was going to see less of her. But she couldn't complain. She was pleased Freya was enjoying being back in Pelican Crossing and happy to have whatever time her daughter chose to spend with her.

'You didn't. There was nothing to spoil. We were just enjoying a few moments of peace.' Gill wasn't sure whether she'd been pleased or disappointed when Freya interrupted the moment when she and Joe had been about to… what? Surely they hadn't been going to…? But the atmosphere had certainly been heated. Joe had left soon afterwards, and Gill had gone to bed to lie there trying to work out exactly what had happened, or been about to happen, or could have happened, if Freya hadn't arrived home when she did. But she had. There was no need for recrimination. *So why did she have this feeling of regret?*

'Didn't look that way to me. But it's okay, Mum. You're allowed to have a relationship, to have feelings. It's not as if Dad and you…' She drained her coffee.

'Leave your dad out of it. It's nothing to do with him. Speaking of which, have you spoken to him yet?'

'No.' Freya's expression was bullish. 'I have nothing to say to him.'

'He wasn't always like this, Freya,' Gill began, not sure why she was defending Max to her. 'When you were small, he loved both of us so much. We had some good times.' It hurt Gill to think maybe it was her fault everything had gone wrong. If she hadn't pursued her career, become so successful…

'It wasn't your fault, Mum,' Freya said, as if reading her mind. 'Dad was always going to be a dick. I know I blamed you for a while but with this last escapade…' she shook her head, '… it's too much, even for him.'

Gill looked affectionately at her daughter. At least Max's latest caper had brought Freya back to her.

But Freya hadn't finished. 'I like the mayor,' she said. 'You make a good couple. I think…'

'Freya, there's no couple. I'm not free. I'm still married, and unlike your father… I do have some principles.' Where were these principles last night, she wondered, when she and Joe had almost… But they wouldn't have, would they? She'd never know, and she intended to make sure the opportunity never arose again. So why did she feel a niggle of sadness at the prospect?

'Well, maybe you should do something about it.'

For a moment Gill, caught up in her own thoughts, assumed Freya was talking about her and Joe. Then she realised it was her and Max she was referring to. 'It's not so simple, sweetheart. Divorce can be complicated, ours more so than most with all your dad's demands. You have no idea.'

'Why don't you tell me?'

'I don't think so.' The dispute between her and Max wasn't something she wanted to share with their daughter. But seeing Freya's concerned expression reminded Gill that her daughter wasn't a child. She was thirty and had had her own troubles to deal with. 'Okay,' she said, and began to enumerate Max's latest litany of demands.

'But he can't do that,' Freya exclaimed, when Gill came to his claim for a percentage of her future income.

'I'm afraid he can… he has. It's what's keeping us from settling things. I don't want to lose this apartment, either.'

'Of course not.' Freya looked around the room, at the sun streaming in through the window, the view of the marina in the distance. 'Couldn't you… I don't know… put it in my name or something?'

'It's a lovely thought, darling, but no, I can't. It's one of our shared assets.' She sighed, reminded again of the burden hanging over her. 'It's not your problem. And I do think you should talk to him.'

'Hmm.' Freya looked thoughtful. 'Maybe I will,' she said, her expression sending a shiver down Gill's spine. What did her daughter have in mind? Perhaps she'd been wrong to be so open with her.

*

Joe couldn't stop thinking about Gill and cursing the fact Freya had interrupted what was promising to be the realisation of his dreams. Or was he mistaken? Had Gill really been about to move their relationship to the next step, or had she been relieved when the light flashed on and broke the mood? Things had been going so well. It had been a perfect evening, the ideal ending to a splendid day. Then Freya arrived, and everything changed. He'd left soon after, recognising Gill's embarrassment at being caught in an almost compromising position. But Freya wasn't a child. Joe was sure she'd understood.

Erica had been in bed when he got home, and after a night when he'd tossed and turned for what seemed for ever, he'd wakened early and left before she returned from her swim. He didn't want to rehash his day with her, preferring to keep his thoughts to himself.

Coco was surprised to be out and about so early, padding happily along at Joe's side as they walked past the marina to *The Blue Dolphin Café* where Joe ordered breakfast and a large mug of coffee. The café had only just opened for the day, and he was its only customer at this time in the morning.

'You're an early bird.'

Joe looked up to see Jamie Whittaker carrying a takeaway coffee. 'Hi, Jamie. Felt like making an early start.'

'Is your sister still staying with you?' Jamie glanced around as if expecting Erica to appear.

'She is, yes. She's joined the group of wild swimmers and is out there enjoying herself right now.'

'She always was one for extreme sports,' Jamie said.

Joe stared at him in surprise. How well had Jamie known Erica back then? He didn't remember too much about what his sister had got up to. He hadn't mentioned Jamie's earlier remarks to Erica. He wondered how she'd react. But she had enough on her plate with her worry about Geoff. The last thing she needed was a shadow from her past.

'I can't stop. I have a group of guys from Melbourne booked in for a fishing trip. We must catch up sometime for a beer,' Jamie said.

'Sure.' Joe was relieved. He'd come here to be alone, to think about Gill, to work out what to do next.

By the time he'd consumed the café's big breakfast, allowing Coco half a sausage, and was wired from two mugs of coffee, Joe headed to the office. He'd decided he and Gill needed to talk. He'd call her and arrange to meet for lunch if her schedule permitted. He was disappointed their evening had been cut short and he needed to discover if she was too.

The office was deserted. Joe ensured Coco had water and settled at his desk. Was it too early to call Gill? When did she leave for the office? Should he wait till she was at work? Wracked by indecision, he looked down at Coco who raised her head. 'What do you think, Coco, now or later?'

Coco merely yawned, her long pink tongue flicking out, then back in again. She was no help.

Joe picked up his phone and stared at it for a full two minutes before pressing Gill's number on the speed dial.

*

Gill had just arrived in the office and was still thinking about her conversation with Freya when her phone rang. Seeing Joe's number on the screen sent a quiver of excitement down her spine. She pressed to accept the call. 'Joe?'

'Gill, how are you this morning? I can't stop thinking about you. Last night…'

Gill didn't reply immediately. His words brought back the previous evening so clearly, that heady moment when they had almost…

'I wanted to ask if you're free for lunch. I think we need to talk.'

'Sounds ominous,' Gill said, trying to still the tremor in her voice.

'It's not. But I think we need to clear the air after…'

Couldn't he form a complete sentence? Gill mentally flicked through her diary. There was the partners' meeting at nine, then she had three client appointments. 'I could be free around one. Does that work for you?'

'Perfect.'

Gill heard him give a sigh of relief. She had the impression any time she'd mentioned would have got the same response. He was such an amenable man, so unlike Max. What on earth was she doing thinking about Max in the same breath as Joe? It was the conversation about him with Freya. It had brought it all back – the betrayal, the evasions, the straight out lies, then the demands… Freya was right about one thing. Joe was one of the good guys, probably too good for her. Gill had never pretended she was anything special. She was good at her job – her success rate spoke for itself – but apart from that, what did she have going for her? It was her turn to sigh. '*Books and Coffee*?' she asked.

'If it's okay with you. I'll have Coco with me, so I'll snag an outside table.'

'See you there.'

After a busy morning, Gill walked along to meet Joe. She was filled with warring emotions. On the one hand, she was looking forward to seeing him again, the memory of the previous evening fresh in her mind, on the other, there was the thought of what had almost happened, how she had almost allowed herself to succumb, to give in to the heat of the moment, to lose the control she fought so hard to maintain.

Coco saw her first and barked excitedly. 'Quiet, Coco.' Joe's calm voice sent tremors through Gill. *How could she have doubted her feelings for him?*

'Hello, Coco,' she said, greeting the dog first, and ruffling her ears. Then she raised her eyes to meet Joe's. 'Hello,' she said.

'Hello, you.' Joe rose to give her a kiss on the cheek.

Gill's heart missed a beat. For a moment, she was tempted to turn her head so their lips met, then she remembered where she was and sat down quickly, before she was embarrassed by making a public exhibition of herself.

'It's good to see you.' Joe took Gill's hand in his, and her heart leapt, making it difficult to remember her decision.

'Good to see you too,' she managed to say, her voice shaking. *This was crazy. She needed to get control.*

'Shall we order?'

'Of course. I'll have a quiche with salad… and coffee.'

'Too easy. I'll leave you with Coco while I order.'

The dog looked up at Gill expectantly, and she leant down to ruffle her ears again. 'Your master is a good man,' she said. 'I don't deserve someone like him.'

Coco gave a sigh, whether in agreement or not, Gill couldn't determine. She was still trying to decide when Joe returned.

'Done,' he said, rubbing his hands together. 'Denny twisted my arm to order two slices of lemon meringue pie too. Hope that's okay with you.'

'Fine.' Gill loved lemon meringue pie but didn't know if she could face it today. 'You wanted to talk,' she said. Best to get it out of the way.

Joe rubbed his chin. 'About last night…' He paused. 'I was sorry when we were interrupted. I was… it was… I thought…'

'I was too, but it was probably for the best, Joe. When Freya arrived home, we were on the point of taking things too far, of letting our emotions take over, of forgetting ourselves.' Even as she spoke, Gill felt herself redden at the memory of how she'd felt in Joe's embrace, his lips on hers, his…

'Would it have been so wrong?'

'I'm still married, Joe. I'm not free to give in to my impulses, even if I want to.'

'So, you admit you wanted to? I wasn't imagining your response?'

'What do you think?' she asked, aware she might be sounding flirtatious.

'I think you're a very beautiful and desirable woman who is making it very difficult for me to think about anything else,' Joe said with a smile which almost took Gill's breath away.

'Oh!' was all she could manage in response.

'But I have no idea how you feel about me,' Joe continued. 'You seem to blow hot and cold. I know you are still married, but you are in the midst of a divorce and, from what you've told me about your husband, he kicked over the traces long ago. You don't owe him anything, least of all loyalty and faithfulness.'

Gill sighed. Joe was right, but… 'You're right, and I'm sorry. I do like you… a lot. And when we're together, I have trouble thinking straight. It's why I don't know if I was pleased or disappointed when Freya broke in on us last night. One part of me was annoyed we'd been interrupted when all I wanted was to finish what we'd started, but another – the more sensible part – was glad we'd been forced to stop in time. No…' she held up one hand, '… I know I'm not some young girl desperate to maintain my virtue, but I'm not sure I'm ready to move on to what would be a serious relationship. I don't do things by halves, Joe, so if we…' she took a deep breath, '… it would have to mean something.'

She looked across the table at Joe who seemed to be struggling with something.

He took her hand in his before speaking. 'I'm with you there, Gill. You already mean a lot to me. After Barb… I never thought I'd find anyone who could replace her in my affections.' He shook his head. 'No, that's not what I mean. I never thought I'd find someone who'd make me feel the way you do. Some people never find the person they want to spend their life with. I've been lucky enough to find a special one twice. I think you may share my feelings, and if you do, there's nothing wrong with expressing them in the most meaningful way possible.'

Gill tried to focus on what Joe was saying, The touch of his hand on hers was sending waves of longing through her, but she was helpless to remove it. She had no idea how to respond and was relieved when Denny appeared with their lunch.

'Enjoy, folks,' he said, placing their meals and coffees on the table, as Joe removed his hand.

Gill was still trying to stop the trembling Joe's touch had set in motion. She picked up her cup and took a gulp, almost choking as the hot liquid burned her tongue. Joe was right. They were two consenting adults. So, why was she finding it all so difficult? 'I do, Joe… share your feelings, but it's difficult for me.' She sighed. 'After Max left, I buried myself in my work. I vowed to remain single and told anyone who'd listen what I thought of all men, and my decision never to allow one into my life again. Then I met you… and all my good intentions flew out of the window. But I can't help wondering if I'm imagining it, if it's all a dream, and I'll wake up to discover I'm back where I started.'

'I promise I'm not a dream,' Joe chuckled, 'not even a bad one.'

A sense of release washing over her at Joe's words, Gill laughed. 'No one could accuse you of that.'

'So, are we good?'

'We're good,' Gill said, not quite sure what she'd agreed to, but relieved to have the conversation over. She hated all this talk about feelings and emotions. They were complicated, and she saw on a daily basis how they messed up people's lives. It was one of the reasons she'd maintained her single status since Max left, avoided the risk of becoming involved again. *And the other? She hated losing control, as she'd been about to do with Joe before Freya's arrival rescued her. But had she really wanted to be rescued?*

'We should eat before this gets cold.'

Joe's words interrupted Gill's thoughts and brought her back to the present. She picked up her cutlery only to discover her appetite had gone.

Forty

Joe was feeling relieved as he and Coco made their way back to the council chambers. For a few moments over lunch, he'd thought Gill was about to tell him she couldn't continue to see him. All her talk about being still married, her vow never to get involved again, had sent his nerves jangling. But it had been all right in the end. She'd agreed to see him again. Though he got the impression she'd do everything in her power to avoid a repetition of the previous evening when they'd been alone in the dark and things had become heated. Maybe it wasn't a bad thing to allow everything to cool off for a bit. She had her daughter staying with her, and he had Erica. Neither of them knew what the future held. But he could live in hope, hope Gill's divorce would be settled, her daughter would find a new life, and Erica would manage to relegate Geoff to the past where he belonged.

The afternoon passed slowly, giving Joe too much time to think about his lunchtime conversation with Gill. Even Coco, lying under the desk, was beginning to make impatient noises by the time Joe closed up his computer and rose from his chair.

When he arrived home, Erica was already there; her shift had finished earlier. Instead of cooking dinner, as she normally did at this time, she was sitting in the living room staring at her phone, an unfathomable expression on her face.

'Is something wrong?' Joe asked, while Coco went up to Erica and laid her head on her lap.

'No, quite the reverse. Look!' She held out the phone.

Joe looked at the black and white streaks on the screen, trying to make sense of what he was seeing. 'That's not…?' he asked, shocked to the core.

'My grandchild, yes. I called Briony. She's fine. Kieren's fine. She said Geoff's ropeable, swearing what he's going to do when he finds me. But she's promised not to let him know I've been in touch. Oh, Joe, it was so good to talk to her.'

'Are you mad? Didn't you listen to what I said, what Gill advised? How long do you think it's going to take Kieren to find out from Briony that you called? And how long before Kieren tells his father?'

'She promised.'

'How much is her promise worth? Kieren's her husband. Do you think she's going to keep it secret from him?'

Erica clutched her phone to her chest and began to sob. 'You're wrong. I know you are.' But she didn't sound as sure as she had earlier. 'I'm going to make dinner.'

'Wait!' Joe was filled with guilt. He was angry with Erica for calling Perth, for putting herself in danger, when both he and Gill had expressly told her not to. Maybe he should have told her about Geoff's call. He could understand how desperate she'd been to get news of home, to talk with Briony about her pregnancy, to check on Kieren. 'I'm sorry I lost my temper, Erica. It's late to start preparing dinner. Why don't I take you out to eat? The Thai's open on Mondays. I seem to remember you enjoy Thai food.'

'Oh,' Erica brightened. 'I'd like that. I don't know when I last had a Thai meal. Geoff always said he couldn't stomach all that Asian muck.' She frowned. 'You don't really think he'll find out, do you?'

'I'm sorry to say I do.'

'But that doesn't mean he'll know where to find me… and there's the AVO.' Her voice began to quiver.

'Well, he's not going to turn up in Pelican Crossing tonight, so why don't you get changed. You can't go out to dinner like that.'

Erica glanced down at the nurse's uniform she was still wearing, the dark blue pants and tunic with her nametag pinned to it. 'No, you're right. I'll shower too. It won't take me long.'

When she had gone, Coco came over to lay her head on Joe's lap and look up at him with her soulful eyes. It was as if she was concerned about Erica's actions too. 'You and me both, Coco. But what's done's done. We just have to hope I'm wrong about Geoff.' But he was afraid he wasn't. He knew his brother-in-law too well. Joe's story about Cairns wouldn't hold him for long. Geoff was a man who'd stop at nothing to bring his errant wife to heel, and once he heard she'd been in touch with Briony…

Forty-one

The day of Gill's monthly lunch date had rolled around again, and she was dreading the inquisition she was sure to suffer, now both Poppy and Liz knew about her and Joe. It was Poppy's turn to host the group, and Gill knew full well her friend would want to know more about how her relationship was progressing, as would Liz – finding her own happy ever after had only dented Liz's love of gossip for a short time. Gill knew she shouldn't malign her friend. Liz had a good heart. But, like Poppy, now she was in a happy relationship, she wanted the same for all her friends. *It had been better when all four of them were single*, Gill thought. At least then, there had been no invidious comparisons. Now, only Rachel and Gill were unattached, and she was seeing Joe, even though there could be no future in it unless… But Gill didn't dare think of the possibility of an amicable divorce settlement. It seemed as far off as ever.

'Guess what, Mum?' Freya breezed into the kitchen as Gill was having breakfast.

What now? Freya seemed to hurtle from one idea to another these days, and she was still spending time with Rory, Gary and Mandy, and insisting she and Rory were only good mates. Maybe she was speaking the truth.

Without waiting for a response, Freya waved her phone at her mother. 'I have an interview in Sydney next week.'

Gill stared at her daughter. She remembered Freya mentioning she was going to check out Australian universities, but had she said anything about making applications? Had Gill been so caught up in her own issues she'd failed to listen properly to her daughter?

'I'm sorry, Mum. I didn't say anything in case it came to nothing. When I checked it out, I found ads for positions in Sydney and Hobart. Sydney have replied first. There was nothing in Queensland,' she added, as if reading Gill's mind.

'Sydney's not too far away, better than California,' Gill said. 'I'm happy for you.'

'If I'm successful, I'd start at the beginning of next year, so you'll still have to put up with me till then,' she grinned.

'I think I can manage it. You were talking about tutoring?'

'I haven't done anything about it yet. Gary suggested I can help him out with admin stuff at the dive school, and with the kitesurfing. I might do that.'

'Okay.' It wasn't what she imagined her daughter doing but would keep her occupied – and in Pelican Crossing – until she could start at the university, always providing she was offered the position.

'I'm optimistic about this, Mum. It's a great school, and my old prof is Head of School, so fingers crossed.' She held up her crossed fingers.

'I hope you're right.' It would be wonderful to know Freya was in Australia, only a plane-ride away. She could come home regularly, and Gill could visit. She liked the harbour city.

'You're seeing your friends today, aren't you?'

'Yes, our monthly lunch… at Poppy's today.'

'Mandy said. You know she's pregnant? Another baby! I can't seem to get away from them.'

'You'll have one of your own one day,' Gill said, picturing the grandchild she'd always hoped for.

'Not for ages. I intend to focus on my career. I told you… I'm done with men.'

'Hmm.'

'What do you mean?'

'You seem to be seeing a lot of Rory.'

'He's only a good mate. I told you. He's not interested in me in that way, either.'

Gill decided it was best not to pursue the conversation. Freya might be telling the truth. 'What are your plans for today?'

'I thought I'd drop over to the dive school to see what Gary had in mind for me to do, then I might go for a swim. I intend to make the most of my time here in Pelican Crossing. Once I start working again in earnest, I won't have much time to relax.'

When Freya had left, Gill made herself another cup of lemon and ginger tea and took it out onto the balcony. She'd thought about Joe a lot since their lunch together, worried she might have ruined what could have been something special. But they had agreed to keep seeing each other, so perhaps all was not lost. She just felt so confused. Now she was alone, she admitted she had feelings for Joe, feelings so strong they scared her. What if, despite what he said, even if he believed it, his weren't as strong? What if his feelings for her paled in comparison with what he still felt for Barb? She'd had enough trouble competing with Max's women. They were alive. She couldn't face competing with one who was dead. Perhaps she should have ended it, finished it before she became any more invested in the relationship.

By the time Gill had finished her tea, she was no further forward in her thinking. She went inside, changed into the bright pink and orange dress that always made her feel good, and applied her makeup, determined to put on a brave face.

*

Liz was already there when Gill arrived at Poppy's house on the clifftop, the two women seated on Poppy's deck with glasses of white wine, Poppy's little West Highland Terrier lying at their feet.

'Here she is,' Liz said, when Gill walked in.

Had they been talking about her? Gill's suspicions were confirmed when as soon as she had poured Gill a glass of wine, Poppy said, 'We were just talking about you.'

Gill flinched. It was what she'd been afraid of. *Why had she come?* But staying away would have sent a worse message. The four of them had been meeting like this for the past thirty years, and it took a major catastrophe for one of them to miss lunch. Liz had missed one earlier in the year when the daughter she'd given up for adoption had appeared in town. But, apart from that, Gill couldn't remember an occasion when the four of them hadn't got together. Even when the other three had been pregnant again, they'd managed to catch up.

Luckily, Rachel arrived just then, so Gill was spared the conversation she knew would take place at some time during their meal. There was a little confusion, while Rachel greeted Poppy's little dog, Poppy poured Rachel's wine, then disappeared to check the oven.

'We were just about to ask Gill about her and our mayor,' Liz said, 'but we should wait till Poppy comes back.'

Gill gave a sigh of relief at her reprieve, but it was short-lived. When Poppy returned carrying a bowl of salad and a dish of pasta, and once they were all seated at the table, Liz asked, 'Well, what do you have to tell us, Gill?'

'I don't know what you're talking about,' Gill said, hoping to buy time while she worked out how much to divulge.

'You and the mayor.'

'Joe? He… we… we're friends. Aren't we allowed to be friends without being a source of gossip?'

'That's not what Poppy said.' Liz glanced across to where Poppy was looking embarrassed.

What had Poppy said?

Poppy shifted awkwardly in her seat. 'I only said how we'd gone sailing together, then had dinner at *Crossings*… and how you and Joe seemed like a good match. I haven't seen him with anyone since Barb passed. It was good to see him looking happy… you too.'

Gill swallowed. She couldn't fault Poppy. It was true. They *had* gone sailing, had dinner at Crossings. It had been the perfect day, then… She blushed at the memory of what happened later, or what might have happened if Freya hadn't returned when she did. *Had it only been three days ago?* 'Not everything's what it seems,' she said, hoping to stave off further questions.

'But…' Liz began.

'Leave Gill alone,' Rachel said. 'Can't you see you're embarrassing her? Remember how you felt when you and Finn started seeing each other, Liz? You weren't so eager to talk about it then, either.'

Liz appeared chastened. 'Sorry, Gill. We're only interested because we love you, but if you don't want to talk about it…' She made the sign of locking her lips and throwing away the key.

Gill was forced to laugh. 'I know that, Liz, but it's a bit too soon to say anything… and remember, I'm still married. You were a free agent when you and Finn got together.'

'But…'

'Liz!' Rachel warned.

'Sorry,' Liz said again.

'How's Mandy going?' Poppy asked. 'She must be what… around six months by now?'

'Due in the New Year,' Liz said, and the conversation moved on to Mandy's pregnancy and grandchildren in general.

Gill was relieved. The conversation didn't annoy her as much as talk about grandchildren normally did. She was just glad she and Joe were no longer the topic of the conversation. But it didn't stop her thinking about him, wondering when she'd hear from him again, and how she'd react when she did.

Forty-two

It was three days since Joe had seen Gill, and he needed to contact her. He was still reeling from Erica's revelation she had called Briony, lacking her confidence that Geoff would never find out. He knew what families were like. Briony would tell Kieren, Kieren would tell Geoff. It was a no-brainer. He should probably have contacted Gill before now; as Erica's solicitor, she deserved to know. But he was still trying to come to terms with his uncertainty as to their relationship and where he stood with her.

He had intended to call her today, to invite her to lunch again. It was a safe bet she'd agree to lunch. But a meeting with Cam when Joe was walking Coco reminded him it was her monthly lunch, the meeting of what Cam jokingly called Poppy's coven. Evidently, it was Poppy's turn to host today. Joe wondered what the women found to talk about.

He hoped he wasn't a topic of their conversation today. He was pretty sure Gill wouldn't say anything, but the others might not be as circumspect, and both Poppy and Liz had seen him and Gill together. He wasn't sure how he felt about being the butt of gossip. It was a long time since anyone had had anything about him to fuel their gossip, not since Barb died. He flinched at the memory of the plethora of condolences, followed by the not-so-subtle advances from women in search of an available man, any available man. He'd soon put them right, told them he wasn't in the market for a new wife, and they'd drifted off in search of more willing partners. What if it all started up again, this time focussing on him and Gill? She'd hate it even more than he would.

Unable to settle to writing the report for the next council meeting, and realising it was lunchtime, Joe took Coco for another walk, choosing to buy a sandwich and a bottle of ginger beer to have by the beach rather than enjoy his usual lunch in the café or the hotel. Coco was delighted with his decision, also with the crusts and remnant of roast beef Joe gave him. He'd call Gill tonight, he decided, tell her about Erica's phone call and make arrangements to see her again. She had agreed to continue seeing him, only refusing to move their relationship to the next level… while she was still married. He respected her decision, even if it left him feeling frustrated.

*

Unwilling to risk Erica overhearing him talking to Gill, Joe waited till he took Coco for her evening walk. He stopped at one of the benches by the beach opposite *Crossings* to let Coco sniff around. The restaurant seemed to be doing a roaring trade, even though it was midweek.

He took out his phone and held it for a few moments, gazing out to sea to where he could see the outline of a large ship on the horizon, its lights barely visible through the darkness, then he pressed Gill's number.

'Hello, Joe.'

The warmth in Gill's voice was music to Joe's ears. He had been worried she might have changed her mind when she'd had time to think about what they'd discussed.

'Gill, how are you?'

'I'm well. You?'

'I'm good.' He shifted awkwardly. 'This isn't a social call… well, it is. I did intend to call you. But there's something you need to know… about Erica.'

'What's happened? Is she all right?' Joe could hear the concern in Gill's voice.

'She's fine, but she went against your advice – mine too – and called Briony. Her daughter-in-law,' he added, when Gill didn't immediately respond.

'I know who you mean. Oh, why did she do that? Okay, I know why, but it was such a reckless thing to do.'

Joe could imagine Gill frowning or biting her lip. He was beginning to know her so well. 'I think she knows, but she was determined. Briony sent her a copy of the ultrasound.'

'Oh, and now I suppose your son will know too, and it's only a matter of time before her husband does.'

'I told her.'

'At least he's in Perth. She did get a new number?'

'So she says.'

'And she withheld it?'

'Yeah.'

There was a moment's silence, then Gill sighed. 'Well, I guess we can only hope for the best. If he does work out where she is and breaches the domestic violence order, he can be charged with a criminal offence and risks facing up to three years in jail. The prospect of that may deter him. What do you think? You know him.'

'Not very well. We've never hit it off. I always thought Erica had made a mistake getting mixed up with him. There was something about the guy that made me distrust him. I doubt it would discourage him, if he thought he could get away with it… and guys like him do.'

'Hmm, you're right. I've seen it happen, and the woman often gets beaten up before the police can act. I wouldn't like that to happen to Erica.'

Joe's stomach churned. Even though Erica had told him Geoff had hit her – and he'd seen the bruises – he hadn't considered he'd engage in more physical violence. Then he remembered Erica's report of what Briony had said. 'Erica told me Briony said Geoff was making threats about what he'd do to her. I thought it was all hot air, but maybe not.'

'You can never tell what some men are capable of, Joe. If Erica hears anything more, let me know right away. I can alert the local police.'

'Will do.' Joe was suddenly afraid for his sister, glad he'd arranged the small car for her so she never had to walk home alone in the dark. He was silent for a few moments, picturing Erica bruised and beaten, then he gave himself a shake. It hadn't happened yet, not here, and he'd do everything in his power to ensure it never did.

'Now, about my other reason for calling. When can I see you again?' He waited with bated breath for her reply.

When it came, it was with a tinkling laugh, which sent his blood pressure soaring. 'When did you have in mind?'

Joe thought quickly. Today was Wednesday. 'How about dinner on Friday? Since our secret's out, we could try the yacht club again.' He remembered she had met her friends for lunch today. 'I hope your friends didn't give you a hard time.'

'It could have been worse. Poppy and Liz have already been there, and I know they only want me to be happy, but I wish they would mind their own business.'

'I get where they're coming from. You've known them a long time.'

'Since Freya was a baby.' Gill sighed. 'They're okay, really. I guess I have to get used to people knowing about us.'

Joe's heart leapt. 'You're sure you're okay about the yacht club?'

'I think so. Everyone's going to find out anyway, and it's not as if I'm ashamed to be seen with you. It might put a few noses out of joint,' she chuckled. 'I've heard you're regarded as quite a catch.'

It was Joe's turn to chuckle. 'So they tell me. But it'll be good to know I'm no longer regarded as available.' Even though he was no longer the target of advances from lonely women, he often caught the odd predatory glance being sent his way.

Coco pulled on her leash, impatient to continue their walk, no doubt wondering why her master had stopped for such a long time.

'Sorry, Gill. I have to go. Coco and I are down by the beach and she's eager to get moving again.'

Gill laughed. 'Give her a big hug from me.'

'I will. And I'll look forward to seeing you on Friday. Can I pick you up at seven?'

'Sounds good. I'll look forward to it too.'

When he finished the call, Joe felt ebullient. There had been something in Gill's voice that told him she'd been pleased to hear from him. After they'd finished discussing Erica, she'd sounded much warmer. He couldn't wait to see her again. Friday couldn't come soon enough.

Forty-three

Despite her reservations about becoming involved with Joe, Gill was looking forward to seeing him again and resigned to them being seen together at the yacht club a second time. She had to accept that Pelican Crossing was a small town. Nothing could remain secret for long. It was probably better to get it over with rather than become involved in a clandestine relationship and ignite a lot of rumours.

Freya was peering at her phone when Gill came out of her bedroom. She was wearing her blue dress again, remembering how Joe had liked it last time she wore it. 'What's up?' she asked.

'Nothing.' Freya closed her phone. 'I spoke with Dad today.'

'Oh, darling, I'm so glad. Did you make up with him?'

'Not exactly.'

'What do you mean?' Gill sat down, dropped her bag on the floor and stared at her daughter.

'I was so furious about what you told me... how he was making all these ridiculous demands on you. I tore a strip off him, told him exactly what I thought of him... expecting you to fund his new life.'

'Oh, honey.' This wasn't what Gill had intended when she suggested Freya needed to speak with Max. 'How did he take it?' She was curious how Max would react to his daughter's anger. They had always been so close.

'Not well. He blustered a bit, tried to tell me you owed him... As if... Then I said if he wanted to see me again, he'd better rethink his position.'

'You what?' Gill's mouth fell open. 'Oh, Freya! What did he say to that?'

'I don't know. I rang off.'

So nothing had been resolved. Gill wondered if she dared hope Freya's words would change Max's mind, if his daughter could achieve what all the solicitor's letters hadn't managed to. 'Oh, my darling,' she said, giving Freya a hug. 'I didn't want you to become involved in our dispute. We both love you and want you in our lives. I don't want to be the cause of you falling out with your dad.'

'Well, it's his problem now,' Freya said, 'and I think that's your date,' she added, as there was a knock at the door.

Gill felt the now familiar butterflies in her stomach as she rose to answer it. 'Have a nice evening, darling,' she said as she picked up her bag and headed for the door.

'You too,' Freya called after her.

When Gill opened the door, Joe greeted her with a lingering kiss on the cheek that had her butterflies swarming.

'Hey, you,' he said, taking a step back and looking her up and down. 'You're looking lovely… wearing that dress again.'

Gill blushed under his scrutiny. 'Shall we go?' she asked. She found it difficult to accept Joe's compliments even though it was why she'd chosen the dress.

'Let's.' Joe took her hand as they went downstairs to where his car was parked. But when they got there, instead of helping her into the car, he said, 'It's a lovely evening, why don't we walk to the club? I can pick the car up afterwards.'

For a moment, Gill hesitated. But what did it matter? Even if they drove, they would both end up here later. And Joe was right. It was a lovely evening. It would be a shame not to take advantage of it.

As they walked along to the loud screeching of a flock of cockatoos overhead, Gill was very conscious of her hand in Joe's, of his warm skin on her fingers. In the sky above them, the stars were just becoming visible. There had been a shower earlier, and as they passed a cluster of lemon-scented gum trees, the air was filled with their distinctive aroma.

Inside the restaurant, Gill peered around cautiously. Only two of the tables were occupied by people she knew – former clients, one with her new partner, the other with her family – but she did notice a few speculative glances being sent in Joe's direction. Had it been like this last time they dined here, or was she especially conscious of it tonight, she wondered, as Joe smiled greetings left and right. As mayor, he was a well-known figure.

With Gill's agreement, Joe ordered the seafood platter for two and a bottle of prosecco, and Gill attempted to calm her butterflies and relax. As they waited for their meal to arrive, they chatted about inconsequential matters, always circling back to Erica and the possibility of Geoff discovering her whereabouts. Gill was very conscious of their underlying attraction and their previous conversation in which she'd laid out her ground rules. *Had she been too demanding, set unreasonable conditions?*

Joe must have been thinking about it too. They had almost finished their meal when, as she'd been describing the challenges of one of her clients, he asked, 'Any progress with your own divorce?'

Gill gulped. She drained her glass. 'Not as such,' she said, 'but Freya has been talking to Max.' She wasn't sure how much of her conversation with Freya to reveal, but Joe was looking at her so intently, his brown eyes filled with such affection and concern, that she continued. 'She's given him an ultimatum. He gives up his unreasonable demands if he wants to see her again.'

'Wow! She's quite a girl.'

Gill smiled at the memory of Freya's words and her determination. 'Yes, she is, but I'm not sure she'll get the result she's hoping for. Max never did like to be put on the spot, and now he's in a new relationship, with a baby on the way...'

'But she is his daughter, and he loves her.'

'Yes,' Gill bit her lip. 'It would be wonderful if it did work, but it could so easily go the other way... make him more determined to extract his pound of flesh, so to speak.'

'Shades of *The Merchant of Venice*, but that wasn't about a divorce settlement. I can't imagine how difficult this must be for you.' Joe reached across the table to cover Gill's hand with his.

'Thanks.' Gill felt her eyes moisten. Joe was such a good man, so compassionate. She didn't deserve someone like him, and judging from some of the glares and nudges she'd seen tonight, a few others agreed with her. But she was the woman he'd chosen to be with and she was grateful. And here she was, burdening him with her problems when he had enough of his own with this latest news about Erica.

'You need to be positive about this,' he said. 'Even someone like Max can change if sufficient pressure if brought to bear. Freya might just be the final straw.'

'I hope you're right.' Gill had a sudden vision of how it would be if Max did change his mind and drop the majority of his demands, especially the one relating to her future income. It would be a weight off her mind and allow her to move forward with her life… and with Joe, she thought, gazing at the man who had come to mean so much to her. She trembled at the realisation which she had refused to accept before now. She was falling in love with Joe Harris.

Forty-four

Having spent most of the weekend with Gill, Joe was feeling good when Monday morning came around. On Saturday, they'd taken a picnic and gone for a drive in the hinterland, while on Sunday, they'd joined Cam and Poppy on a dive trip. Gill had managed to gain her certification as a diver a week earlier so there was no need for Gary to accompany them.

The previous evening, over dinner at Gill's, Freya had let slip the fact she was off to Sydney for a job interview this week, so Gill would be alone. Joe tried to hide the anticipation which flooded him at her news, knowing nothing had really changed. Gill was still determined to keep their relationship on the same footing, regardless how much they might both yearn for more intimacy.

Since Joe had no meetings today, the morning passed slowly. He was about to take Coco for a walk when his phone rang. He was surprised to see Erica's number. She wasn't rostered on at the hospital today so at breakfast had told him she planned a lazy day. A date had finally been set for her to speak to a group at the *Bellbird Women's Centre* and she intended to put together some notes for her talk. She'd been researching coercive control, shocked to discover it was what she'd suffered for most of her married life.

'Hi, Erica, what's up?' he asked.

'Joe,' Erica sounded distraught, 'I need to talk to you. Kieren just called and…' Her voice broke.

Joe's heart sank. *Was this what he'd been dreading? Had Geoff discovered*

Erica had been in touch with Briony? If so, it might only be a short time before he worked out where she was. He hoped he was wrong. 'Steady on, sis. Look, I was about to leave the office to walk Coco and get some lunch. I could come home. How would that be? We can talk then.'

'Oh, Joe, would you?'

'I'll see you soon.' Joe picked up his keys and Coco's leash. 'Sorry, Coco, no walk today. Erica needs us.' On the way out he stopped by Debbie's desk. 'I'm heading home. Family problem. Don't worry if I'm not back today. You can contact me by phone if anything urgent comes up. Otherwise, I'll see you tomorrow.' By which time Joe hoped he'd have this sorted, and Erica would be on a more even keel.

When they reached the car, Coco leapt into the passenger seat and waited till Joe opened the window so she could stick her head out as she always did. Joe wasn't sure why she liked it so much, maybe it was the feeling of the wind on her face, though he'd read somewhere it was to do with the dog's sense of smell, or so they could check out their surroundings. Whatever the reason, Joe knew Coco loved it, her tongue hanging out to show her delight. He turned on the engine and headed for home.

Erica was seated at the kitchen table twisting her fingers, an untouched cup of tea on the table, when Joe and Coco walked in. Seeming to sense her distress, Coco went straight up to her and pushed her nose into her lap. Erica's hand immediately fell onto the dog's head. 'Oh, Joe, thanks for coming. I don't know what to do.'

'What exactly did Kieren say?' Joe asked, taking a seat next to his sister and clasping her free hand. He could feel her tremble, and her eyes were red. She'd been crying.

'He… Briony told him I'd called,' Erica began, gulping back the tears. 'He wanted to know why I'd left Geoff, where I was. I didn't tell him, but I think he may have guessed. He knows how close we were. He didn't say he'd told Geoff, but…'

'You think he would?'

'They're close. He'd want to keep his dad informed about… Oh, Joe, what am I going to do?'

'I thought you'd called Briony from a silent number.'

'I did… but then, she wanted to send me the photo of the ultrasound…' Erica's voice trailed off as she clearly realised what she'd done.

Joe thought quickly, but he didn't have a solution, unless… 'What about the women's refuge in Bellbird Bay, the one Gill has talked about, the one that Ali woman runs. You were planning to give a talk down there.'

'But not as one of the women who seek refuge.' Erica seemed stunned Joe would mention it. 'Anyway, I suspect they don't have room. Places like that often have a waiting list. I know from my research there's been a rise in the demand for crisis housing. I probably wouldn't qualify because I have you.' She pulled her hand away from Joe's to wipe her eyes.

'Let's make you a cup of tea. It looks like yours has gone cold.' He gestured to the cup sitting on the table which was still full. 'Have you eaten?' he asked, as he was filling the electric jug.

'I couldn't face anything.'

'Well, troubles always seem better when you have something in your stomach, as Mum used to say.'

Erica managed a teary smile at this reminder of their mother who'd had a wealth of such sayings which she trotted out regularly when they were growing up, much to their annoyance.

Joe opened the pantry and, finding a can of vegetable soup, emptied it into a pot, before taking a packet of muffins from the fridge, splitting two and dropping them into the toaster. He was hungry, even if Erica wasn't and he always thought better on a full stomach. Mother hadn't been too far off the mark.

By the time the soup was ready and he'd added slices of cheese to the toasted muffins, Coco had left Erica and was sniffing around Joe's feet. 'Not for you, Coco,' he said. Then he took pity on the dog and gave her a dog biscuit from the box Coco knew Joe kept in the pantry.

Joe was pleased to see Erica managed to have some of the soup and took a few bites out of the muffin before laying down her cutlery and saying, 'I can't eat any more.' But she had drunk the camomile tea Joe had prepared, thankful Erica had bought in supplies of the herbal teas she liked. He seemed to remember camomile was calming. He hoped it worked.

'Do you need to go back to the office?' Erica asked, when Joe was clearing the dishes.

He had intended to, but seeing his sister's expression, Joe decided to stay home. 'Not today,' he said. 'Coco and I can stay home and keep you company.'

But his words failed to comfort Erica who was trembling again. 'What should I do?' she asked Joe again, 'What if…' Her eyes widened with fear.

Joe felt helpless. What should they do? Now Kieren had been in touch, there was a strong possibility he'd tell Geoff and…

Erica's phone rang.

Before Joe could warn her to be careful, she picked it up and answered it. Then she dropped it on the floor as if she'd been stung.

'What…?' Joe began as a familiar voice emanated from the phone. Although he couldn't distinguish the words, he recognised the voice.

'It's Geoff,' Erica said in a tremulous voice

Joe picked up the phone on which he could still hear Geoff's voice. He ended the call and turned off the phone. The silence was deafening. Even Coco was silent, and had wandered off to lie under the table, her head on her paws.

'Sorry,' Erica said.

Joe pulled his sister into a warm hug. She'd been foolish, but it was done now, and they had to think about what to do. After a few minutes he thought of Gill. As Erica's solicitor, she might have a solution. 'We should contact Gill,' he said.

*

Gill gazed at the tearful woman sitting beside Joe in her living room. When he'd called her at the office, she'd had back-to-back appointments so had suggested they come around to the apartment after she got home. Freya was in her bedroom packing for her trip to Sydney, so it was just the three of them. Joe had left Coco at home.

Joe had just finished explaining Erica's predicament, and Gill had poured glasses of wine in the hope of making it feel like an ordinary evening, though she knew it was anything but. She had bitten her lip to stop her from calling Erica all sorts of a fool for giving Briony her number. But perhaps she'd have done the same, given the prospect of seeing an ultrasound of her first grandchild. Who knew how they would react in a similar situation?

'Maybe we're worrying unnecessarily,' Joe said, in a clear attempt to reduce the tension in the room. 'Perhaps Geoff won't figure out where Erica is.'

But Gill was doubtful. 'You're Erica's only other relative, Joe. Where else would she go? The wonder is that he hasn't worked it out before now, even given your attempt to mislead him.'

'I wondered about the women's refuge you talked about,' he said. 'But Erica wasn't optimistic they'd have a vacancy.'

'She's right. Ali said they were chock-a-block.'

Just then, Freya popped her head around the door. 'I'm off now, Mum. Rory's giving me a ride to the airport. I'll see you later in the week. I may stay down for a few days to look around.'

'Excuse me,' Gill said to Joe and Erica, an idea forming in her mind as she accompanied her daughter to the door. 'Good luck with the interview, darling. I hope it goes well if it's what you want. And take your time in Sydney. It's a lovely city. I think you'd enjoy living there.'

'Thanks, Mum. You're the best. No word from Dad?'

Gill shook her head. She didn't expect to hear from Max. They'd said all they had to say to each other long ago. In recent years all their communication had been through their solicitors.

There was the sound of a car horn.

'That's Rory now. Bye, Mum.'

Gill hugged her daughter. 'Safe trip and let me know how it goes.'

'I will, Mum. Bye,' she said again and she was off, running out to where Rory was waiting for her.

With a sigh, Gill closed the door and returned to the living room where Erica was sobbing, her head on Joe's shoulder. At the sight of Gill, she made an effort to pull herself together, wiping her eyes with a tissue. Gill refilled their glasses, then said, 'I think I have a solution. Freya will be gone to Sydney for a few days. Why don't you move into her room here, Erica? It will give you some breathing space, and if your husband does arrive in Pelican Crossing, he'll never think of looking for you here.'

Both Erica and Joe stared at Gill. 'Do you mean it?' Erica said, the relief in her voice unmistakable.

'Of course. I wouldn't offer, otherwise.' Although it went against all her rules to offer accommodation to a client, Erica was Joe's sister, a friend.

'It's very kind of you,' Joe said, 'and you're right, Geoff wouldn't find her here. What do you think, Erica?'

'I think it sounds like the perfect solution,' Erica said. 'If you're sure, Gill.'

'I'm sure.' It would also ensure she and Joe wouldn't be tempted to take advantage of her being alone in the apartment, Gill thought, before dismissing the thought as unworthy. 'I'll give you a key and you can move in anytime.'

'Thanks.' Erica rose, and to Gill's embarrassment, gave her a hug. 'You won't regret it.'

Gill hoped she was right. But what possible harm could there be in providing Erica with a safe place to live?

Forty-five

When Gill arrived home from the office next day, Erica was already there. She looked different, dressed in her nurse's uniform, less distressed, more confident.

'Thanks so much for this, Gill,' Erica said. 'I feel a lot better, knowing Geoff can't find me. Do you really think he'll come looking for me in Pelican Crossing?'

'Probably.' Gill had enough experience of men like Erica's husband to understand something of their thought processes. She'd seen it all before, the difference being, this was the first time she'd offered sanctuary to one of her clients. She wasn't sure how her partners would view her action, but she couldn't have allowed Joe's sister to be in danger, as she could have been if she'd remained with Joe. She tried to ignore the shiver which ran down her spine at the thought Joe might still be in danger, though what benefit would there be to Erica's husband in harming Joe?

'I feel safe here,' Erica continued, 'and at the hospital. He'd never think of looking for me there. He hated it when I was working. As long as I'm either at the hospital or here, everything should be fine, until we know…'

'I've alerted the local police, but there's nothing they can do unless he arrives here and tries to breach the AVO. Hopefully, if he does come and finds you're not with Joe, he'll go back to Perth and all will be well.' Gill tried to sound upbeat, more upbeat than she was feeling. If, as she suspected, Erica's husband was one of those men who beat, then took things to the extreme and murdered their wives, he wouldn't stop if he didn't find her at Joe's. But there was no point in making Erica more afraid than she was already. And Erica was right, he couldn't guess she was here. So why did Gill feel uneasy?

'Why don't you have a shower and change?' Gill said. 'I talked with Joe earlier and he's joining us for dinner. You haven't used that phone again, have you?' she asked with the sudden fear Erica might have taken it into her head to contact Briony again.

'No,' Erica shook her head. 'Joe has it. He turned it off after Geoff's call and wouldn't let me have it again. I feel naked without it, and the hospital can't contact me.'

For a moment, Gill considered suggesting Erica give the hospital her number, then thought better of it. Best no one but Joe knew where Erica was staying. 'Hopefully, it won't be for long,' she said, 'and your husband will give up looking for you.'

Gill could see from her expression, Erica didn't believe her, but she went off to change anyway.

By the time Joe arrived, the apartment was filled with the aroma of cooking. This time Joe was accompanied by Coco at Gill's request. She thought the dog's presence might help calm Erica so was willing to make an exception to her no animals in the apartment rule for once, and Joe had assured her he'd give Coco a firm talking to first, to ensure the dog behaved herself. In recognition of Erica's first night in the apartment, and that this was the first time she'd cooked a meal for Joe, Gill had pulled out all stops. She hoped the roast leg of lamb with accompanying vegetables would tempt Erica's tastebuds and prove to Joe she could cook when the occasion demanded it.

'Wow,' he said when he walked in, 'something smells good.'

Coco evidently thought so too, immediately making her way to the kitchen and positioning herself by the stove.

'Sorry,' Joe said. 'She doesn't often get the opportunity to smell roast lamb.'

'It's okay. There's plenty for her to have some too, if it's okay with you.'

'She'll love you for ever.'

'Joe!' Erica joined them, looking refreshed after her shower and dressed in a casual outfit. She hugged Joe, and Coco left her position by the stove to greet her. 'Hello, Coco,' Erica said, ruffling the dog's ears. 'I'm glad you brought her,' she said to Joe.

'Wine?' Gill asked, taking a bottle from the fridge.

'Let me do it.' Joe took the bottle from Gill and poured three glasses. 'To a fast resolution,' he said, holding up his glass.

'I'll drink to that.' Gill took a sip of wine.

But Erica held her glass without drinking. 'Do you think it's possible?' she asked, sounding worried again.

'We have to believe it,' Joe said. 'We're doing all we can. If Geoff comes, he comes, and there's nothing we can do to stop him. But if he does breach the AVO, the police can arrest him. That's right, Gill, isn't it?' He turned to Gill for confirmation.

'It is, Joe. So, you see, Erica, you can relax.'

'I don't think I'll ever be able to relax until I know he's safely in Perth… or locked up. But that would mean…' She shivered and took a gulp of wine.

To Gill's relief, the lamb was cooked to perfection. Joe carved the joint, dropping a few slices into a bowl for Coco along with a bit of veg, much to the dog's delight, then carried the meat out to the balcony where Gill had set the table.

It was a cool night, but not too cool to sit outside, and the view was amazing, the lights of the marina twinkling and reflecting in the ocean, a match for the stars above. Having satisfied her hunger, Coco took her place under the table, ready to rescue any food which was dropped.

Gill was pleased Joe steered the conversation away from Erica's husband, instead focussing on sharing amusing anecdotes about the exploits of him and Erica growing up here in Pelican Crossing, even managing to make his sister laugh and, hopefully, forget her troubles for a time.

They had just finished the individual cups of Häagen-Dazs ice cream Gill had found in the freezer – something Freya must have purchased – when Erica yawned and said, 'I think I'll turn in. I didn't get much sleep last night, and I have to work again tomorrow. Thanks again for having me stay, Gill, and thanks for this lovely meal. I don't expect this every night. I'm happy to cook for you. I'd enjoy it.' Giving Joe a hug, and Gill a peck on the cheek, she disappeared. Coco rose to follow her, but a stern look from Joe stopped her in her tracks and she lay down again.

'Coffee?' Gill asked. 'Don't worry about the dishes, I'll do them later,' she said, when she saw him start to collect them.

'If you're sure?'

'I'm sure.'

Now Erica had gone to bed and she was alone with Joe again, the butterflies which had been dormant all evening made their presence felt.

When Gill carried the coffee into the living room, Joe was seated on the sofa, Coco at his feet. She placed the two mugs on the coffee table and joined him, his arm immediately snaking around her shoulders. 'Thanks,' he said. 'I know Erica has already thanked you, but I needed to. I suspect this is way above what you normally do for your clients.'

'Erica's more than another client,' Gill said, as Joe put one finger under her chin and lifted her face to meet his. As their lips met in a deep kiss, and before she was lost to all sense of time and place, Gill reflected it was lucky Erica was in the next room... and Coco was snoring at their feet. Otherwise, all of her good intentions might have flown out the window, as Joe's closeness made Gill yearn for an intimacy she'd never imagined she'd ever want again.

Forty-six

It had been two weeks since Erica moved in with Gill, and they were all beginning to feel complacent, reasoning, if Geoff hadn't come here by now, they were safe. Freya was still in Sydney, her old professor having suggested she stay around and sit in on a few classes to get the feel of the place. She was confident she'd be offered the position and had even started looking around for accommodation. But she was planning on coming back later in the week, and Erica was making noises about moving back to Joe's.

'What do you think?' Gill asked, when Erica had gone to bed. Since his sister had been staying there, Joe had joined the two women for dinner most evenings, Coco too, and Erica had developed the habit of tactfully disappearing to bed leaving the couple alone. But Joe's awareness of his sister's presence only a few metres away, plus Gill's determination, kept him from taking their relationship any further.

'I think possibly enough time has passed. If Geoff was going to travel all the way from Perth, he'd have done it by now. My guess is the AVO, and the risk of possible jail time has made him cautious. He's a businessman, used to taking calculated risks, but also evaluating the potential of failure. He's not stupid, and it would be stupid to risk the loss of his liberty – and his business – by pursuing Erica and breaching the AVO.'

'You may be right.'

'You don't think so?' Joe was surprised by Gill's tone.

She sighed. 'I've probably seen more of these cases than you have.

Men like your sister's husband often don't consider the consequences of their actions when their wife is the one they're pursuing. But I hope you're right. Erica has suffered enough, and she's only just beginning to feel secure again. I wish Freya wasn't coming home so soon, even though I'll be pleased to see her again.'

'Erica will be right with us, won't she, Coco?' Joe nudged the sleeping dog with his foot, only to have her grunt in her sleep, her ears twitching as she doubtless chased a pelican in her dreams.

'I hope so. I guess she can't stay in hiding for ever. She does seem to have settled into Pelican Crossing.'

'We both loved it here when we were growing up, and the town hasn't changed too much since then. I could never imagine leaving.' Joe stretched out his legs, this time ensuring his feet avoided Coco's sleeping body.

'I love it too. It's one thing I have to thank Max for. If it hadn't been for him accepting a teaching position at Pelican Crossing High, who knows where we might have ended up? I always thought he'd choose to be in the city, and I'd join some high-powered legal firm.'

'Instead of which…' Joe turned to look at the woman who had come to mean so much to him. 'You've never regretted it?'

'Maybe a little, when things got bad between Max and me. But by then I had my practice. I love what I do, Joe, helping women, women like me… and Erica. I sometimes wish I could do more. I look at what Ali Wells is doing in Bellbird Bay and…'

'Don't sell yourself short. You do a lot. Pelican Crossing would be the poorer without you.'

'Thanks, Joe.' Gill smiled and snuggled into him. 'You've done a lot for Pelican Crossing too.'

'Now we've decided we're both essential members of the community, why don't we enjoy our time together? If Erica moves back with me, and once Freya is home, we'll have no excuse to spend so many evenings like this.' As Gill opened her mouth to speak, Joe pulled her into his arms to silence her with a kiss, and for the rest of the evening not another word was spoken.

*

Next day, Joe had just arrived home from the office and was preparing to take Coco for a walk before heading to Gill's for dinner. Although she had only been there for two months, Joe had become accustomed to Erica's presence in the house and had missed her since she moved to Gill's. He'd be glad to have her back, though sorry his time with Gill might be curtailed. Perhaps he could persuade her to spend some evenings here with him and Erica… and Coco. As if reading his mind, Coco let out a woof of what Joe took to be agreement. He chuckled.

Joe had taken Coco's leash from its hook, and the dog was bouncing around in anticipation of her walk when there was a loud pounding on the door. Fearing the worst, Joe instructed Coco to stay and went to answer it. When he saw the red-faced, bloated figure at the door, the first thing that hit Joe was how much his brother-in-law had changed since they last met, when Geoff had been in Pelican Crossing for Barb's funeral two years earlier. Then he'd been fresh-faced and if not the trim-figured man Erica had married, at least looking fit and healthy. The man facing him seemed to have aged prematurely. He didn't look well.

'Where is she?' Geoff blustered. 'I know she's here. Where else would she go other than to her brother? The pair of you were always as thick as thieves. You lied to me about some friend in Cairns, but you're not getting away with it this time.'

Joe stared at his brother-in-law. He wasn't making any sense. But he knew better than to question him. 'If you mean Erica, if you're looking for your wife, she's not here.'

Behind Joe, Coco started to growl.

'Quiet, Coco,' Joe said, putting out one hand to silence the dog.

'Where is she?' Geoff repeated, making to push past Joe.

Coco growled again.

This time Joe ignored her. Coco recognised Geoff wasn't a friend. 'You can come in,' he said, 'but you won't find Erica here.' He was glad Erica was still with Gill, and that she'd taken all of her meagre possessions with her, leaving no sign she'd ever been there. If it had been later in the week… but Joe didn't want to think of that.

Geoff pushed his way in, past a snarling Coco, only Joe's hand on her collar preventing the normally mild-mannered dog from attempting to bite him. He blundered through the house, going from one room to another in his fruitless search, while Joe stood in the hallway with Coco. 'Satisfied?' Joe asked, when Geoff finally returned. 'She's not here.'

'What have you done with her? Kieren told me…'

Joe's heart sank. What had Kieren said? He couldn't know his mother had come to Pelican Crossing, could he?

But Geoff didn't elaborate. 'I'm not done with you yet,' he yelled as he barrelled out the door and made his way to what Joe recognised as a rental car sitting by the kerb.

'No, Coco,' Joe said, as the dog made to follow him, her teeth bared. 'He's not worth it.' His eyes followed the car as it disappeared around the corner. Maybe Geoff would go back to Perth now he'd failed to find Erica. But Joe wasn't sure he'd managed to convince his brother-in-law. Before heading to Gill's, he made a call to one of the local police officers he knew quite well. Gavin was married to Megan, one of Poppy's daughters, and was a keen local athlete. He knew Gill had apprised him of Erica's situation and wanted to update him. It was as he'd expected, there was nothing the police could do. As yet, Geoff hadn't actually breached the domestic violence order.

Too upset to take his normal walk, Joe attached Coco's leash and headed to Gill's. He kept an eye out to ensure Geoff wasn't following him, but there was no sign of the dark blue SUV.

Joe was still feeling shaken when he reached Gill's apartment to find the two women enjoying a glass of wine on the balcony.

'What's up?' Gill asked, when he walked in, Coco at his heels. The dog immediately went over to lay her head on Erica's lap, as if understanding she was about to receive bad news.

'I had a visitor,' Joe said with a pinched expression.

'Not…?' Erica's face paled; her hands clenched.

'Geoff paid me a visit. He was looking for you.'

'Of course he was,' Erica said bitterly. 'Oh, I knew this would happen. What am I going to do?' She began to tremble.

'Stay calm,' Gill said. 'He doesn't know you're here. What did you say?' she asked Joe.

'I told him the truth. You weren't there. He blundered through the house, but there was no sign of you, or any of your belongings. Lucky you brought everything here with you.'

'That was Gill's advice.' Erica looked gratefully at Gill.

'It was only the sensible thing to do,' Gill said. 'But now he's here in Pelican Crossing, you need to be doubly careful.' She seemed to think for a moment. 'It's probably a good idea if you stay in the apartment for a bit, call in sick at work… just in case.'

'But I was going to move back to Joe's. Your daughter is coming home,' Erica said, her face now ashen.

'You can't go back yet. When Freya gets home, we'll work something out. I can always make up a temporary bed in the study, for a few days at least, until we know what your husband is up to, or we know for sure he's left town.'

'Gill's right. And I need a drink,' Joe said, discovering he was shaking. It must be the result of delayed shock at the way Geoff had pushed his way in and stormed through his house.

'Coming up.' Gill disappeared to fetch a glass of wine for Joe.

Joe gave Erica a hug. 'It'll be fine, sis,' he said. 'Geoff can't stay here for long. He has a business to run back in Perth. If, as Gill suggested, you lie low here for a few days, he'll realise he's made a mistake. Then, once he's returned to Perth, you can come back to live with me and Coco and go on as before.'

'If you're sure.' Erica didn't sound convinced, but Joe couldn't imagine Geoff hanging around if he couldn't find her.

'I am,' he said, trying to sound more positive than he felt, remembering the anger in Geoff's voice. He'd sounded deranged but surely even he wouldn't want to waste his time here if there was no sign of Erica?

By the time Gill returned with Joe's wine, Erica seemed calmer and was sipping her wine. 'Thanks. Gill,' she said. 'I don't know what I'd have done if you hadn't offered to have me to stay.'

'Not a problem,' Gill said, reddening. She met Joe's eyes, and his heart flipped at the thought of being alone with her later. Then he felt guilty for focussing on his own emotions when his sister was in such trouble.

'I contacted Gavin to let him know Geoff was in town,' Joe said. 'But, as I thought, there's nothing they can do.'

'Gavin?' Erica asked.

'He's a local police officer, one I happen to know pretty well. Gill, too.'

'He's married to the daughter of a friend of mine,' Gill said. 'I was in touch with the station earlier, and Gavin said he'd keep a look out. Sadly, they can't take action until…' she corrected herself, '… unless Geoff actually tries to make contact with you. Accusing Joe doesn't count.'

Erica shivered.

'It's okay, sis.' Joe hugged her again. 'We're not going to let that happen.'

Forty-seven

The previous evening had been difficult. When Joe arrived with the news Erica's husband was in town, it had taken Gill and Erica by surprise. And Gill wondered if her suggestion Erica stay in the apartment till he had left town had only made things worse. But it was the only thing that made sense.

Joe had been good. He'd supported her, telling Erica it wouldn't be for long, and she'd be safe in Gill's apartment. Gill hoped he was right. By the time Erica retired for the night, she had seemed calmer, but Gill doubted she'd got much sleep. Her eyes had been bleary at breakfast, and she'd been disappointed to miss her early morning swim. Even though it was doubtful her husband would be on the beach at sunrise, it was best to take care.

After Erica had gone to bed, Gill had curled up with Joe on the sofa, but for once, they had shared nothing more than a cuddle, both worried about what Geoff might do next, and neither willing to speculate. Before he left, earlier than usual, they'd agreed to continue to spend their evenings together to keep things as normal as usual for Erica in these days which were far from normal. Even Coco had sensed the tension in the atmosphere and had stayed close to Erica until she went off to bed.

'I wish you didn't have to go to work,' Erica said nervously, as Gill prepared to leave. 'What if…'

'He's not going to find you here,' Gill said. 'And I need to go to the office. I have meetings, appointments… I'd stay if I could,' she said, seeing Erica's eyes moisten. 'You'll be fine. Call me or Joe if you're worried about anything. Either of us can be here in minutes.'

'I know… It's just…'

'I'm sorry. I understand you're worried, afraid Geoff will somehow find you, but there's no way he could know you're here. How could he?'

'I know. You're right.' Erica sighed. 'I'm sorry I'm being so difficult. You've been so good to me.'

'No, *I'm* sorry,' Gill said. 'I do understand your concern. I see it every day in the women I meet. I see their fear, their doubt, how it fills their minds so they can't think of anything else. But it won't last. I can promise you that.'

'It was okay when I could go to work. Caring for other people helped me forget about my own troubles. But being here all day, alone, with nothing else to think about… It's going to do my head in.'

'Why don't you try watching a movie, or a series on Netflix? I know it's not a real solution, but it might help take your mind off Geoff for a bit. I'll give you a call when I'm between appointments, and Joe said he'd drop in at lunchtime, didn't he?'

'Thanks. You're right. You're both so good to me.'

'Now I must go. I'm sorry. Take care and don't answer the door unless it's Joe or me.'

As soon as she'd spoken, Gill regretted her last words when she saw how Erica flinched. But it was too late to retract them. 'See you tonight,' she said as she headed for the door.

*

Gill had a busy morning but she made time to call Erica a couple of times to ensure all was well with her. She still sounded troubled but assured Gill she was okay and apologised for being such a wimp.

It was close to lunchtime. Gill was between clients and about to send out for a sandwich, which was all she was going to allow herself today, when her PA appeared in the doorway.

'There's someone to see you,' Josie said nervously.

A large man, overweight with a florid appearance was standing behind her.

Gill knew who he was immediately. Erica had described her husband to her over coffee one morning, when they'd returned from their early morning swim. What was he doing here?

'You,' he said, pushing past a surprised Josie and pointing a finger at Gill. 'I know about women like you, you and your like. You think you're so smart, don't you? Encouraging women to leave their husbands, telling them they have rights, fabricating laws to make them think they can get away with it. You're no better than those witches they used to burn at the stake. Bitches, the lot of you. You deserve to be…'

'Enough!' Gill said, pushing to her feet.

The man practically snarled, nostrils flaring. 'Where is she?' he said, 'I know you've hidden her away somewhere.'

Gill took a breath, trying not to show how much she was trembling. 'I don't know you, or the person you're looking for, but you need to leave right now before I call…'

'Call who? The cops? For what? Demanding my rights? You're nothing but a waste of space, just like the rest of them, holier than thou, think you're God's gift…'

'Josie, call the police, right now,' Gill said, backing off to the side when Geoff stepped up to her.

As Josie went to pick up the phone on a nearby desk, Geoff strode over and batted it off the desk, sending it clattering off the wall.

'Now,' he said, turning back to Gill, 'I know my rights. You need to tell me where my wife is, right now, or so help me I'll…'

Gill reached for the phone on her desk, but he was there in a flash, snatching the receiver from her hand and slamming it down.

'You don't get it, do you?' he said, right up in her face.

'Oh, I get it alright,' Gill said, 'you're nothing but a coward who doesn't think twice about hitting a woman. You have no rights here, and certainly no right to be in my office. Get the hell out!'

'You've got some bloody nerve,' he yelled, the fierceness in his eyes making Gill wish she'd kept her mouth shut. 'Last chance, you bitch, tell me where she is or I'll…'

His loud tirade suddenly stopped, he put up one hand to clutch his chest, uttered something between a moan and a groan and collapsed with a thud to the floor.

'Josie!' Gill yelled to the woman who was still standing by the desk, a shocked expression on her face. She fell to her knees and put a finger to his neck. Thankfully, there was a pulse. 'Josie!' she yelled again, seeing her PA hadn't moved other than to put one hand to her mouth, 'call an ambulance. I think he's had a heart attack.'

For Gill, it seemed as if everything happened in slow motion, but it was only a few heart-pounding minutes before two paramedics appeared to join her and manoeuvre her out of the way as they checked Geoff for signs of life. She and Josie watched on while they opened his shirt, performed CPR then attached sticky electrodes to his skin before lifting his body onto a stretcher and carrying him off.

'Who the heck was that?' Josie asked when they had all left.

'A client's husband.' Gill wondered what had brought him to her office, but it wasn't too difficult to work out. He must know Erica had consulted a solicitor to arrange the AVO. It wouldn't have taken too much asking around to discover she was the most likely one for her to have consulted. Anyone in Pelican Crossing could have told him she was the most popular divorce lawyer in town. She couldn't recall if her name had appeared anywhere on the documents, but even if she hadn't been his first port of call, he'd have found her eventually.

She collapsed onto her office chair.

'Tea?' Josie asked and, without waiting for a reply, went off to make it.

When she returned, Gill realised she was shaking. 'Thanks,' she said, taking a gulp of the hot liquid, and grimacing at its sweetness. How much sugar had Josie added?

'Do you want me to cancel your next appointment?' Josie asked, clearly seeing Gill's distress.

'No, I'll be fine in a few minutes. But could you go out and get me a sandwich?'

'No problem.'

When she had gone, Gill took another gulp of tea and picked up the phone. She had to let Erica know what had happened.

Forty-eight

Joe had just arrived at Gill's to check on Erica as promised, when the phone on the kitchen wall rang. Erica almost jumped out of her skin, and Coco's ears pricked up at the unfamiliar sound of the ring tone of Gill's phone. She was more accustomed to the sound of Joe's mobile.

'You answer it,' Erica said to Joe.

'It's just the phone, Erica,' Joe said, but went over to answer it. 'It's probably Gill.'

'She's already called me twice. She can't be calling again so soon.'

Cursing his brother-in-law for turning Erica into this nervous wreck, Joe picked up the receiver. 'Hello?'

'Joe?' He was relieved to hear Gill's voice, though he didn't know who else he'd expected. *Were Erica's jitters beginning to affect him?*

'I just got here. What's up? Erica said you only just called.'

'It's Geoff.'

Joe's heart sank.

'He was here.'

'At your office? What did he want? He couldn't have expected to find Erica there.' Joe shook his head at his sister who was reaching for the phone, her eyes wide with fear.

'No, it was me he wanted to rant at. But it's not why I'm calling. He was in full flow when he collapsed, a probable heart attack. We called an ambulance, and it took him to hospital. I wanted to let Erica know.'

Joe could see Erica trying to work out what they were talking about. 'I'll tell her.' he said, 'and see you later.'

When he hung up, Erica stared at him. 'It was Geoff, wasn't it? What's he done?'

'I think you should sit down.' Joe took Erica into the other room and made sure she was sitting down before he joined her and took both of her hands in his. 'Geoff turned up at Gill's office.'

Erica gasped. She turned pale. Her eyes widened with fear.

'He'd no doubt discovered she was a divorce lawyer, maybe even the one you'd consulted. He went there to rant at Gill.'

'Where is he now?' Erica's voice quivered.

'In hospital.'

'What?' Her eyes widened even further. 'How...?'

'It seems he had a heart attack, and they had to call an ambulance. Right now, he's either in or on his way to Pelican Crossing's Emergency Department.'

'Oh!' For what seemed like a full minute, Erica was silent as she digested the news, then, 'I should go to see him.'

'Steady on, Erica. I don't think that's a good idea. Right now, Geoff doesn't know for sure you're here. If you turn up at his bedside...'

'But he's still my husband. It's my place to...' Then the significance of Joe's words seemed to hit her. 'But then.... Oh, Joe, what a mess.'

'You're right there.' Looking at his sister, he could see she was shaking. He didn't feel too flash himself at the thought of what Gill had been through. 'I think we need a drink. Will you be right if I leave you for a minute?'

Erica nodded. She wrapped her arms around herself and began to rock back and forth. Coco laid her head on her lap.

Joe headed to the kitchen, hoping Gill kept some strong drink in the apartment. He went to the pantry and, sure enough, almost hidden at the back of a shelf, he found a half-full bottle of scotch. Perfect! He poured two small measures and took them through to where Erica was still as he'd left her. He handed one glass to her and laid one hand on Coco's head. The dog seemed to sense all was not well.

'I thought you meant tea,' she said.

'I think we need something stronger than tea. I can make some after we have this.'

'Poor Geoff,' Erica said at last. 'He'd been having trouble with his heart. The doctor told him to take things easy, to change his diet, get more exercise. But he wouldn't listen. Maybe if I hadn't...'

'Stop! It's not your fault, Erica. Don't ever think it. Whatever has happened to Geoff, he brought it on himself. It's nothing to do with you. This could have happened anytime, anywhere. He didn't look well when I saw him yesterday, and today, he obviously went too far. It's Gill you have to feel sorry for, if anyone.'

'You're right again. How did I come to have such a bright brother?' she managed a weak smile.

'You've only just noticed?' Joe joked. He drained his glass. 'Now I'll make us some tea, and something to eat. I did intend to have lunch with you.'

'Oh, I'm sorry. I was going to make some. I don't know what happened.'

'It's okay.' Joe knew she'd been traumatised by the knowledge Geoff was in town. 'I'm sure I can whip up a couple of sandwiches and maybe open a can of soup.' He remembered seeing some cans in the pantry when he was looking for the scotch.

'Sounds good. Do you know, I think I'm actually feeling hungry.'

Coco's ears pricked up at the prospect of food.

*

Gill was relieved it was Joe who answered the phone, glad he'd be there to support Erica when she heard the news. She couldn't imagine how the other woman would feel – anger that he'd burst into Gill's office, relief he was no longer a threat?

It wasn't the first time Gill had come face-to-face with a client's husband, but it was the first time she'd felt to be in physical danger. Although a shock, it had been almost a relief when he collapsed.

She only managed to take a few bites of the sandwich Josie brought her, throwing the rest into the bin. Then she took a few deep breaths to prepare herself for her next client. Fortunately, this one and the one after proved to be straightforward with no hints of violence from their partners, so Gill was able to end the day on a more positive note. She was looking forward to getting home and finding out how Erica had coped with the news about Geoff. While his heart attack wasn't a cause for celebration, surely it would put her mind at ease and allow her to resume the new life she was making for herself here in Pelican Crossing. Though there was always the risk Geoff would continue to pursue her once he was discharged, if the police didn't lay charges.

'Feeling better?' Josie popped her head through the door.

'Yes, thanks. It's been quite a day. I'm glad our clients' husbands don't make a habit of coming to berate us.'

'Will he be all right?'

'I hope so. I should call the hospital.' It suddenly occurred to Gill it's what she should have done before now. She picked up the phone, only to be told the patient was as well as could be expected. She sighed, knowing it was the standard response since she wasn't a relative. Next, she called Gavin to find out what the police intended to do, but again she was frustrated. It appeared that unless she was prepared to press charges, he'd be free when he left the hospital, free to terrorise Erica. But Gill really couldn't lay a complaint. Yes, he'd burst into her office uninvited and ranted at her. He'd acted violent, scared her, but hadn't made any actual physical contact. She had no reason to ask the police to charge him. Perhaps it would have been better if he had raised his fists, Gill thought, then shuddered, berating herself.

By the time she arrived home, she was feeling angry and frustrated, so the sight of Joe sitting there with a glass of wine was welcome, as was Coco's now familiar presence at his feet.

'Hey,' he said, rising to greet her and pulling her into a warm hug. 'You look beat. How about I pour you a glass of wine? I found a lasagne in the freezer and put it in the oven, and Erica's made a salad.'

'Oh, Joe! It's so good to see you, to be home.'

'Gill!' Erica appeared, looking pale, but smiling. 'It must have been awful for you. How did Geoff know I'd consulted you?'

'I don't know that he did.' Gill accepted the glass of wine Joe had poured and took a gulp. It hit the spot, helping to release the tension which had been building up ever since Geoff walked into her office. 'He just wanted to lash out at someone. It would have been easy to discover I was the local go-to divorce lawyer. Guess it's what I get for being so well-known. But there's still no reason to believe he knows you're in Pelican Crossing.'

'I want to visit him… in hospital.'

'What?' Gill looked from Erica to Joe and back again.

'I've told her it's a bad idea,' Joe said with a sigh, 'but…'

'He's my husband,' Erica said. 'And I want to see for myself he's really had a heart attack and isn't faking it.'

'He definitely didn't fake collapsing in my office,' Gill said. 'He went down like a ton of bricks. Does he have a history of heart disease?'

'He was told to take care at his last checkup, but he thought he knew better than the doctor. He's put on a lot of weight over the past two years, too much beer and fast food. Geoff has never been one to listen to advice, and with the hours he puts in at the car yard…'

'Sounds as if it's all caught up with him,' Joe said. 'I can't say I'm sorry, after the way he treated you, Erica, but I wouldn't wish a heart attack on anyone.'

'You have a son,' Gill said, suddenly remembering. 'Have you let him know about his dad?'

Joe and Erica exchanged glances, and Gill realised that if Erica contacted her son, it would reveal where she was.

'Maybe we can get the police to do that,' she suggested, to see Erica's face lighten.

'Good idea,' Joe said, 'or I could do it. Geoff did come to see me first. And Kieren knows me.'

'Even better,' Gill said. 'Now, you mentioned food?'

While Gill and Erica were setting out the lasagne, salad and some crusty bread, Joe called his nephew to let him know his father was in hospital in Pelican Crossing.

'Kieren had no idea his dad was here,' he reported when he joined Gill and Erica at the table. 'He's going to fly over when he and his wife can get a flight, but he's worried about leaving the car yard, something about invoices?' He looked at Erica.

'Don't look at me, Joe. I was never privy to anything to do with Geoff's work. He told me I wouldn't understand.'

'Well, not our problem. I asked him to let me know when they get in. I can meet them.'

Gill could see from Erica's expression how she was torn. It would be difficult for her to know her son and daughter-in-law were in town and she couldn't see them, but that if she did, her husband would know she was here.

'I'm going to the hospital,' Erica said in a determined voice. 'If he's still unconscious, he won't know I'm there, and I have to see him for myself.'

'And if he's not?' Joe asked.

'I still want to go.'

'Okay,' Joe sighed, 'if you're determined, I'll go with you.'

'I don't think it's a good idea,' Gill said, 'given he's already been to your house. I'll go with Erica. As her solicitor, I can say I'm there to protect her interests, and if he does regain consciousness, I can be a witness to anything that occurs.'

Coco, clearly tired of being ignored, let out a whine of annoyance.

'Sorry, Coco,' Joe said, dropping a crust down for her, which she snapped up eagerly.

After dinner, when they went through to the living room with coffee, Gill could see Erica was still distressed. She didn't say much, only coming to life when Gill asked her about making arrangements to visit the hospital next day.

'I still don't think it's a good idea,' Gill said, 'but if you're determined.'

'I am, and thanks. I'm sorry for all the trouble I've put both of you to.'

'Don't be,' Joe said. 'We both want what's best for you. It's no trouble.'

'Thanks,' Erica said again.

Erica was still sitting there when Joe rose to leave. Gill accompanied him to the door, sorry they weren't to have any time alone together that evening, but still feeling shaken from her encounter with Geoff.

'Let me know what time you're going to the hospital tomorrow and I'll meet you there,' Joe said, pulling Gill into a warm hug.

'But...'

'I won't go in to see Geoff with you, but I want to be there. Erica's my sister. I need to support her in this... and you.'

'Okay.' Gill understood his concern. It was so like Joe to want to be there for them both. 'I'll call you in the morning.'

'Maybe once this is all over, we can think about us,' Joe said, taking her in his arms.

'Maybe.' It would be good to have Erica's problem resolved, but there was still Max to consider, and Gill knew she couldn't move on till that was settled. Then Joe's lips met hers and once again she was transported into a world where none of it mattered.

Forty-nine

Gill went swimming alone next morning. When she peeked into the spare room, Erica was asleep, though from the way the covers were tangled, it was obvious she'd had a restless night.

As always, it was good to be out in the fresh air, to feel the water on her skin, to greet the new dawn. It always felt like a new beginning to spend time in the ocean at this time of day, when most of Pelican Crossing was still asleep.

As she floated on her back, Gill relived her encounter with Geoff the previous day. She dreaded to think what might have happened if he hadn't collapsed. He was a big man, strong too. She'd have been no match for him if he'd decided to use his fists. Even though Josie was there, she'd have found it difficult to be of any help. Gill had been really scared, realising exactly what had prompted Erica to leave him. And now she wanted to visit him in hospital, to see the man who'd been physically abusive to her. The least Gill could do was accompany her and hope he didn't regain consciousness while they were there.

When she came out of the water, Gill was surprised to see Joe and Coco waiting for her on the beach. Coco immediately ran up to her. 'Good morning, Coco,' she said ruffling the dog's ears, and looking up at Joe questioningly. Why was he here? Had there been a development with Geoff's condition?

'Hey.' Joe pulled her into a hug, despite her protest she was all wet.

'No worries,' he said, handing her the towel at her feet.

While she dried herself, and Coco stayed close, Joe filled her in.

'I called the hospital early this morning and managed to have a word with the cardiac surgeon. I know him from a couple of committees we're both on. It seems Geoff is scheduled for surgery this morning, but Erica will be able to see him before he goes to theatre. I still don't think it's a good idea, but she seemed determined and I know from growing up together that once she gets an idea into her head, she won't be swayed.'

'I'll be with her, and I'll try to make sure she's okay, though if Geoff's conscious…'

'He'll know she's here, and that I lied to him. But what can we do?' He shrugged.

'Do you want to come back for breakfast? Luckily, I only had a couple of meetings arranged, and I contacted Josie last night to reschedule them. If Geoff's having surgery this morning, we should get there early.'

'Good idea, and breakfast sounds good.'

'Woof,' said Coco, obviously recognising the word.

'She's already been fed,' Joe said, 'but she's always alert to any mention of food.'

Gill pulled on her clothes, and they set off back to her apartment.

When they arrived there, Erica was in the kitchen, looking as if she had just got up, the dark circles under her eyes evidence she hadn't slept well. 'Sorry I didn't get up in time to go swimming, Gill,' she said. 'I must have been awake half the night, thinking about Geoff. No matter how I feel about him, what he's done, he doesn't deserve this. Any word from Kieren?' she asked Joe.

'Not yet, but I did hear Geoff's having surgery this morning.'

The colour drained from Erica's face. 'Oh, no!' she said, putting a hand up to her mouth. 'So I won't be able to see him?'

'If we get there early, we should make it. You're still of the same mind?'

'Of course. He's still my husband, despite…'

'Let's eat, then,' Gill said.

'Why don't I rustle up some eggs while you two shower and dress. It'll save time. You stay here, Coco,' Joe said to the dog who looked undecided which of the women she was going to follow. At Joe's words, she slunk under the table.

Less than an hour later, they were on their way to the hospital.

*

Leaving Joe and Coco in one of the landscaped courtyards which formed part of the hospital surrounds, Gill and Erica hurried inside and made their way to the cardiac unit where they were greeted by one of the nurses on duty.

As soon as they said they were here to see Geoff Masters and that Erica was his wife, they were admitted to a side ward where Geoff was lying very still, a number of tubes attached to him.

'Geoff!' Erica said in a tremulous voice, moving close to the bed. Gill remained by the door.

At the sound of his wife's voice, Geoff opened his eyes.

Gill flinched. They shouldn't have come. She and Joe should have persuaded Erica to stay away. But it was too late now.

'Erica? You *are* here. That damned brother of yours lied to me. I should have known. Where else would you run to? You're too…' He seemed to lose track of what he was saying then, 'Well, now you've made your point, when I get out of here, you can come back home to Perth. Your place is with me, with your family, not with that milksop of a brother of yours.'

Gill was desperate to say something but knew she had to remain quiet. She doubted Geoff had even noticed she was there; his attention was fixed on his wife. Surely Erica wouldn't agree?

But before Erica could speak, several staff members in blue scrubs pushed past Gill. 'Sorry, you need to leave now. We need to prepare Mr Masters for theatre.'

'How long…?' Erica asked in a broken voice.

'Difficult to say,' one of the nurses replied, giving Erica a sympathetic smile, 'Cases like this can take up to six hours. It's best if you can go home. We'll give you a call when your husband's in recovery.'

Erica seemed reluctant to leave, so Gill took her by the arm. 'There's nothing we can do here, Erica. Let's join Joe and Coco and find something to do till the hospital rings.'

'They don't have my number,' she said.

They stopped by the nursing station where Erica gave the nurse in charge her new number, the one which was meant to keep her safe from Geoff. Then they took the lift down to meet Joe.

Joe and Coco were sitting near the doorway. He rose when they saw Erica and Gill. 'How is he?' he asked.

'He's going to surgery now,' Erica said. 'They promised to call when we can see him again. I need my phone back.'

Joe raised an eyebrow in Gill's direction. She shrugged. She had no idea what Erica was thinking. This was the man who'd exerted coercive control over her for years, who'd physically abused her. He was her husband, but… Gill tried to imagine how she would feel if it was Max lying there, but there was no comparison, Max had another woman who'd be the one at his bedside.

'Why don't we go back to my place,' Joe suggested. 'Your phone's there. Coco can be in the yard, and we can have some tea. You didn't eat much at breakfast, Erica. Maybe you'll feel more like something now?'

'I don't know, Joe. I'm not really hungry.'

They piled into Joe's car, Coco leaping into the front passenger seat before anyone else could and making them all laugh… even Erica. 'Sorry,' Joe said, 's he thinks it's her spot.'

By the time they reached Joe's house, Gill was pleased to see Erica had a little more colour in her cheeks. This was the first time she'd been in Joe's home since Bev had passed away, and it felt strange. When Joe's wife was alive, the book club had often met there and, glancing around, Gill could see little had changed. It gave her a weird feeling to be here, knowing the woman who had lived in this house was no longer alive to enjoy it.

'Let's have some tea,' Joe said, clearly unaware of Gill's feelings. 'And how about a boiled egg with toast and vegemite. That's what we used to have as children when we were under the weather.'

'Maybe,' Erica said, sounding a little more cheerful. 'I think I could manage that.'

'Gill?'

'Just toast for me.' Gill had eaten breakfast, but toast and vegemite sounded good.

Coco seemed to think it sounded good too, as she followed Joe around the kitchen.

They took the food out into the yard to sit at the wooden table there, while Coco could have more freedom, but the dog, seeming to sense all was not well, chose to stay close to her master.

Erica drank her tea and managed to eat a boiled egg and a slice of toast. She didn't join in the conversation when Joe asked Gill when Freya was returning from Sydney and they shared their experiences in the harbour city.

Then, out of the blue, Erica began to speak, her eyes downcast. 'I'm sorry I've caused everyone so much trouble,' she said. 'And now Geoff's in hospital. It's all my fault.' She began to cry, loud, gulping sobs.

Clearly surprised by her outburst, Coco rose and padded over to put her head on Erica's lap. As if in a dream, Erica dropped her hand to the dog's head.

'It's not your fault,' Joe said. 'None of it's your fault. Geoff brought this on himself, all of it.'

'You don't understand,' Erica said. 'If I hadn't left, I'd maybe have been able to make sure he took more care of himself, cooked him proper meals, tried to…' Her voice trailed off.

'No, Erica,' Gill said in a gentle voice. 'Joe's right. You did the right thing, the right thing for you. You've nothing to blame yourself for.'

But Erica didn't appear to hear her.

'I need to go back to Perth,' Erica said. 'As soon as Geoff gets out of hospital. He'll need someone to look after him. And there's Kieren, and Briony and… did I tell you she's having a girl? My granddaughter. I want to be there to see her grow up.'

Behind Erica's back, Gill met Joe's eyes and shook her head. Now wasn't the time to argue with his sister. Her guilt was fuelled by grief, by the shock of Geoff's heart attack. Hopefully, given time, she'd be able to think more clearly and realise a return to Perth, to Geoff, was a crazy idea. But for now, it was best to go along with her.

Joe nodded. 'Why don't you have a rest?' he suggested to Erica. 'It's not likely we'll hear from the hospital for hours yet. You'll want to be fresh when they call. I got a text from Kieren, and I said I'd pick him and Briony up.'

To Gill's relief, Erica nodded, rose and headed to her bedroom. Coco followed her, seemingly unwilling to let her out of her sight.

'She didn't mean it,' Gill said, when she and Joe were alone. 'She's still in shock.'

'I'm not so sure,' Joe said. 'Erica can be pretty pigheaded, and if she's got it into her head it was all her fault, there's no telling what she might do. But I hope you're right. I'd hate to see her back in the thrall of that bastard.'

'We'll just have to do what we can to ensure she doesn't.' Gill hugged Joe tightly. 'You're a good man, Joe Harris,' she said, with a break in her voice.

Fifty

Gill looked up when Joe walked into the kitchen. They had been trying to find ways to pass the time while they waited to hear from the hospital and had resorted to making an attempt at a jigsaw Joe had unearthed, but neither could focus on it properly. Joe had just gone to check on Erica.

'She's asleep,' he said, 'with Coco lying beside her. I didn't have the heart to move the dog. I'm guessing Erica didn't get much sleep last night.'

'No, I suspect she didn't. When does Kieren arrive?'

Joe checked his watch. 'In half an hour. Will you be right here, while I go and pick them up?'

'Of course. It must be worrying for them. I'll see if I can rouse Erica before you get back.'

'Thanks. That would be good.' Joe dragged a hand through his hair.

Erica was lucky to have him as a brother, Gill thought, *so lucky*. Not many men would do so much for a brother-in-law like Geoff Masters. How she hoped Erica would change her mind about returning to him. As Gill knew, he'd never change – a leopard didn't change his spots – and next time, and there would be a next time, Erica might not be so lucky. Gill remembered stories she'd read, cases she'd seen on television, women Ali Wells had told her about. Domestic violence was out there in the community in epidemic proportion, and Erica was a victim of it. Gill hated how so many women didn't seem to learn, how for a number of reasons they were drawn back to these abusive men. Hopefully, they could persuade Erica not to go down that track. Maybe her son could help, though Erica had said he was in his dad's pocket.

After she'd farewelled Joe with a hug and a kiss, Gill was at a loose end. She wished she'd brought her laptop with her and could get on with some work. It felt strange to be in Barb's house on her own – even with Erica asleep in the next room. It would always be Barb's house to Gill, the house where she'd enjoyed so many book club gatherings. Barb Harris had been a lovely woman, kind, generous, a perfect partner for Joe. The whole town had been devastated by her death. But life went on, and now Joe and Gill… Gill shook her head. She couldn't think of that in this house.

Gill turned on the electric jug to make tea. She'd be swimming in it before the day was over, but it gave her something to do. She heard a sound behind her and turned to see Coco padding in. 'Hello, Coco,' she said, bending down to hug the dog, the warm, furry body providing comfort. 'Is Erica awake?'

The dog didn't answer, but in a few moments, Erica appeared, rubbing her eyes, but looking rested. 'Where's Joe?' she asked, looking around the kitchen.

'He's gone to meet Kieren and Briony at the airport. Would you like tea? I was just making some.'

'Oh, I must have fallen asleep. I should have gone with him. They'd expect me to be there. Tea? Yes.' She slumped into a seat. 'Thanks, Gill, but shouldn't you be at work?'

'I thought I'd be more use here.' *But was she?* Gill made two cups of camomile tea, glad to find a box of teabags in the pantry. She suspected it was Erica's doing, as she couldn't imagine Joe buying them. 'Shall we take these outside?'

'If you like.' Erica seemed to have lost the impetus which had led to her announcement she was going to return to Perth with Geoff. Gill hoped she had changed her mind. 'Any word from the hospital?' she asked when they were seated outside, Coco at their feet, chewing on a bone-shaped dog biscuit.

Gill shook her head.

Then, as if suddenly remembering, 'Joe still has my phone,' Erica said frowning. 'The hospital was going to call me.'

They were still there when Gill's phone rang. 'Hello,' she said when she saw Joe's number.

'The hospital just called. Geoff's in recovery. Can you take Erica there? Kieren's plane's just landed. I'll bring them and meet you there.'

'Okay. Erica's right here. Do you want to speak to her?'

'Not now. I need to…' Gill heard the sound of voices, and the line went dead.

'What is it?' Erica asked, a tremor in her voice.

'It was Joe. Geoff's in recovery. We need to get to the hospital.'

'Oh!' Erica began to tremble.

'It'll be fine. Joe will meet us there, with Kieren and Briony.'

'Oh!' Erica said again, but her face brightened at the prospect of seeing her son with the pregnant Briony. 'I'll just wash my face.'

Coco, sensing something had happened, leapt to her feet.

'Sorry, Coco, you can't come with us this time. You'll have to stay here and mind the house.' At the word *stay*, Coco padded inside and went to her favourite spot by the door. 'Good girl,' Gill said, ruffling her ears. Since knowing Joe, she'd grown to love the dog. *It was odd*, she thought, *how it was easier to acknowledge her feelings for the dog than for the man.* She sent that thought to the back of her mind to consider later.

*

When Gill drew into the car park, she saw Joe's car sitting there. The doors opened, and Joe got out along with a younger man, who looked so like him he could have been his son, and a pregnant blonde woman.

'Kieren!' Erica called and rushed over to give the young man a hug.

'Mum! What were you thinking of to leave Dad? You knew his heart…'

'Now's not the time, Kieren,' Joe said, signalling to Gill, who moved closer. 'This is Gill Dickson. She's a friend of mine and Erica's solicitor.' As soon as he spoke, it seemed he realised his mistake, when Kieren swung round to face him again.

'Solicitor? What does Mum need with a solicitor?'

This time it was Erica who spoke up. 'Can we just go inside, Kieren?

We're here to see your dad. We can sort out everything else later.'

Kieren's eyes clouded, and he seemed about to speak again, but Briony took his arm. 'Let's go in, honey. I need to sit down.'

'Sorry, sweetheart.' Kieren patted her hand. 'I forgot. You must be tired.'

Gill could see the lines of exhaustion on the young woman's face. The pair had just suffered a five-hour flight leaving late last night, Perth time, to arrive here after midday. She suspected the pregnant young woman had found it difficult to get any sleep on the trip. Taking pity on her, she said, 'Would you like to come for a cup of tea, Briony, while the others head to the ward? It may be some time before your father-in-law is out of recovery.'

Briony gave her a grateful look, then glanced at Kieren, as if for approval.

'On you go, sweetheart,' he said. 'She's right.' He didn't give Gill her name, and his tone made it sound as if he was reluctant to agree with her.

Leaving Joe, Erica and Kieren to go to check on Geoff, Gill and Briony headed to the cafeteria where they ordered mugs of hot chocolate and blueberry muffins which smelt as if they had just come out of the oven.

'Yum,' Briony said, biting into her muffin. 'It feels ages since I've eaten, and the food on the plane wasn't up to much. I'm always hungry these days.' She rubbed her stomach.

'Erica says you're having a girl?' Gill said, trying to keep the conversation on a positive note and away from the wife-beater who was recovering from major surgery. She could remember what it was like when she was pregnant with Freya.

'Yes.' Briony smiled and her face lit up. 'We've painted the nursery pink. I can't wait. I'd hoped Mum would be there to help. So, do you think she'll come back home with us?'

For a moment, Gill was puzzled, then she realised Briony was referring to Erica. 'I'm not sure,' she said warily. 'We'll have to wait and see. What about your own mum?'

Briony's eyes clouded. 'Mum and Dad are both gone. It's why Kieren's folks are so important to us. They'll be little Ava's only grandparents.'

'I see.' Gill did. Briony would most probably feel the loss of Erica more than the others, if she decided to stay in Pelican Crossing.

'Shall we go now?' Gill asked when they had finished their hot chocolate, and all that remained of the muffins was a collection of crumbs.

'I guess.' Briony hoisted herself out of her chair, and they headed up in the lift to join the others.

When they reached the cardiac unit, Joe and Erica were sitting in the waiting area, Kieren pacing impatiently up and down. 'They told us to wait here,' Joe said.

'Why won't they let us see Dad?' Kieren fumed.

Joe rolled his eyes. Clearly this was nothing new.

'They'll allow us in when they bring your dad up,' Erica said. 'He must still be in recovery.'

'How long does it take? When did they call?' Kieren asked Joe.

Joe frowned and caught Gill's eye. It had been some time since he received the call. *Should they be worried?*

At that moment, a man, wearing blue scrubs, a stethoscope poking out of one pocket, who gave the impression of being someone in charge, came hurrying towards them. 'Which of you is Mrs Masters?' he asked.

'I am,' Erica said in a trembling voice, rising so quickly she almost overbalanced.

'I'm her brother and this is her son,' Joe said, stepping forward to put an arm around Erica's shoulders.

'What…?' Kieren began.

'Can you come this way, please?' the man gestured to a door leading into a small room.

'We'll wait here,' Gill said, when Briony made to join them.

Joe signalled his thanks.

They were gone for some time.

'Do you think…?' Briony asked, clearly reluctant to put into words what they were both thinking. *It wasn't good news.*

Gill and Briony didn't speak as they waited, while members of staff went about their business around them, and other visitors arrived to enter the ward proper. Then the door to the small room opened and the others came out, followed by the doctor. Erica was in tears, and

Gill could see Kieren was having trouble keeping his in check. Joe shook his head.

'What's happened?' Briony rose and went to Kieren. He didn't reply.

It was Joe who said what Gill had already figured out. 'Geoff's dead. He didn't survive. The doctor said the surgery was successful, but he didn't make it out of recovery.'

Fifty-one

The pall of death hung over the house. Even Coco was more subdued than usual, as if recognising the sombre atmosphere. It reminded Joe of when Barb died, only this time the body of the deceased wasn't lying in the next room, but in the hospital morgue.

Gill had gone straight home from the hospital, saying she didn't want to intrude on the family's grief, but Joe wished she was here to help him handle the awkward silences combined with Kieren's accusations to his mother. Wisely, Briony stayed out of it, pleading the need to rest, and disappearing into the bedroom. Joe had no such excuse and tried to mediate between mother and son with little success. He knew Erica was still consumed with the guilt she'd expressed to him and Gill earlier, now greater than ever and overlaid with grief. While he knew much of Kieren's anger was a result of *his* grief, his similarity to his dad was worrying.

Now, two days after Geoff's death, the argument revolved around Geoff's funeral, with Kieren insisting his body be returned to Perth and the funeral held there, and Erica wanting to have it in Pelican Crossing and get it over and done with.

Joe couldn't see them coming to an agreement. He decided to bow out of it and headed out with Coco, hoping to catch up with Gill. They hadn't seen each other since that dreadful moment at the hospital, though he had spoken to her on the phone.

It was good to get out of the house. The place which had been his comfort all those years, which had provided him with solace when Barb died, had turned into a battleground. He wanted to do something to help Erica, but Kieren was Geoff's son, and he had rights too. Joe had often heard it said that a death could bring out the worst in families. He was witnessing it firsthand, and it wasn't pretty.

Coco was glad to be out too, her nose to the ground as she sniffed out all the new scents since her last walk.

Joe wandered down to the marina, stopped for a few moments to admire the rows of boats berthed there, then moved on in the direction of Gill's apartment. It was a Saturday morning. She didn't work on Saturdays. But there was no guarantee she'd be home. He couldn't believe how much he wanted to see her, to hear her voice, to be with someone unconnected with death and its attendant grief, grief for a man he'd despised, a man who didn't deserve the outpouring of grief Joe had been expected to share.

Taking a deep breath, the thought of seeing Gill filling him with a sense of anticipation he hadn't been prepared for, he made his way to her door.

*

Gill was feeling restless. Since returning from her early morning swim, she'd showered, changed and eaten breakfast. Now she was sitting on her balcony with a second cup of liquorice tea, wondering what was happening across the town in Joe's house. Freya was due back today but not till late afternoon. She had a whole day to fill.

Gill's mind went back to that moment in the hospital when Joe had told her Geoff was dead. It had been a shock, and she felt guilty at her initial feeling of relief, relief Erica would no longer have to be afraid of her husband. But her relief was soon tempered with sadness that Erica's son had lost the father he idolised. Death was never pleasant, and this one had happened so suddenly, been so unexpected. Now the family would be grieving, and although she'd spoken to Joe on the phone, she had no idea what their plans were.

Draining her cup, she took it into the kitchen, rinsed it and set it on the draining board. She often didn't bother with the dishwasher when she was on her own. She missed having Erica there, missed

Joe dropping in with Coco. The dog had such a comforting presence. Gill was sure she was providing comfort to Joe's family, aware of their distress.

Deciding these thoughts were unproductive and wanting to keep busy, Gill went into her study and fired up her computer. She had plenty of work to do, and she was sure Joe would contact her again when he could. She was looking forward to Freya coming back and to hearing all about her time in Sydney.

As her computer came to life, Gill saw a new email from her solicitor. Her heart sank. Max had been surprisingly quiet since Freya called to issue her ultimatum, but knowing him, he'd manage to get around it somehow. She opened the email.

Gill blinked, unable to believe her eyes. Freya's tactic had worked. Not only had Max withdrawn his demand for a percentage of her future income, he'd agreed she could buy him out of the apartment using a fair market value. She stared at the email again, to make sure she wasn't seeing things. But the words were still there. She was flooded with a sense of exhilaration. After all those years, after all the angst, all the recriminations, the divorce could finally be settled. This called for a celebration.

Gill was looking in the fridge and wondering if it would be too self-indulgent to open a bottle of champagne and drink a glass by herself at this time on a Saturday morning, when there was a knock on the door. Closing the fridge door, grateful she'd been saved from making a decision, she went to see who was there.

As soon as Gill opened the door, she was greeted by a wet nose and a tongue licking her hand. She raised her eyes to see the dog's master. 'Joe,' she said, staring at him in surprise, her heart racing.

'Can we come in?'

'Sorry. Of course.' Gill realised she'd been standing there as if turned to stone. 'I didn't expect to see you today. I thought you'd be busy arranging…'

'Thanks.' Joe walked in, following Coco who was already making her way to the kitchen. 'It's a madhouse at my place. Kieren and Erica are at loggerheads over the funeral. I had to get out. I was hoping you'd be home.'

'Where else would I be?' Gill smiled. She was so pleased to see him.

She wanted to share her good news, but was it appropriate when he was so mired in grief… or was he? She knew he didn't have much time for his brother-in-law when he was alive, and Joe wasn't one of those hypocrites who suddenly changed their attitude to a person once they were dead.

'Freya not back yet?' Joe asked glancing around the room.

'She gets in later today.' Gill couldn't keep the grin off her face.

'You're looking very pleased about something. Dare I think it's about seeing me?'

Gill suddenly felt guilty. Of course Joe would jump to that conclusion. 'Actually, I just received some good news,' she said.

'Let me guess, you've won the lottery?'

Gill laughed. 'Almost as good. Freya's ultimatum worked. Max has taken back most of his ridiculous demands. My divorce can be settled.'

'Well, that does call for a celebration.' Joe pulled Gill into a warm embrace, their lips meeting.

Gill clung to him. She felt her senses swim. But, as their embrace deepened, their passion mounting, she realised they were alone in her apartment. Freya wouldn't be back for hours. If she gave in to her emotions, if she and Joe made love, there would be no turning back.

What was wrong with her? Gill slid out of Joe's embrace, seeing his expression of disappointment. Coco mirrored her master's feelings, her eyes filled with sadness as she dropped her head onto her paws.

'What's the matter?' Joe asked, clearly puzzled by Gill's withdrawal. 'You've got what you wanted, haven't you?'

'Ye…es, but…' Gill bit her lip. She wanted to consummate their love. She did, she knew she did, but something held her back. *Would it always be like this? Would she always draw back, too afraid to allow herself to enjoy a proper relationship?*

'I'm sorry,' she said, feeling like a rabbit caught in headlights.

'Sorry for what?' Joe said, frowning.

She wanted to grab him, kiss him. Instead, she took a step back.

'What is it?' Joe persisted, 'Has something happened?'

Yes, something has happened. I've fallen in love with you.

'Sorry,' she said again, 'I just… it's… I'm not sure I can do this, Joe…'

Joe sighed and shook his head. 'I can't do this right now. It's too much. Come, Coco.'

Gill's eyes misted as she watched him leave. Coco padding silently behind him. She wanted to call him back, to tell him… But she didn't. *What had she done?*

Fifty-two

It was a week since Gill had made the mistake which had cost her Joe's friendship. She'd never forget his expression when she pulled out of his arms and backed off from him. He'd left soon afterwards and hadn't been in contact since. Gill knew he'd been busy. She'd heard on the grapevine that his nephew had finally prevailed, and his brother-in-law's body had been transported back to Perth. Erica had gone too, and Gill regretted she hadn't had the opportunity to say goodbye and wish her well.

So now Joe would be alone again, with only Coco for company. Gill missed him, missed him more than she thought possible. And she missed Coco too. She'd become attached to the labrador, her wet nose and friendly manner.

Gill was alone too. Now Max had retracted his demands, Freya had been persuaded to visit her dad, and was spending the weekend with him and his new partner.

'Don't expect me to like her, Mum,' she'd said before she left. But Gill knew Freya was looking forward to seeing her dad again, and she was glad her daughter was going to be reconciled with Max.

Looking around her empty apartment, Gill was filled with regret. If nothing else, Geoff's sudden and untimely death had shown her how short life could be, how you never knew what the future held. She was no spring chicken and every time she looked in the mirror, it seemed her face was more lined, and there were more streaks of grey in her hair. She sighed. What was to become of her? Freya would soon be off to Sydney – she was confident she'd be offered the position there – and Gill would be left alone again. It hadn't seemed to matter before… before she met Joe. She'd been perfectly content with her life, telling anyone who'd listen how she didn't need a man to feel fulfilled. *When had that changed, and why hadn't she realised?* And now it was too late… or was it? Maybe, now Erica had left, Joe would contact her, forgive her erratic behaviour, and they could begin again.

Suddenly, she felt the need to get out of the apartment. The home she loved with its Scandinavian design felt alien to her. Pulling on a jacket, she picked up her hat, and slipping her phone and wallet into her pocket, headed to the beach.

Once there, with the breeze on her face, the smell of the sea in her nostrils and the sound of the seagulls overhead, Gill felt better, energised. Pulling off her sandals, she wandered along the hard-packed sand by the water's edge, happy until she spied a couple standing chatting some way ahead. They were accompanied by two dogs who were cavorting together in the ocean.

As Gill came closer to them, she realised the man was Joe. She didn't recognise the woman. The couple appeared to be enjoying each other's company, laughing together at the dogs' antics. Gill was struck by a shaft of… jealousy. Who was the woman with Joe? How could he have moved on so quickly? It was only a week ago when he and Gill were… She'd been a fool. She hadn't appreciated what a good man Joe was, even though she'd said so several times.

As Gill approached, the couple turned towards her. Joe smiled. 'Gill, have you met Kate Warren? She's the new town planner, and this is her dog, Bear. Kate, this is Gill Dickson. She's our local solicitor *par excellence*.' Gill managed to smile and say hello, before moving on, her thoughts in a whirl, her fists clenching and unclenching in her annoyance with herself and what she'd thrown away.

By the time Gill had walked to the end of the beach, turned and was on her way back, she had managed to calm down, but her memories, and images of her and Joe together continued to fill her thoughts. So much so that she thought she was imagining it when she felt Coco's warm body against her, and a wet tongue lick her toes.

Looking up, she saw Joe. He was alone, his companion nowhere in sight.

'Hey,' he said.

'Hey,' Gill said shyly. Was she going to have another chance? 'I'm sorry,' she said, 'for last week. I don't know what came over me. I shouldn't have…' Her eyes met his, those brown eyes belonging to the man she now realised she loved dearly. Today, his expression was inscrutable, maybe because of the sun in his eyes. She couldn't tell what he was thinking. She took a deep breath, deciding to take a risk. He could only refuse, and she wouldn't be any worse off than she was right now, and perhaps…

'I have a bottle of champagne at home,' she said. 'It's the one we should have opened last Saturday.'

For a few moments, Joe didn't speak, and Gill thought she'd made a dreadful mistake. Then he smiled, the smile she'd become familiar with, the smile that sent her stomach fluttering, and said, 'Better late than never. Let's go,' and taking her hand, and with Coco lolloping beside them, the pair ran along the beach.

Back at Gill's apartment, she took the champagne from the fridge, while Joe fetched two glasses. He poured the wine, then asked, 'What are we celebrating?'

'The future,' she said, then… 'No… *our* future. It's time to move forward, Joe. If that's what you want, of course.'

'To our future together.' He raised his glass. 'I love you, Gill. I think I always have, ever since Coco and I bumped into you outside the medical centre when you were so upset. After Barb died, I never thought I'd fall in love again, but I was wrong.'

'I love you too. I always vowed never to let another man into my life, but somehow you – and you, Coco,' she said as the dog nudged her – have managed to sneak under the barriers I'd erected. I missed you all this last week, but I think it was only when I saw you with Kate, and I thought…' she blushed. 'It's when I realised I didn't want to live another day without you. To us.' Gill raised her glass to meet Joe's.

Seeing her humans happy, Coco sighed and lay down to watch them.

After downing one glass of champagne, Joe went to top up their glasses, but Gill stopped him, looked him in the eye.

Words weren't needed.

Joe took Gill in his arms and kissed her. She responded with fervour, shivering as Joe kissed his way down her neck, desire flooding her as his hand moved to the buttons on her shirt.

'Wait,' she said, clamping a hand over his.

Joe gave her a worried look.

She grinned. '*Not in front of you know who,*' she said in a whisper and jerking her head towards Coco.

Joe grinned right back. 'You're right,' he said, scooping her up in his arms and carrying her to the bedroom.

*

Next morning, after a night of wonderful lovemaking and very little sleep, Gill rose at her usual time, but before she could decide whether or not to go swimming, she found Joe at her side.

'Stay with me,' he said.

Gill needed no further urging. The ocean could wait. Joe couldn't. She allowed him to pull her back into bed.

Later, they stood together on the balcony watching the sky change colour, the rosy glow of a new dawn over the ocean. *And a new dawn for us too*, Gill thought, as Joe's arms tightened around her. She lifted up her face for his kiss.

The End

If you've enjoyed Gill and Joe's story, I'd love if you could leave a review on Amazon and/or Goodreads. A few words will suffice, no need for a lengthy review. It will mean a lot to me and help other readers find my books.

I'm thrilled so many of my readers are enjoying this series set in Pelican Crossing and are making friends with my characters.

The fourth book in the series, *A Christmas Surprise in Pelican Crossing* is Rachel's story.

Christmas is coming to Pelican Crossing, brinsging with it a host of surprises.

Fifty-eight-year-old widow *Rachel Mason* thought she had her life all figured out – running her quaint Bed and Breakfast, spending time with her grandkids, and keeping her loyal West Highland Terrier by her side. But when her son announces a Christmas surprise, Rachel's world is turned upside down.

Luke Findlay, widowed, retired, and looking to check off items on his bucket list, suddenly finds himself back in his hometown of Pelican Crossing, where he is tasked with temporarily running the local vet clinic.

When the new vet turns out to be Rachel's teenage crush, and her son's Christmas surprise is very different from what she anticipated, her life becomes unexpectedly complicated. But then, Luke receives a surprise of his own.

As Rachel and Luke reconnect, sparks fly, and old feelings resurface. But with Luke's impending departure and Rachel's unforeseen responsibilities, can their newfound connection survive?

Fans of heartwarming romances will love this story of second chances and unexpected love.

You can order here https://mybook.to/ChristmasSurpriseinPC

From the Author

Dear Reader,

First, I'd like to thank you for choosing to read *A New Dawn in Pelican Crossing.* I hope you've enjoyed visiting Pelican Crossing as much as I've enjoyed creating it.

Like all my other books, although it is part of a series, it can be read as a standalone.

If you'd like to stay up to date with my new releases and special offers you can sign up to my reader's group.

You can sign up here

https://maggiechristensenauthor.com/subscribe/

I'll never share your email address, and you can unsubscribe at any time. You can also contact me via Facebook, Twitter or by email. I love hearing from my readers and will always reply.

Thanks again.

Acknowledgements

As always, this book could not have been written without the help and advice of a number of people.

Firstly, my husband Jim for listening to my plotlines without complaint, for his patience and insights as I discuss my characters and storyline with him, for his patience and help with difficult passages and advice on my male dialogue, and for being there when I need him.

John Hudspith, editor extraordinaire for his ideas, suggestions, encouragement and attention to detail, and for helping me make this book better.

Jane Dixon-Smith for her patience and for working her magic on my beautiful cover and interior.

My thanks also to early readers of this book – Helen, Maggie and Louise for their helpful comments and advice, and to my daughter, Jolene, and granddaughter, Lara, for helping me understand scuba diving.

And to all of my readers, reviewers and bloggers. Your support and comments make it all worthwhile.

About the Author

After a career in education, Maggie Christensen began writing contemporary women's fiction portraying mature women facing life-changing situations, and historical fiction set in her native Scotland. Her travels inspire her writing, be it her trips to visit family in Scotland, in Oregon, USA or her home on Queensland's beautiful Sunshine Coast. Maggie writes of mature heroines coming to terms with changes in their lives and the heroes worthy of them. Maggie has been called *the queen of mature age fiction* and her writing has been described by one reviewer as *like a nice warm cup of tea. It is warm, nourishing, comforting and embracing.*

From the small town in Scotland where she grew up, Maggie was lured to Australia by the call to 'Come and teach in the sun'. Once there, she worked as a primary school teacher, university lecturer and in educational management. Now living with her husband of over thirty years on Queensland's Sunshine Coast, she loves walking on the deserted beach in the early mornings and having coffee by the river on weekends. Her days are spent surrounded by books, either reading or writing them – her idea of heaven!

Maggie can be found on Facebook, Twitter, Goodreads, Instagram, Bookbub or on her website.

https://www.facebook.com/maggiechristensenauthor
https://twitter.com/MaggieChriste33
https://www.goodreads.com/author/show/8120020.Maggie_Christensen
https://www.instagram.com/maggiechriste33/
https://www.bookbub.com/profile/maggie-christensen
https://maggiechristensenauthor.com/